'A first class terror story with a relentless focus that would have made Edgar Allan Poe proud'
New York Times on *The Cormorant*

'Gregory writes with the hypnotic power of Poe'
Publisher's Weekly

'Gregory's voice and vision are wholly original'
Ramsey Campbell

'Intelligent and well-written'
Iain Banks on *The Cormorant*

'A considerable delight... the quality of the prose and the economy of expression are particularly impressive'
Time Out on *The Cormorant*

'An extraordinary novel - original, compelling, brilliant'
Library Journal on *The Cormorant*

First published 2013 by Solaris
an imprint of Rebellion Publishing Ltd,
Riverside House, Osney Mead,
Oxford, OX2 0ES, UK

www.solarisbooks.com

ISBN: 978 1 78108 151 8

10 9 8 7 6 5 4 3 2 1

A CIP catalogue record for this book
is available from the British Library.

Designed & typeset by
Rebellion Publishing

THE
Waking
THAT
Kills

Stephen Gregory

SOLARIS

for Broo Doherty at Wade & Doherty
and Jonathan Oliver, Solaris

Prologue

'LAWRENCE LUNDY,' MY father said, blurring the words oddly in his mouth.

Then, to try and remember where he'd heard the name before, he pretended, with an invisible chisel in one hand and an invisible hammer in the other, to carve it onto an invisible gravestone. He stared at the empty space, reading and re-reading the letters as he cut them.

This time it didn't come back to him.

He'd always said he had a head for names: he'd been a monumental mason for forty years, staring at a name for hours on end as he cut it into the stone. He claimed he could remember exactly where and when he'd carved each one.

But this one wouldn't come.

'Lawrence Lundy,' he said, and he started to carve the name again, shaping each letter with his lips as he tapped it carefully, painstakingly, into thin air with his invisible tools.

I told him it didn't matter, but he ignored me. He carried on working, in the same way he'd ignored me when, as a boy, I'd sat with him on a frosty morning in a country churchyard or a hot afternoon in a military cemetery. I watched him. He seemed to have forgotten I was there, although I'd flown over seven thousand miles to visit him. I imagined I could hear in my head the knock of the hammer on the handle of the chisel, the nick of the blade into stone.

The room was small and stuffy, already cluttered with the few books and pictures he'd managed to bring with him. It smelled of him and his clothes, although he'd been there less than a fortnight and the window was wide open. There was an impressive view: the nursing-home was on the promenade and his room was on the top floor. For a man who'd worked outside since the day he'd left school, suddenly confined in such a narrow space, it was good that he'd be able to breathe the sharp salt air and watch the changing moods of the estuary.

Now, quite oblivious of me, he was still chipping away. He was tall and very thin, all bumpy joints and jutting angles; strong fingers with swollen knuckles, horny nails, glasses slipping to the end of a bony nose... my stricken father, mouthing the letters of a name he'd heard somewhere but couldn't quite remember.

He looked very tired. His face, indeed his whole demeanour, was lop-sided. He'd tried talking to me, but his tongue was wet and heavy. He'd listened to my brief account of another year overseas and my plan for the summer. When I told him I was going to stay not far away, that I'd taken a tutoring job for a couple of months and could come into town by bus to see him every week, he'd rummaged in his bedside drawer and pulled out a ring of keys.

'Use the car,' he mumbled, and when he saw me wince at the suggestion, he shrugged and added, 'See if she'll start, take her round the block a couple of times, it's up to you.' He pressed the keys into my hand, and in doing so he held my fingers between his. 'So soft,' he smiled, 'not a day's work in all your life.'

His eyes were drooping. A trickle of saliva shone on his chin. I stood up and made softly for the door, meaning to let myself out and tiptoe down the corridor.

But he heard me and shook himself awake again. He stared at me as though I'd just come into the room and he didn't know who I was. Startled, smearing at his mouth with the back of his hand, he tried to say that name again. For a moment, as he blinked at me in bewilderment, he seemed to think that I, a stranger he'd never seen before, was Lawrence Lundy. And suddenly – I could see from a flicker of fear in his eyes – suddenly he remembered the name... yes, he knew it, he'd seen it somewhere, he'd read it somewhere, and at last it had come back to him.

But his tongue and his lips refused to work. He writhed in his chair, infuriated, impotent.

'No, Dad, it's me,' I said, 'it's me, it's Christopher,' and I moved across the room again, to try and calm him.

He recoiled from my touch. His face twisted into a grimace of revulsion. 'Bad boy... bad boy...' he was blubbering through numb, wet lips, and he squirmed away from me.

I left. And as I closed the door and moved along the corridor, I could still hear him trying to get the words out, spluttering with anger and frustration.

Chapter One

I WALKED ALONG the promenade, past holiday hotels, bed-and-breakfasts and old people's homes. I reached the town and turned into a narrow side-street. The air was shrill with the ill-tempered cries of gulls, and the sky was grey and cold, lowering onto the chimneys and slatey rooftops of the town.

I felt fidgety in England after more than a year away. It prickled on me. It was an itchy old coat I hadn't worn for a long time, unwashed, stale, with forgotten oddments mouldering in its pockets. In five minutes, I saw things I'd never seen in the gently complacent country I'd left behind: homeless teenagers huddled in blankets, a drunken woman yelling in a pub car park, a man in an ugly confrontation with a traffic warden, shop doorways blocked by bags of rubbish, the pavement sticky with chewing-gum. I rounded a corner into a cobbled alley and came to my father's lock-up garage. As soon as I slotted the key into the big padlock, snicked it easily and then withdrew the key with a sheen of oil on it, I knew that the car would start and I'd have no choice but to roll it out and drive it dutifully, foolishly, around the town for a mile or two.

I swung the garage door up and open. The car bulged out of it, huge and slabby, mottled grey, like the carcase of a whale.

It was a Daimler hearse. My father had bought it from a local undertaker when I was seven, and for more than twenty years he'd used it as his everyday transport, as his workshop and even as a place to sleep when he was away from home. My mother had hated it, but he'd insisted it was both useful and distinctive, appropriate for his line of business. Now it loomed out of the garage, as though it had been swelling and bloating in the darkness, pressing against the walls and the door to get out. I eyed it with a curious mixture of dislike and irresistible nostalgia. It was ridiculous, the embodiment of my father's pig-headedness, and yet it was a real, tangible piece of my childhood and adolescence.

Sure enough, when I slipped onto the worn leather of the driver's seat, turned the ignition key, waited for a moment and pressed the starter button, the engine stirred into a lazy, rumbling rhythm. It ticked over almost silently when I took my foot off the throttle. I eased the car out of the garage and into the alley, left it running while I went around and opened the back door. The smell hit me straightaway, and I blinked into the gloom of the space that my father had converted for all his tools and materials, a place to rest and read, even a little stove on which he'd made soup and brewed tea in a hundred cemeteries from one coast of England to another. It was the smell of my father, of my youth, of well-oiled tools, well-worn raincoats, work-gloves and work-boots and pipe tobacco: the smell of all the days and nights he'd spent in and around the hearse and the times I'd spent with him. His tools were there, a mahogany chest of hammers and chisels and brushes, the rags and oils he'd used to maintain them, and a cardboard box full of old newspapers. He'd installed a couch for himself, now with its rugs and pillows neatly folded. There were books and maps, and the floor was covered with a green carpet.

I slung my bag inside, the only luggage I'd brought across the world with me. A few minutes later, the hearse was rolling through the town centre.

A dull, squally Sunday afternoon. Grimsby, on the north-east coast of England. Along the prom to Cleethorpes, grimmer than Grimsby.

A gust of wind from the estuary slapped into the side of the hearse. It creaked and swayed, and a spatter of spray fell on the windscreen. People turned to look as I drove by. An elderly couple, arm in arm for a bracing walk, swivelled their heads and stared, a look of sullen resentment in their eyes. A group of youths simply guffawed, a horrid braying noise. A very fat, middle-aged man, drinking beer on his own in a seaside shelter, pulled himself to his feet and stood, head bowed, in mock respect. And when I stopped at the traffic-lights at the end of the promenade, two small boys who'd been kicking a football on a patch of waste ground ran up and pressed their faces to the back window, curious to see if there was a coffin inside. When I accelerated away, they left smeary fingerprints and a mist of hot breath on the glass.

Lawrence Lundy. The name was lodged in my head too. I'd arranged to meet him the following day. I had a night to kill.

I manoeuvred the car back into town, and with some difficulty reversed it into the garage. Six o'clock, that dreadful, deadly hour on a Sunday evening. When a church bell started to ring, and the gulls screamed around the rooftops more defiantly than ever, I slipped into a pub and tucked myself into the darkest, deepest corner I could find.

The beer was flat and warm. The place filled up with people determined to ward off the looming approach of another Monday. Suddenly very tired, after an eighteen-hour flight and then six hours on the train from London to Grimsby, I stayed where I was, now and then struggling to the bar and into my corner again, and I let the beer salve the itch of being back in England. When I emerged at eleven o'clock, the chilly air hit me, I swayed unsteadily and looked around to find my bearings, and I realised I hadn't found anywhere to stay the night. I'd left my bag in the hearse.

It was raining. I had the uncomfortable feeling that someone was following me as I turned into the alleyway and crossed to the lock-up garage. I fumbled with the lock and snicked it open. When I pulled the door up and over and the enormous chromium grille of the hearse gleamed in the darkness, I saw the shadowy movements of three or four figures hurrying down the alleyway towards me. I ducked into the garage. Swinging the door shut behind me, I managed, in a slit of light from the wet cobbles outside, to ram the bolts into place. Just in time. There was a cannonade of fists and boots, hammering on the door, rattling it on its hinges.

I backed away, into the dark depths of the garage. My pursuers couldn't get in, although they bellowed and hammered for a few minutes. At last they gave up, urinating long and noisily onto the door before they moved away and the alleyway outside fell quiet.

A soft green light came on, when I opened the back of the hearse. I climbed inside. It was warm, and the familiar smells were a comfort to me. I sat on the couch, meaning to wait and listen for a while until it was safe to go out and try to find a side-street bed-and-breakfast. But when the silence grew around me and every bone in my body ached with tiredness, I kicked off my shoes and lay down, pulling my father's blankets over me.

Twenty-four hours. From one side of the planet to the other, from one world to another. From the balcony of my spacious, sun-filled house in Sarawak, to a couch in the back of a hearse, in a lock-up garage in Grimsby...

The weight of sleep folded around me. My eyes closed and my head pressed deeper onto my father's pillow. His face came to me. He was struggling to speak, gagging and grimacing, mouthing a name whose meaning he was powerless to explain.

Chapter Two

I ARRIVED AT Chalke House at noon the following day. It took two hours to drive there. The countryside changed and softened as I drove inland from Grimsby, away from the bleakness of the coast, across the plains of Lincolnshire and into the wolds.

I'd decided to use the hearse after all. After a night of untroubled sleep, I'd stepped outside, into the cool sunshine of a May Monday morning. Over a bacon sandwich and a mug of tea in a cafe next to the bus station, I considered the advantages of taking the ridiculous machine, as my transport and as a base in case things didn't work out with the job: the hearse was working, it was comfortable, it would save the expense of hiring a car or the inconvenience of public transport.

I regretted my decision every mile of the way. People stared, from one border of Lincolnshire to the other. Everybody, every single person who happened to see the hearse go by, took a lingering second or third look. It was a relic of all the graveyards it had sat in: blistered by the seasons it had endured, weathered and worn down, not so much a car as a tomb on wheels. It had carried hundreds of coffins, but now it seemed, when I glimpsed its reflection in the window of a shop or a car showroom, as though the hearse itself was doomed to its final resting-place. Hollow, vacant, it was ready to be rolled into a barn and colonised by chickens, or crushed in a breaker's yard.

I came closer to Chalke House, in the wolds. The lane narrowed and twisted, dipping deep into a wooded valley. At last I saw the sign at the foot of an overgrown drive. I had an impulse to roll the car into the shade of the trees and conceal it. How? More and more eccentric, all but impossible, to hide such an enormous, incongruous thing in the dappled sunlight of a Lincolnshire woodland... I turned into the drive and drove very slowly, crunching over gravel. The car wallowed through long grass. Thistles swished along its flanks and belly.

There was a tremendous crash on the windscreen.

The glass imploded. I felt a spatter of splinters onto my face, as something big and very heavy thumped into the soft leather of the passenger seat.

I jammed my foot on the brake. Swiping at my forehead, sensing a smear of blood on the palm of my hand, I opened the driver's door and tumbled out.

I'd stopped in the shade of a Scots pine. There was a cry from overhead. The sunlight dazzled through the branches, and as I squinted upwards a figure dangled into view. Like an elf descending on a cobweb in a children's pantomime, a woman slipped silently to the ground and stood there, blinking, staring at me and the car, brushing the hair from her eyes.

Neither of us spoke. When she stepped forward and the look in her eyes suggested that she'd guessed who I might be, she reached to my face and touched my forehead with one fingertip. Her touch was very cool. She withdrew her finger, with a tiny drop of my blood on it.

'I'm so sorry,' she said, a bit out of breath. 'How awful. I think it's just a scratch, but I'm so sorry. Are you Mr Beal? Christopher Beal? I'm Juliet Lundy, Lawrence's mother...'

She wiped my blood onto her shirt, brushed again at the hair which fell over her forehead. Without realising it, she left a smudge of bark and proceeded to smudge and smudge the rest of her face by running her hands around her nose and mouth – as distractedly and naturally as a kitten cleaning itself. She was tiny, in a man's shirt and a pair of faded blue jeans, with a pointy, questing, twitchy face and a shock of foxy-russet hair. Now that her skin was smeared with the dust of the Scots pine, she had the look of a whiskery wild animal, a squirrel or a marten which had skittered to the ground from high in the branches.

'Your car,' she said, and she bent inside it to pick up the thing she'd dropped out of the tree. It was a claw-hammer. She hefted it from hand to hand, and her face twitched and puckered as she looked at the broken windscreen. 'I was up in the tree, trying to fix Lawrence's tree-house. Your car kind of startled me, the hammer fell out of my hand...'

'Your hammer kind of startled me too,' I said. 'Yes, I'm Christopher Beal. Don't worry about the car right now. Can I leave it here?'

For a moment, a queer shadow seemed to pass across her. She shivered and glanced up into the tree from where she'd appeared. She craned her neck, shaded her eyes with her hand and peered up and up to the very highest branches – back down to the car, then back up again, as though, for some reason, she was measuring the distance and angle between the two points – perhaps the trajectory of the claw-hammer. At last she said, with another shudder of her narrow shoulders, 'Yes, leave it here. A good place. Come along to the house, and we'll get you cleaned up...'

I followed her through the garden... or rather, a piece of woodland through which the ghostly outline of a long-ago garden was just discernible. Beech trees, their scarred grey trunks towering into the foliage of early summer. A pond the size of a tennis court, a mirror of peaty, unfathomable water. A derelict greenhouse, built against an overgrown chalk cliff, from which an ancient vine forced its tendrils through broken panes, crumbling and lifting the brickwork with its roots. Everywhere, a dense cover of bramble and nettle and cow-parsley.

Once or twice the woman glanced over her shoulder to see that I was following her. I heard her saying indistinctly that she was glad I'd come, that she'd been worried I might not come, that I might have changed my mind about coming... I was going to say I'd never thought of not coming, that I had nowhere else to go in the whole of England, no friends or relatives and only the prospect of staying in a bed-and-breakfast in Grimsby or sleeping in the back of an old hearse... but I nodded back at her and, ducking through the low branches of ash and silver birch, followed her slim, quick figure through the glade.

She was thirty-something, five or eight years older than me: a pixie-woman who'd dropped out of a tall, dark tree, all scuffed and smudged by twigs and moss and lichen. When we broke out of the shade and into the light of a lawn, when she turned to me again and said, gesturing with a sweep of her arm, 'Let's go in and I'll get us a drink...' a flicker of cloud ran the length of the building in front of me, so that it seemed to shudder as the shadow passed over it. Chalke House: an old hunting-lodge, chalky white and gently rounded like a slab of boulder which had tumbled from the ridge of the wolds and come to rest in the deep, wooded valley. I had time, before we stepped from the lawn and through the wide-open French windows, to look up at the house and see its curiously angled roofs, an eccentric parapet and a kind of tower with crumbling battlements. The shadow of the cloud crawled up and up the tower like a live thing and moved higher and higher across the woodland behind the house. For a second, there was a movement in the window of the tower, the flash of a white face pressed to the glass... and then I was inside, blinded by the darkness of a big, dusty living-room.

The curtains were drawn. In the gloom, she was a fragile, fey figure. She had the advantage, as I dropped my bag and tried to make out the shape and dimensions of the space around me, to press an ice-cold glass into my hand and then sit me down on a soft shabby sofa. One taste of the drink – a gin and tonic – and she was perched so close to me that our knees were almost touching... and she was opening the envelope I'd handed her, my CV and a couple of references, murmuring, 'Borneo? How extraordinary...' and then she was reading aloud, line after line, glancing at me from time to time to see if the impressive, glowing words matched the reality of the person who'd just arrived at her house...

Christopher Beal, a twenty-eight-year-old English teacher, six years in a government secondary school in a logging-town called Marudi, on the Baram river, Sarawak. The reality was me, a tousled ex-pat, jetlagged and a bit hung-over, whose hands shook a little and rattled the ice in the gin and tonic.

She smiled, a sudden snarl of pointed little teeth. It was an odd response to what I'd just told her, that I'd flown home at short notice because my father had had a stroke and moved into a nursing-home. 'He's been a monumental mason all his life,' I was saying, 'carving the names on headstones, re-carving the names on war-graves. That's his car, he converted it into a workshop and...'

But she didn't seem to be listening to me, and I realised that the snarly smile was directed past my face and over my shoulder. I glanced around, thinking that someone had come into the room and was standing silently behind me. But there was no one.

Her eyes flickered beyond me. The smile quivered and vanished from her mouth. 'I'm so sorry,' she said. 'I thought I heard... I mean, I'm sorry to hear about your father.'

She was herself again. She'd been distracted, she'd been elsewhere, somewhere in a dim corner of the dark room. She folded my papers and slipped them back into their envelope. 'So, your father... now that he's settled reasonably comfortably, and you'll be able to go and visit him as often as you like, you can stay here for the summer and be a friend for Lawrence.'

She pulled herself together. A cliché, but that was what she did, she seemed to tug at the outermost corners of her concentration and draw them tightly in, excluding, shutting out, blinkering out anything else which might distract her from the reason I was there.

'That's what Lawrence needs,' she said, 'not a counsellor or an analyst – he's had so many of those that we've lost count and none of them's been any good – and not really a tutor, although that's what I put on the advertisement. He needs someone nice and kind and patient, to be his friend, a kind of brother...'

Her voice tailed away. She swigged from her glass and then swirled the ice cubes round and round at the bottom. We both stood up. She was a head shorter than me, so she tilted her smudged, anxious little face up towards me. She dipped a piece of tissue into the ice-water in her glass and dabbed deftly at the scratches on my forehead. I could smell the gin on her breath and the scent of soap from her skin, as she cleaned my negligible wound. And at the same time she was whispering, 'I don't know how much you've heard about Lawrence. I mean, do you get the news out there, the newspapers? In any case, whatever you've read, whatever you've heard, just be a friend for him. Please, that's all I need, that's all he needs.'

She took me upstairs to meet Lawrence Lundy.

Chapter Three

'HE LIVES IN the tower,' she said.

On the first floor landing of the house, she beckoned me to follow her and disappeared into a narrow spiral staircase. It was cool and dark in there, just wide enough for one person to be going up or down, and the white-washed walls had dropped a powder as fine as talcum on every step. Her little body swayed above me, up and up, and her footsteps were almost silent, just a slip and a slither of friction on the velvet dust. I put out a hand to steady myself against the wall of the staircase, as it wound and wound around me, and I felt the dry powder on my fingertips – indeed, when my arm brushed the wall, the whiteness glimmered on the material of my shirt. It grew darker as we climbed further away from the landing below us, but then, all of a sudden, the woman reached up, pushed open an arched wooden doorway and a pale wash of daylight, clouded with chalky dust, flooded the staircase.

'Lawrence,' she called out, and then drew me up and into a big, sun-filled room. 'Are you there, Lawrence? He's here, the gentleman's arrived...'

The boy turned to face us. He'd been standing at a window with a pair of binoculars pressed to his eyes, but he lowered them on a strap round his neck and crossed the room towards me.

He was as unlike his mother as any son could possibly be. Almost as tall as me, Lawrence Lundy was a sinewy, lanky fifteen-year-old with purple-black, mole-dark hair. His face, unusually narrow and gaunt for a teenage boy, was downy; at least, the light from the window from which he'd been staring shone on the down as he angled his face one way and another. His Adam's apple bobbed and bulged as he said, 'Hello,' in a manly voice, and his handshake was bony. Beside him, his mother looked even smaller than she had before, a pantomime elf clutching the hand of a pantomime ogre. He was dusky-dark, his hair like a pelt, the bristle of his eyebrows and the gleam of his incipient whiskers... while the sunlight caught her bright quick colours as she looked from her son to me with an imploring smile, with the unmistakable plea in her eyes that we should straightaway like each other...

The boy seemed less interested in me than in the smudges on his mother's face. He loomed over her, and, although she tried to fend him off with exasperated swipes of her hands, he feinted at her cheeks and her forehead with his long white fingers. The tower-room was a grand airy space, with wide windows on all four sides, and the views of the woodland valley, right up to the distant ridge of the wolds and further to a hazy, blue horizon, gave the sensation of being in the eyrie of some huge bird of prey. The windows were open, and a breeze was moving and tinkling dozens or even scores of model aircraft which hung from the rafters of the high ceiling... a hundred planes of different shapes and sizes and colours, a myriad squadron which swerved and banked in such a chill wind that it might have come all the way from the faraway coast of the North Sea. A door opened directly onto the odd parapet I'd glimpsed from the lawn – and just then, before I could comment on the unusual, marvellous room and interrupt the woman and her son in their teasing play, there was a sudden commotion...

An orange cat sprang from the parapet and into the room, holding a pigeon in its jaws.

The bird, a wood-pigeon which seemed to be as big as the cat itself, was beating and thrashing with all its strength, and yet the cat tiptoed between the three of us as though we weren't there, sprang effortlessly from the floor onto the boy's unmade bed and pressed the struggling creature deep into the rumpled sheets. In the few seconds it took for any of us to react, the pigeon fought itself out of the jaws of the cat and sculled across the bed, was pounced on and recaptured, shaken violently and pinioned...

The boy, Lawrence, took two long strides to his bed. His mother gave a little squeak, with both her hands pressed to her mouth. He took the cat by the scruff, lifted it from its prey and dropped it unceremoniously onto the floor. Straightaway he had the exhausted pigeon in a close, firm grip. Unable to move, it hissed and panted and stared around the room with bulging, red eyes. In another moment the boy had crossed to the open door, and before his mother could say more than, 'No, Lawrence... I don't think it can...' he'd tossed the bird off the parapet and into mid-air.

'Lawrence, no... it can't...' his mother said again, but it was too late.

Whether the boy had meant to rescue the pigeon by enabling it to flutter into the nearest tree or had simply dumped it out of the tower, it made no difference. He leaned over the parapet and chuckled hoarsely, a dry rasping sound in the back of his throat, 'Go on, fly... go on, fly!' I followed the woman outside, in time to see the bird falling and falling, beating one of its wings pathetically in a futile attempt to remain airborne, wheeling and tumbling until it landed upside down in a nettle-bed and sank into the undergrowth.

Out of the corner of my eye, I saw a flash of brilliant orange... the cat shot out of the tower-room and down the spiral staircase. A moment later, as the boy and his mother and I craned over the parapet, we saw the cat reappear far below us. It sprang out of the house, through the open French windows. It paused on the lawn, long enough to sense and locate the flutter and flap of the broken bird... it must have sensed, in the way that perhaps only implacable killers can do, that the pigeon was fatally crippled... and it strolled nonchalantly across the grass, head down, swaying its hips like a lioness, and slunk at last into the nettle-bed from which the sound of the fluttering was coming.

I was watching the boy, whose friend I was going to be. Lawrence Lundy. The name still meant nothing to me, although I'd seen my father almost apoplectic in his efforts to tell me where he'd heard it or read it before. Quite oblivious of me – indeed, he'd spoken only one word to me and barely glanced in my direction for more than a second or two – the boy now lifted the binoculars to his face and pointed them down to the spot where the bird had crash-landed, where the cat had disappeared.

He was holding his breath. Then he licked his lips and swallowed, so that the bulge in his throat rose and fell and was still again. The smile on his mouth was like a scar. I saw a prickling of tears in his mother's eyes.

Chapter Four

I'D SEEN THE advertisement pinned up in a newsagent's stall on Lincoln station.

I'd got off the train there to make the connection to Grimsby. With a few minutes to spare, I'd bought a newspaper and a chocolate bar and scanned the notice-board for the possibility of renting a bed-sitting-room or a cottage or even a caravan to use as my base while I was settling my father into his home. There was a hand-written note on water-marked paper, large, cursive letters from the broad nib of a fountain-pen: 'Home tutor needed for a teenage boy, to live as part of the family in a comfortable, quiet, country house. Chalke House, 0392 0897.' Straightaway, on an impulse, I'd used the handful of change the newsagent had given me to make the call from the telephone kiosk on the platform.

The Grimsby train was pulling in. The station loudspeaker started blaring. The call-box swallowed coin after coin. I shouted my name and the purpose of my call into the receiver and could barely make out the breathless voice of a woman suggesting I visit as soon as I could make it, even tomorrow, Monday, and some directions for me to find the house... 'Lawrence, my son's name is Lawrence Lundy, he's fifteen and...' The voice was so faint I could hardly hear it. My coins ran out. The train was going to leave. No more than a minute since I'd first read the advertisement, I was scrambling onto the train for Grimsby, with the dim notion of a job and even a home for the coming summer months.

*   *   *

'YOU WERE VERY brave to come at all,' the woman was saying.

Juliet Lundy, the imp from the tree-tops, had bathed and changed into a loose cotton robe. I'd showered in my own bathroom, adjoining a spare bedroom which looked across the dark brown pond and into the woodland. A cool twilit evening... the French windows were still open, and she was nestling on the sofa with her feet tucked underneath her. It was a large, untidy, comfortably dusty lounge; the inside of the house was covered with a powdering of chalky dust which sighed and sifted with every breath and movement of the building's inhabitants. After a sherry, we'd eaten lamb sandwiches, apparently the leftovers from the previous day's Sunday lunch, but delicious with a minty salad and a bottle of red wine.

Dusk gathered around the house. The darkness crept out of the surrounding woodland, folded onto the tower, the battlements, the obliquely angled roofs of Chalke House and all its softly rounded corners. The room was pleasantly gloomy. The only light was a shaded lamp in the corner and a paraffin lamp just outside, where the boy was sitting and reading.

'I meant it when I said I didn't think you'd turn up,' the woman went on. 'Yesterday, on the phone, you could hardly hear a word I was saying, and you were shouting over that awful loudspeaker. When you didn't try to call again, I thought you weren't interested. But you came, so thank you for that.' She made a vague gesture of toasting me with her wine glass. 'If you want to stay for a few days or a week and see what we're like, that's all I can really expect.'

I frowned, about to demur, genuinely puzzled by her insistence that I'd performed some unexpected feat of bravery by turning up at her house. She glanced across the room and caught the eye of her son. Lawrence had been poring over an old aviation magazine, he hadn't seemed to be listening at all. But all of a sudden he prickled himself upright in his chair and was staring hard at his mother... as if he was assessing the implications of everything she was saying and was ready to stop her if she said something wrong. So now she pulled a face at him, turned back to me and tried a joke. 'I mean, you hadn't even got out of your car and I'd thrown a hammer at you. Not very welcoming, but not entirely my fault. It isn't every day a hearse comes rolling into the garden...'

The boy bent over his magazine again. Earlier, I'd had some success with him. Through mouthfuls of cold lamb and mint jelly, in answer to my gentle questioning and encouraged to answer by his mother, he'd told me he'd been at school in Alford, not so far away from Chalke House; he hadn't liked the teachers or his fellow pupils, he'd asked and then persuaded his mother to take him out of school. 'Just before last Christmas,' he was mumbling, 'I made a mess of my exams, I failed them all, and then there was a bit of trouble with some other boys and I...'

She'd stopped him in mid-sentence, with a gentle hand on his arm. 'Don't try to eat and talk at the same time, dear. There'll be plenty of opportunity for Christopher to get to know you properly.'

It was a mutual, reciprocal thing. They watched each other and they listened, almost breathless with waiting, waiting for a slip-up or a giveaway. That was what it sounded like, on that long, slow, first evening at Chalke House with Juliet and Lawrence Lundy. Now, leaving the lamp burning outside, the boy came in. I talked about Borneo, the weeks and months of an ex-patriate teacher in a small town in Sarawak, the kind of boys and girls I was teaching, their hopes and expectations, their lifestyle, their lives... Another bottle of wine, the windows wide open on a cool, black night, the wind in the high trees and the bubbling call of a tawny owl... and as I talked a little more, the woman and her son sat side by side on their sofa and sank deeper into the soft, shabby cushions.

They wanted me to talk. And I started to understand why. Not because they were fascinated or even mildly intrigued by my descriptions of another world so many thousands of miles away, but because it saved them from talking. They could relax. They didn't have to guard what each other was saying. Whatever secrets they were keeping from me – and I kept seeing, from time to time on the blank screen of my mind, an image of my father's tormented face, the gleam of fear in his eyes as he scoured his memory for the meaning of the name I'd given him – while I was talking they were safe in their own silence.

I was suddenly very tired. A cockchafer whirred through the window and butted noisily against the lampshade in the corner of the room. For a moment, my mouth was ready to begin a sensational account of the bugs and beetles, snakes and crocodiles I'd encountered along the banks of the Baram river, but my head was too weary. The boy was watching the cockchafer, his mouth curiously agape. The lamplight accentuated the unusual swarthiness of his face. He looked somehow nocturnal. He was scenting the air, tasting it, as though the beetle had brought the spirit of the night into the house. Indeed, he opened his mouth and his tongue shone with saliva, as if he might snap at the insect and swallow it down. His eyes gleamed as he followed its erratic, bumbling flight, as it bashed and buzzed around the room and back to the inescapable lure of the lamp.

And then he stood up. In a couple of loping strides he'd crossed to the lamp and caught the cockchafer in his hands. He cupped it there, held his hands to one ear and then the other, and he listened as it roared and raged in its prison. He didn't offer it to his mother or to me, as an adult might do by way of a conversation piece. It was nothing to do with us, nothing to do with anybody except himself. He was curiously alone, alone with the beetle, as though they were the only living things in all of that soft spring night.

He crossed to the French windows. He stepped outside. As if to release the creature into the darkness.

No. He opened his hands and dropped the beetle into the glass bowl of the paraffin lamp.

For a mad second, it fizzled furiously around the flame. Then it ignited. An explosion of green and gold, it plopped into the paraffin and fizzed into a whiff of blue smoke.

THE TORPOR OF the house was on me, and the weight of all the hours of travelling. I could hardly remember going up to my room, escorted to the door by the solicitous woman. I slept so deeply that a kind of vacuum sucked all my thoughts and dreams away and left me lying in a state of death-like nothingness...

And yet, when I awoke in the middle of the night and stared around the room, unable to remember where on earth I was, I was suddenly and utterly conscious. Not a shred, not the tiniest cobweb of sleep clung to me, as I swung my feet out of bed and stood up. Something had woken me, aroused me from the deathliness of my sleep.

There was a movement at my window and I crossed the room to look out.

It was a movement I'd seen the previous afternoon, when I'd first arrived at the house. Not the flash of a falling, metallic object... not the dazzle of sunlight through the branches of a tall tree... but a crawling shadow, the shadow which had crawled like a live thing across the building and over the hills. Now, the same movement led my eyes from the sill of my window into the garden below me.

Bright moonlight. A moon-shadow. Cast by a rag of cloud, it slid across the sky and dissolved into nothing.

The moon quivered in the dark waters of the pond. The cloud-shadow had gone. It had become a figure, which moved across the lawn in stealthy silence.

The boy. He stopped, and his own shadow was a pool of blackness, lapping around his feet. I froze at the window when he turned his face upwards. But he didn't look at the house, he didn't look at me, he stared at the moon until the whiteness of it blanched his skin. Then he trod swiftly across the lawn, the shadow flickering around and beneath him, until he came to the deep cover of a nettle-bed.

It was the very spot where the pigeon had fallen. As lithe as the cat which had pursued its stricken prey, as smoothly as though his own shadow were a coating of oil, he simply folded himself into the undergrowth and disappeared completely. He was gone. I waited for him to emerge, looked for any swaying or stirring of the tall nettles, but there was no movement and he did not reappear. He was gone, as if he and his shadow were drowned forever.

But, just as I was turning from the window to collapse onto the bed, the boy reappeared from the nettles. He was carrying something, a loose grey bundle which overflowed his hands as he walked with it towards the edge of the pond.

He paused there, the moonlight on his face, and a big silvery moon floating in the black water. When he coiled himself like a spring, wound himself up and then uncoiled and hurled his bundle high into the night air, I could see for a second that it was the remains of the pigeon... a rag of grey feathers and a hollow carcase.

It splashed onto the water, and the moon was shattered into a million shimmering fragments. Only for a moment... exerting its mighty magnetic pull upon its own pieces, the moon drew itself splendidly together and was whole again. It folded and rippled for another minute, until the surface of the water was still.

From my upstairs window, I watched it happen. The boy stood and watched it from the edge of the pond. The bird floated, sinking slowly as the mat of feathers and gristle became waterlogged...

But then, before it sank completely from sight, there was a sudden, sinewy swirling in the pond.

A whirlpool... no, a kind of black hole appeared and gaped and sucked and... and the pigeon was gone. The pond, or something greedy and muscular from deep inside it, swallowed the remains of the bird.

The boy had gone too. When I drew my heavy eyes from the moon in the water to the place where he'd been standing, there was nothing. No boy, no shadow, only a few grey feathers which had fallen from his hands.

I blinked and stared. I must have been dreaming. As sudden and as sweet as morphine, once more the deathliness of sleep was on me. The weight of my limbs and my head was almost too much to support.

I crossed back to the bed and fell onto it.

Chapter Five

THE BOY WAS still scratching at the blebs on his hands and wrists a few days later. He had a swipe of white blisters across his face too. I knew where and when he'd got the nettle stings, but he'd fended off his mother's questions by telling her he'd been looking for birds' nests in the garden; he said he thought there was a flycatcher starting to build on the brick wall of the derelict greenhouse, and he'd been pushing through the undergrowth to get a closer look. The boy and I were in his room in the tower. We'd started, rather shyly and hesitantly at first, to do some of the 'home tutoring' that ostensibly I'd been hired to do. He fidgeted and itched, and he read aloud to me from *Lord of the Flies*, a text he'd been studying at school before he'd persuaded his mother to take him away.

He read beautifully. Odd, because he was still very curt, off-hand, when I tried to engage him in conversation about himself and his home, his family, school and so on. When I asked him to suggest some of the themes of the book, he looked at me as though I was the most predictable and boring of all the teachers he'd ever had, stifled a yawn and started to drawl contemptuously, 'War, survival, isolation, the loss of innocence, death...' a list he'd had to learn at school and trot out for homework or exams. I managed to stop him with my own loud theatrical yawn. And then, when I asked him to choose a passage in the book, a crisis which illustrated one of these themes, he turned straightaway to a well-thumbed page and read slowly, relishing the brilliant clarity of the words... the death of Piggy, the fat little boy hit by an enormous boulder, his body falling and falling through space and smashing onto the rocks below...

He itched at his wrists. The blebs were tiny white blisters on the purpling of his veins. Beside him, on the rumpled bed where he was sprawling, the orange cat sprawled too. It lay flat on its back, ridiculously asleep: legs splayed, eyes tightly closed, head thrown back, its breath whistling through bared fangs. I watched the boy and listened to his reading: he and the killer-cat side by side, accomplices in the capture, defenestration and death of the gentle pigeon.

He finished reading. In my mind's eye, Piggy lay broken on the rocks, until a wave rolled over him and the sea sucked his body away.

Now, a cool breeze blew through the open windows of the tower. The squadrons of aircraft clattered together, and for the first time in the few days I'd been at Chalke House, Lawrence volunteered to speak to me. If only to divert me from the book – a book he'd done to death in a classroom he'd hated, with boys he'd hated, with a teacher he'd hated – he glanced up to the ceiling and said, 'That's a Phantom, the green one, the fighter with the RAF roundel... it's what my Dad flies, out of Coningsby.'

Of all the hundred planes hanging from the rafters, I could only have identified a handful. Never an enthusiast as a boy, never interested in planes or cars or steam engines, I glanced up too and said, 'I haven't got a clue, Lawrence. Let me see...' I pointed with my thumb. 'That's a Lancaster bomber, and there's a Spitfire, and is that a Mosquito? Oh, and the airliner, the white one with the blue stripe, is that a Comet?' I scanned around the rafters of the high room. 'Green one? I don't see it... which one do you mean?'

He reacted explosively. One moment he was a drawling teenager lying limp and exhausted on his bed... and then he bounced onto his feet, reaching up, reaching up, his face suddenly clouded with a rushing of blood into his cheeks. The cat was out of the room in one long orange streak. The boy grabbed one of the planes, wrenched it off its thread and flung it onto the floor. It smashed into pieces.

'Green!' he was hissing at me. 'Didn't I say the green one? The Phantom he flies out of Coningsby!'

He was calm again. The blood drained out of his face. His skin was as white as before, with only a residual blotchiness where the nettles had blistered him. He stepped off the bed and busied himself picking up the pieces of the shattered aircraft. 'I can fix it, I can fix it,' he was saying to himself, and then he turned to look at me over his shoulder, as though he'd suddenly remembered I was there, and he said more loudly, 'I can fix it, I'm good at fixing things, it's only a model.'

He sat on the bed with the fragments in his hands. He spread them across the blanket and rearranged them, the bits of a puzzle, like an archaeologist about to reassemble the fossilised bones of a dinosaur he'd unearthed. His calmness was rather unnerving. I watched his hands, the long, white, bony fingers, as if I would detect a tremor or a twitch, some aftershock of anger. There was none. There was no quaver in his voice, when he said to me, 'My mum will tell you. She'll explain it all, I guess. I get angry. That's why I'm here right now, that's why I'm at home and not at school. That's why you're here.'

Indeed. I wanted to tell him – to counter his burst of anger with a show of my own resentment of what he'd said – that I was there because I'd chosen to come, that I was staying of my own free will and not because I'd been summoned by his mother to take charge of her spoilt, solitary son. But I held my breath and didn't say anything. For one reason, I knew from my experience of teaching how a few cross words too soon in a new relationship with pupils could make things prickly for weeks or even months; and furthermore, the matter-of-fact way the boy had spoken, without a trace of rancour in his voice, made me hold my tongue.

As though he could read my thoughts, he turned his face towards me as he re-aligned the pieces of the plane on his bed, and with a quick, charming smile he said, 'I'm sorry. I get angry. That's all you need to know about me for the time being.'

I followed him across the room to the open window. He picked up the binoculars and handed them to me. I held them to my eyes, readjusted the focus and looked as far as the silvery horizon. 'On a clear day you can see the sea,' he was saying, 'and sometimes the planes taking off and coming back to Coningsby, where my Dad flies from...'

I instinctively dipped the glasses when the top of the Scots pine blurred my view of the further distance. I changed the focus and followed the bristly blackness of the tree down and down to the very base of the trunk. The orange cat was sunbathing on the bonnet of the hearse. For a second, a spangle of light from the crazed windscreen dazzled me so that I held the binoculars away from my face and rubbed my eyes. It gave the boy the chance to take the glasses from me and put them back on the window-sill.

'The garden and everything, I'll show you. Come on.' He gestured me to follow him out of the room and down the stairs.

It was May. The woodland was busy with birdsong, and everywhere was bursting with the fresh greenery of brambles and nettles and sweet new grasses. And yet, somehow, a whispering uneasiness seemed to lie among the rambling acres of Chalke House. Despite the fanfare of the wren, despite the watery song of the robin and the fluting of the blackbird, the morning threw a smothering gauziness among the trees and across the overgrown lawns. The songs of the birds were oddly muted by something in the air... and as the boy and I strolled further from the house where the cover of the trees grew denser still, I began to feel it was he, the boy, who wore a cloak of stillness, his own space, his own quietness, which damped all the sounds around him.

We paused at the lake, whose edges were fringed with a bed of reeds.

'Pike...' he said, and his eyes flickered over me as if he'd almost forgotten I was there and he couldn't remember who I was. 'My Dad told me there's a pike in the lake, a monster, maybe a hundred years old... he told me he caught it once, when I was a baby, and he put it back into the water because it was so huge, so old, such a marvellous monster he couldn't not put it back where it belongs.'

He stared across the still, green water.

'So deep,' he said, more to himself than to me, 'no one knows how deep it is, no one knows how big the pike is now, how old it really is.'

He turned and looked at me. With a defiant cast in his eye, as though to pre-empt a display of schoolteacherly knowledge from his new tutor, he added, 'But I know that the pike is there, and it's a monster, and it's a hundred years old, because my father's seen it and he's told me. I don't need to see it for myself or read about it in books.'

'We won't just read books, Lawrence,' I reassured him, as we walked away from the pond and closer to the Scots pine. 'Your mother didn't want me to come and do lots of the same old schoolwork with you, all the stuff you've been doing at school. I'll just stay a while, just as long as you're both happy to have me here, and as long as I'm happy to be here, and we'll talk, or not talk, and maybe we'll get to know each other a bit better. Or maybe we won't.'

I took his elbow to make him stop walking ahead of me, to make sure he was hearing what I was saying. 'Lawrence, you don't have to tell me anything about yourself, either you or your mother, that you don't want me to know.'

He looked at me with his head slightly on one side – a dark beady eye, the pelt of his hair as dense and glossy as an otter's – oddly unsure of what I was saying. So I added, 'Lawrence, I haven't come here to try and solve you, like a puzzle. If we get on alright, that's good. If we don't, then I'll move on. A few days ago I'd never heard of you or knew you existed.'

'I don't believe you,' he said. 'Everyone's heard of me.' He glanced down at my hand so that I let go of his arm, and he spun away from me, through the shade of the woodland.

Lawrence Lundy. I remembered how my father had struggled to recall the name, how he'd chiselled the letters onto thin air, seen them hovering in front of his eyes as though they were carved onto cold, hard stone. Lawrence Lundy. The name meant nothing to me.

The cat stood up on the bonnet of the Daimler. It stretched luxuriously as the boy stroked it from the top of its head to the very tip of its tail. Then it had had enough. It slipped off the car and slunk into the long grass, parting the tall blades with its nose and snaking its hips deeper in and in and disappearing. The boy fingered the shattered windscreen, the edges of the hole which the hammer had smashed into the car.

'What was your mother doing up there?' I asked him, with a jerk of my head up into the branches of the pine tree. She had already told me, the previous evening. So he answered, with that odd curl of a smile on his lips, not quite a sneer, 'You mean you didn't ask her? You arrived here and she dropped a hammer onto your car from high up in a tree and you didn't ask her what she was doing up there?' The smile slid off his mouth, as sudden as the slither of the cat from the bonnet of the car. 'She told me she was hoping you'd ask me. She knew you would. She was up there trying to fix my tree-house. I think she already thinks you'll have a go at helping her.'

I did a deliberately comic blink at the roundabout way in which the information was being imparted. 'I like to go up there,' he went on. 'It's the view from my tower, only better. Not really a tree-house, but a kind of platform right at the top. My Dad built it so that I could see the planes as they take off from Coningsby and come back in. He likes to know that I'm watching him. He waggles his wings a bit when he comes in, so I know it's him and he's back safe and sound from manoeuvres...'

I was opening the back of the hearse, for no real reason except to let in a bit of air or maybe intrigue the boy to keep on talking. He'd been talking about his father, so I thought he might be interested in mine, not a dashing daredevil who hurtled himself through the skies in a million-pounds worth of jet plane, but a cranky old man who'd spent his life hunched over the gravestones of a hundred cemeteries or peering over the huge black steering wheel of a hearse.

Lawrence leaned into the gloom of the car and he sniffed. Then he inhaled very slowly, holding each breath in his chest for a second before letting it out of his nose again... slowly, as though to capture the scent in the whiskery tunnels of his nostrils. He inhaled and exhaled a few times, like a bear or a badger investigating the lair of another creature it had discovered on its territory, almost as though, having gathered all the information he could from the smells in this strange dark den, he would cock a leg and piss onto the mottled paintwork of the hearse...

He didn't, of course. He cocked his head, politely, like a jackdaw listening to an unfamiliar sound – or, for me just back from Borneo, like a mynah trying to catch the strangeness of a sound in order to mimic it – as I told him about my father's work as a mason and the purpose of having the Daimler as his workshop and hidey-hole and home-on-wheels. The boy was attentive and deferential. Indeed, he affected the mannerisms of a grown-up so exactly that I wasn't sure whether he was really interested or just humouring me... he examined the tools in the tool-box, handling them very carefully as if they were my most precious family heirlooms, he hefted them from hand to hand and sniffed the oil on their blades and the decades of sweat ingrained into their wooden handles, he stroked the nap on the leathery gloves and...

When he unfolded the flaps of the cardboard box – a boring old cardboard box which had been shoved into a corner by the couch – he recoiled from it as if there was a cobra coiled inside it.

And then he was off. Before I could come out with a sudden 'What's up?' or 'Hey Lawrence, what's the matter?' he'd spun away from the car and was striding very fast and purposefully through the woodland, back towards the house. He paused and turned once, as though he'd bethought himself for being rude, and he shouted... not words, but a braying kind of noise such as grown-ups make when they leave a room to answer a telephone or switch off a forgotten frying-pan. In any case, he was gone in a moment.

The grasses and nettles swished where he'd hurried off. And then the woodland was utterly still.

I peered into the cardboard box which seemed to have startled the boy so much. No cobra. Only a heap of newspapers, a glimpse of headlines about a miners' strike, a sensational murder, a Hollywood divorce...

I swung the door of the hearse shut. It was so heavy, the hinges so sweetly oiled, that it closed itself with a click. There was no other sound in the fragrant shade of the Scots pine.

Except... except... another sound I hadn't heard for more than a year. A favourite of mine, which I didn't know I'd missed so much during my sultry perpetual summer in Borneo. A favourite sound of an English summer.

The swifts. I peered up and up through the branches of the pine. High in the pale blue sky, the swifts were hurtling and screaming, screaming their lungfuls of screams in giddy, madcap flight.

Chapter Six

'YOUR FACE IS better.'

I was in the kitchen with Juliet. She'd made me coffee and toast for breakfast and she was doing some baking. She'd taken two rings off her wedding finger and dropped them into an egg cup on a shelf behind her, and she was spreading flour all over the big wooden table. She'd already managed to dab her face with powdery smudges, and now she was starting to make her mixture in a glass bowl.

I hid a smile in my mug of coffee. Everything she did, since I'd first met her dangling out of the tree with moss and pine needles in her hair, seemed childishly untidy and slapdash, in the way that a puppy or a very young kitten might leave its own trail of untidiness. But nice. I liked her and I liked the house, its carelessly comfortable, lived-in feeling. And now, in her country-kitchen, as she stood at the wide table and swept it with flour, she looked again like an elf or a pixie of the household, somehow too small for the place, but busy and quick and... and messy. I couldn't help smiling, managed not to burst out laughing, at the way she pushed the hair out of her eyes and left her forehead ghostly with flour, her hair like a mist of cobwebs. And yet, despite the mess she was making, there was a cavalier expertise in her movements... she'd done it all many times before, and the end result, the scones she was assembling, would no doubt be delicious.

She blinked at me, frowned. She knew I was amused. 'Your face is better,' she said, to change the focus of attention from her to me. 'It was just a scratch. Could've been a lot worse, if you'd got some glass in your eyes...'

She crossed the kitchen towards me and peered closer. She had flour on her lashes. 'You're alright now. But I don't suppose you'll ever get the windscreen fixed, will you? I mean, how do you find parts for a car like that? What year is it? Something from the 50s or 60s?'

'Don't worry about the car,' I said. I finished off my coffee and toast and carried the mug and plate to the sink. I was going to go upstairs and try to engage Lawrence, or at least see if he was awake and out of bed. After all, it was a bright morning at the end of May, it was going to be a hotter and hotter day, and that was why I was there, in Chalke House in Lincolnshire, to engage a troubled teenage boy and be some kind of mentor for him. I couldn't just sit in the kitchen watching an attractively fey, dizzy woman making scones. 'Don't worry about the car. It's not going anywhere, not at the moment. And my father's never going to need it again.' I added, to smooth over any guilt she might be feeling about the damage she'd caused and also just to sound helpful, 'You must have a car here, if you ever want me to run out and get anything...?'

She'd made the scones and put them on a tray, into the oven. She said, 'It's round the back of the house. I go out as seldom as possible, just to do a big shop that'll last us for weeks. I don't want to go out, nor does Lawrence. And anyway, the car's a mess.'

As I rinsed my mug in the sink, she stood beside me and rinsed the flour off her hands. We shared the same flow of water from the cold tap. Our hands touched. Our hips touched. A bit awkward, so I thought of something to say, 'I could take a look, if you like? Check the oil and water and stuff?'

'No.' She said it too sharply. 'No, don't.'

She turned away. I watched her as she reached for the egg cup and slipped her rings back onto her finger. It prompted me to ask, 'And where is your husband? Lawrence has mentioned his father a few times...'

'Sit down,' she said. 'I'll make you another coffee. Lawrence won't be up yet. You don't have to clock in and start work, like you do in your school in Borneo.'

So we sat opposite one another at the table and drank coffee. It didn't take long for her to tell me what had happened, only long enough for me to take a few sips and burn my lips and for the smell of the cooking scones to fill the kitchen. Last autumn, her husband had taken off on a routine training flight, a Tuesday morning, the 13th September, with two other Phantoms... and as she talked she drew into the flour on the table with her left forefinger, to illustrate what had happened. A dot in the flour for the air-base at RAF Coningsby, a line in the flour to the coast, the line continuing across a powdery white sea, and then a sudden angry squiggle where her husband's plane had impacted with the water, smashed into pieces and sunk.

She looked across the table at me. 'Missing, presumed dead. One moment he was on a regular sortie... the other pilots said it was a clear, calm day and they were going out to sea and up the coast... and then he was gone.' Again she squiggled into the flour, to mark the spot where the plane had vanished. 'They couldn't explain it. They'd circled back to see what had happened, seen nothing on the surface but a slick of oil... he'd just gone. There was a lot of searching. They opened an enquiry.' She made one big circle around the scribble into which her husband had disappeared. 'Missing, presumed dead. The enquiry was closed.'

There was a long silence. We both sipped our coffee. The kitchen door opened and the boy came in. He was tousled and bleary, in a t-shirt and shorts, straight out of bed. He paused for a moment to appraise the scene and then went across to where his mother was sitting and stood behind her. As he squinted and frowned at the mysteriously chaotic diagram on the table, he put his hands on her shoulders, moved them closer to her neck. He looked very big, his face pale and unsmiling. She looked very small, more like a little sister than his mother, and somehow vulnerable. He loomed over her and his white bony fingers tightened near her throat. She didn't cringe, at the weight of his hands or the sinewy maleness he was exerting over her, but neither did she relax as one might relax at the first caress of a masseur.

'So what's all this?' he said. He bent so close to her that her hair fluttered when he whispered the same words again. 'So what's all this, Mummy? What've you been telling my new teacher? Telling him a story?'

He took an enormous breath, inhaling long and slowly and holding the air in his chest for a long time. And then, at last, he blew with all his strength. The flour puthered up and up from the table. For a few seconds, until his breath ran out, there was a white powdery haboob in the middle of the room. He stopped and the dust settled.

'End of story,' he said. There was nothing but a smooth film of flour on the table: a ghostly palimpsest.

He crossed to the oven, opened it, snatched a tea-towel and lifted out the tray of scones. They looked perfect, they smelled delicious. Juliet slid some of them onto a plate and told us to take them upstairs to the tower.

I WAS PUZZLING over what the woman had told me, unsure whether or not to broach the subject with the boy, feeling a knot of nervous apprehension in my stomach as I climbed the narrow stairs behind and followed him into his room. I didn't know what we were going to do that morning, if we were going to read or listen to some music or share some ideas from a newspaper or magazine; the account of his father's death had left me quite unready for any kind of structured tutoring of the boy. So I was relieved when he just gestured me to sit down in an old armchair by the open balcony window, and he set about re-assembling the model aeroplane he'd smashed the other day.

I watched him and I wondered what he was thinking. He bent his head and gulped his Adam's apple and examined the shards of plastic he'd spread all over his bed. Obviously he didn't want to talk to me or listen to me talking. Perhaps, as he applied himself to the rebuilding of the toy, he was imagining the wreckage of the real Phantom which would never be mended, which had disappeared to the bottom of the North Sea with the body of his father.

I ate a scone. I looked out of the window, past the Scots pine and the spars of the tree-house in it, towards the horizon where the coast might be, where my father would be. I pictured him so vividly in his room in the nursing-home that I could conjure the smell of him and his things. How odd, I thought, for me to be sitting in this strange tower, in this strange house, with a strange boy I'd never met until a week ago... to have flown thousands of miles from Borneo to settle my own father, and now to find my head fuddled with someone else's worry and frustration. For a moment it rankled with me, the unfairness. I should've done it myself... I mean, before the boy had come into the kitchen and erased the complicated mess his mother had made on the table, I should've done it myself. I should've stood up and stopped her talking. I should've swept the flour from the table with one swipe of my hand and reminded her I'd come back to England to comfort my own father, not her, not her son...

Screaming. Screaming outside. So high-pitched that it was more like a whistle than a scream. An alien sound. Inhuman.

Something, a black projectile, hurtled through the open window and into the room.

The boy leapt off the bed and scattered the splinters of plastic onto the floor. I clenched my hand on the scone so suddenly that it exploded into crumbs.

A swift. The bird had swerved through the window, and now it was battering and beating hopelessly among the model planes which dangled from the ceiling. And screaming a pathetic rasping scream, so hoarse and high that it scratched at the very limit of human hearing...

The boy stood up on his bed. Like a silly kid in his t-shirt and pants, he bounced up and down and flailed his hands at the bird, as though to swat it like a shuttlecock. He clapped at it, as though he might catch it, or crush it. 'Leave it, Lawrence, leave it...' I was calling to him, 'just leave it and it'll find its way out...' but he bounced like a child and giggled in a manic high-pitched way, a sound as alien as the weakening screams of the swift. The bird snagged its long black wings among the invisible threads of nylon. Entangled for a moment, it writhed and freed itself and cut at the wings of the green and grey toys. The planes clattered together. There was an oddly musical clacking of hollow plastic and the mad, feeble fluttering of the bird.

'For heaven's sake, Lawrence, just leave the thing!' And as he sprang off the bed and loomed towards me, his eyes flaring with anger, the bird flopped from the ceiling. I'd seen a split-second of an uncontrollable threat in his face... but the fall of the swift, the way it spiralled softly down and crash-landed on the bed with nothing but a puff of sound, made both of us turn and stare and forget each other.

We sat on the bed and leaned over it, the two of us.

Exhausted. Dying? The swift lay on the bed-cover, heaving so hard that its little chest might burst. Black, uniformly black... no, the darkest, deepest brown, its plumage as smooth as the richest, most expensive chocolate... sooty-black, as we bent over it and took away the light. A slim tubular body, perfectly aerodynamic. Wings so long, longer than its body, like scythes for cutting and carving and slicing the air. The swift: the ultimate flying-machine, more exquisitely refined for flying than any device a man could ever dream.

I glanced at the boy. He was aghast. I don't think he was breathing. Every part of his being, apart from his eyes which goggled at the creature which had hurtled into his room and bedazzled the pathetic plastic things he'd hung on his ceiling before exhausting itself almost to death... every other part of him was stopped. I don't think he was breathing. I think his heart might have stopped beating.

Then he touched the bird. With the tip of one finger he felt where the breast was heaving. He stroked the length of one wing. He touched the feet, the nothing-feet, almost nothing but the feeblest of claws. He stroked the wide whiskery mouth, from which the screams had come until all of its breath was gone. He marvelled at the swift, for it was truly marvellous.

And, before our eyes, it seemed to fill itself with life again. It was a kind of miracle. Somehow, by a strange magic of its own, a kind of magnetism of the life-force which it could feel in the air of an English springtime, the bird drew into its tiny, mighty body the energy it needed to live again.

Like an injured butterfly, it manoeuvred its wings free and clapped them above its body. It tried to take off, but maybe the bedding was too soft beneath its belly, too yielding of even its almost-weightlessness, and it was too cosily sunk into it. Again, and a third time, the bird clapped its wings. But it couldn't get any purchase on the air.

So I made to pick it up. The boy, remembering to breathe, said, 'No, I want it.'

I ignored him. I cupped the bird very gently, allowing the wings to fall clear of my fingers, stood up and carried it towards the balcony window. The boy, so close behind me that I could smell his sleepy unwashed body, said again, 'No, I want it... what are you doing?'

And when I placed the swift on the parapet outside, high above the garden and the pond and level with the foliage of the trees and the towering pine, he clamped his hand onto mine. He was very strong. He was as tall as me. His eyes stared into mine, empty, blank, and his breath was stale. I felt a lurch in my belly, as though I'd been picked up and dropped into a place I hadn't been for as long as I could remember. Fear... a small dark space in my being... a feeling I'd almost forgotten in the comfortable years of my lucky life.

His hand was heavier still. It was clammy and cold. 'I want the bird. It came into my room, in my house.'

'Yes, it's your room, Lawrence, and it's your house,' I said, 'but it isn't your bird.' I heard a tremor in my voice. I licked my lips and went on. 'So take your hand off my hand, and we'll let the bird go free. If you're interested in the swifts there's a lot we can talk about, and we can watch them, we can learn about them from up here in your wonderful tower. But this little thing, this lovely living thing has the whole of the summer ahead of it and then a long way to go in the autumn.'

He lifted his hand off mine. He stepped back. I lifted my hand away from the swift.

It had had time to gather its energy, to steady its breathing and calm the air in its lungs. As though it was the most natural thing for a living creature to do, it simply rolled off the parapet. It fell like a rag for a yard or two, and then scissored its wings. This time, with nothing to hinder its perfection, the bird rocketed up and up into the blue until it was no more than a speck.

A speck, beyond our vision. A scream, beyond our hearing.

Lawrence watched it go. Then he spun away from me and back into the room. Over his shoulder he muttered something. I half-heard what he said, half-understood.

'What did you say, Lawrence? I didn't catch...' He shrugged and sat on his bed again, feeling on the floor for the broken pieces of his model plane. Above his head, the toys on their nylon threads were swaying silently in the breeze, never touching, as though their make-believe air-space had never been invaded.

I went out of the room. As I trod down the stairs from the tower, I suddenly realised what he'd said to me. The words came to me so clearly that I stopped in the shadows and listened to them inside my head. 'I'll tell my father what you did. When he comes back, I'll tell him.'

Chapter Seven

NEEDING TO GET out of the house and away from the woman and the boy, I went down to the bottom of the garden.

When I left Lawrence in his tower, I'd first of all gone to my room, thinking to sit and think in my own space, or to lie on my bed and wonder at what she and he had said to me that morning. But it wasn't my space, it wasn't my room, it wasn't my bed, it was a bedroom assigned to me by a couple of strangers in their strange house. I needed to connect myself with something that was really mine, away from this muddle of dusty back-stories and muttered half-secrets.

So I flung myself out of the room and downstairs. I tiptoed past the kitchen where Juliet was clattering so noisily at the sink that she couldn't possibly have heard me go by, and outside through the French windows of the lounge.

Down the garden, to the car. My father's car.

Nothing to do with the Lundy family, nothing to do with the otherworld of Chalke House buried in the folds of the Lincolnshire wolds. I needed, for a short while, to touch – yes, physically touch – the reason why I'd come back to England.

Even in the week or two since I'd arrived, the grasses had grown fast and thick around the wheels of the Daimler. The bodywork, already so matt and dull, a grey-green patina where the paint had long ago been black, was dusted with a fall of bark and twigs from the Scots pine. I passed a hand over the windscreen, where the glass had been smashed by the impact of the claw-hammer, and picked off clumps of needles. The car looked very tired, and oddly disconsolate.

The enormous chrome radiator had bloomed a rash of rust, and the orbs of the headlamps were like tearful eyes.

'Hey, what's up, old girl? Did you think I'd left you here for good? Hey, you got a long way to go yet...'

But my voice sounded small and unconvincing. There was a quaver of uncertainty. I looked up into the blackened gantry of the pine, through the scaffold of branches which jutted from the towering trunk. I swivelled and stared high into the overwhelming foliage of the beech trees, the mature oak and chestnut which blotted the sky... and all around me, into the suffocating tangle of undergrowth, the dense barricades of nettle and cow-parsley and formidable bramble. The bottom of the garden? No, not a garden, but an acre or three of ancient English woodland, a shut-in world of its own, shutting out the rest of the world. But yes, the bottom. No wonder the car looked so forlorn, so crushed... as I looked up and around me, I remembered the last few miles of our journey, the descent from the clarity of the Lincolnshire farmland and its marvellous sky, down into the shadows of the wooded wolds, and down and down as though we'd stumbled into a hole and it was sucking us deeper...

At last, my own space. I opened the driver's door and slid onto the seat, behind the big black steering-wheel. When the door fell shut with a snick of its well-oiled hinges, when I closed my eyes and inhaled the familiar scents of the old car, I had my own space again: thousands of miles from Borneo, and a long way from the puzzles of Juliet and Lawrence Lundy. Everything I touched in the car, the soles of my shoes on his pedals, through the seat of my pants and my spine on his leather upholstery, to my hands on his wheel... it was the touch of my father.

I could smell him. I could feel him. His son – me – I was sitting exactly in the place in the world he had made and claimed for himself.

But what was the good of that? I shook myself out of my cosy daydream. I hadn't flown back so I could sit in a hearse and think about my father. He was alive and breathing and real and only a few miles away. 'Hey old girl... hey, we gotta look after you, make sure you're good to go. Maybe not today, or even tomorrow, but let's make sure you're up and running. We might want to get out of here.'

In a moment I'd felt for a lever under the steering-wheel and pinged open the bonnet. I slipped out of the car, moved around to the chromium radiator and heaved the bonnet open. A cavernous space, sooty and oily... the mighty engine, lovely, ugly, a mysterious mass of machinery, a Daimler which had swished hundreds of dead bodies to be buried or burned and swished my father from cemetery to cemetery all over England and France. I knew enough to find the dipstick and check the oil; of course it was fine, my father's meticulous maintenance. I unscrewed the radiator cap, and of course the level of the water was fine. And so, leaving the bonnet yawning open, I slipped back into the car and turned the key.

Tick, tick. Tick – the fuel pump. Wait a few seconds. I pressed the ignition button. The engine shuddered and coughed... sweetly slumbering, stirred into life.

Silent, almost silent. A whisper in the woodland. Hardly a sound. No one could have seen or heard what I was doing. But, as I got out of the car and walked around to watch the engine throbbing like open-heart surgery, a haze of blue smoke rose from the exhaust pipes and into the surrounding trees...

Chapter Eight

'COLOUR-BLIND? You took Lawrence out of school because he's colour-blind?'

Juliet had had a bit too much to drink. My fault really. It was quite late at night and we'd been sitting and talking in her living-room. The three of us had had dinner together, fillets of white fish she'd dug out of the freezer and done very simply with a few potatoes and peas, and then Lawrence had gone up to his tower. He was still sulky with me since the incident with the swift in the morning, and he'd looked sideways at me and his mother as we shared a bottle of white wine. So, after the meal, he'd sloped off to his own room.

And then Juliet and I had moved to the comfy old sofa near the open French windows. As dusk dissolved into twilight and became a deep, almost purple-black night, as the darkness of the trees gathered like a blanket around the house, we sat and talked. In the afternoon, during my communion with the car, I'd felt that I'd descended into a lower world, a soft and suffocating underworld... and now it was as though the woman and I were sinking deeper still and drowning in our cosy cushions.

Perhaps it was the gin. She'd made me a gin and tonic when we first sat down together, but I'd made the second one and the third. I'd been telling her about my life in Borneo. She listened with real interest, her pointy face close to mine, her squirrel face with its anxious eyes and quickly nibbling movements of her lips, her twitchy nose. She blinked a lot and she laughed abruptly. I told her about the school I'd been teaching in: a government secondary school in a logging-town called Marudi, miles inland from the coast of the South China Sea, on the banks of the enormous Baram river; I described my students, teenage boys and girls from the *kampongs* in the forest and along the forest tributaries, how they sat in their dusty classrooms with the fans stirring lazily overhead, the boys in the front rows in their neat white shirts and black *songkoks*, the girls in their crisp white *tudungs* in rows at the back. An Islamic school, in a strictly Islamic society, in which every lesson, every meeting and function was started with a prayer and finished with a prayer... where the boys and girls studied together but couldn't sit side by side in the same classroom and had to be segregated into different rows.

'They call me Mr Chris. I'm the only *orang putih*, the only white man in the school. When I go into class they all stand to attention and they chant in unison "Good morning, Mr Chris!" and stay standing until I tell them to sit down. Lovely kids, nice and smiley and well-behaved... the boys have names like Farouk and Faisal and Abdul Aziz and there's about six Mohammads in every class... the girls are cute and funny and shy, Siti Hanisah and Nurul and Rokiah and Qistina and Rabiatul...'

She took a longer swig at her drink, tipping the glass so much that the ice slipped and bumped onto her upper lip. Gulping the mouthful down, she licked her lips with a slow swipe of her tongue and then, setting down the glass, she dabbed her chin, squirrel-like with the back of both hands. Time for a top-up...

I went on. 'And because we start early in the mornings – I get up at five and I'm clocking in at six-thirty – school's all over by one o'clock in the afternoon. I go home, a lovely big house on wooden stilts on the bank of the river, I have a shower and lunch and maybe take a nap because in the afternoon it's sweltering hot, then at five I'm out running or on my bike, getting a bit of exercise once the day starts to cool down.'

I finished my drink too. The dregs were just ice-water. 'And then,' I said, waving my empty glass and picking up hers, 'home again for another shower and feeling very thirsty after all the exertion. At six-thirty, exactly at sunset, the call to evening prayer comes wailing out of the mosque – it's called the *maghrib* prayers – but for an infidel like me it means something else... time for a great big, hefty big, swirly big gin and tonic.'

I stood up, with a glass in each hand. 'Juliet, the ones you make are nice, don't get me wrong, nice and refreshing like lemonade or barley water. But shall I make the next one? The kind I make for myself in Borneo?' I moved across the darkening room, in the direction of the drinks cabinet. 'Have you read Somerset Maugham's stories from South East Asia, when they have a *"gin stengah"* in the club in the evening? Well, *"stengah"* is the Malay word for half. So I make my gin and tonic the old-fashioned way, half tonic and half gin.'

And so we'd had a second drink together, and then a third. I made them. A tall glass half full of gin. Drop in a handful of ice, so that the level comes close to the top of the glass. Oh dear, not much room left, only enough for a splash of tonic. My fault. Later, when the night was so velvety-black that it seemed to oily-ooze from the woodland and through the French windows into the room itself, Juliet's little frame was snuggled into the softness of the sofa. And I was feeling comfortably weightless, boneless, the alcohol loosening and dissolving my skeleton...

And loosening our tongues. I'd told her about the swift in the tower bedroom and how Lawrence and I had dealt with it, although I hadn't mentioned the confrontation we'd had or the strange thing he'd muttered to me. I hadn't told her, I thought I would never tell her, that for a bewildering moment I'd been afraid of her son. When the conversation had shifted from my cheery, uncomplicated students in Marudi to my first impressions of Lawrence and my inklings of the kind of progress we might make in forming a relationship, I'd recounted the earlier incident, when he'd lost his temper and smashed the model plane into pieces.

'He gets angry,' she said, 'that's the issue.' She had a bit of trouble with the word, the sibilance on her tongue. 'He gets angry. How did you make him so angry?'

'I don't know. He just exploded. He was trying to show me the kind of plane his father flies... the kind he used to fly... and I didn't get which one he was talking about. The green one, the grey one... I don't know, he's got so many hanging on the ceiling up there, and they all look the same to me.'

She pricked up at something I'd said. Her face, which had fuddled and lost some of the sharpness of its features, flickered back into focus. 'Look the same? That's an issue with Lawrence. The colours, they all look the same to him. He's colour-blind. What did you say to him? The green one, the grey one? Is that when he got so angry?'

'Now you mention it, yes. That was when he lost his cool and yelled at me and smashed the plane.'

I shrugged at her and swilled some more gin. It was so strong that it caught the back of my throat and made my eyes water. A real Borneo *stengah*, the kind I'd drink on the balcony of my house with a saucer of olives... and my binoculars ready for the crocodiles which eased their bulk out of the undergrowth and into the river as the light was failing.

'He over-reacted a bit, don't you think? I mean, quite a lot of people are colour-blind, red and green and brown, that's the commonest kind. I had an uncle, I remember my Dad telling me about him, he found out he was colour-blind during the war because he wanted to join the RAF or something and it meant he wouldn't be able to...'

I stopped myself just in time. I made a pretence of spluttering on my gin. Juliet was suddenly very composed again, as though the alcohol had pickled her by now and she was preserved in pristine condition.

She levelled her eyes at me. 'Think about it, Christopher. Yes, that's why he gets angry. They told him at school he's colour-blind. Usually it's a trivial thing, it's just one of those things, it's nothing but a curiosity. But think about it. For a boy who idolises his father, who idolised his father, and who wanted more than anything else in the world to be like him, to be a...'

She paused, lifted her glass to her lips. But then she sniffed at the intense perfume and set it down. 'Too strong for me.' She made a smile with her lips, but it slipped off almost straightaway. 'But now you know why I keep him at home, out of school.'

I frowned at her. 'Because he's colour-blind? Alright, so he gets angry, I understand all that. But is there anything more you want to tell me?' I tried to lighten the mood again, because I'd seen her eyes welling with tears. 'Hey, do you want another drink? I can make one of your nice lemonade versions, if you like?'

She started to stand up. Me too. It took us two or three attempts, because the sofa and all its cushions were as difficult to escape as the pitcher-plants I had in my faraway garden. At last we wobbled together, giggling a bit, and for a few moments she took hold of my arms to steady herself. Then she looked up at me and sniffed and said, 'There's a bit more to tell you, Christopher, yes. You'll get the story from me or from Lawrence. But not now. Right now I need to go to bed and sleep off your great big, hefty big, swirly big gin and tonics...'

I closed the French window. She turned off the lights. I followed her to the foot of the stairs, waited, and she went up ahead of me. She turned at the top, on the first landing, where it was so dark I could hardly see her. Her disembodied voice floated down to me.

'Don't go away, Christopher,' she said softly. I heard her take a long breath, and then it all came out in one breathless release of words. 'I know you're concerned about your father and you're thinking about slipping away and leaving us to our own devices... me and Lawrence, we were in the tower this morning, I came up with more coffee for you and he said you'd gone out and we saw the smoke in the trees and guessed what you were doing... we thought you were going, going for good without even saying anything to us...'

She stopped. No more breath. There was a long empty silence. I couldn't see her at all. I thought she might have vanished into her bedroom. But then her voice came again, even more quietly, no more than a whisper in the benighted house.

'Don't go away just yet. We both need you. We all need you.'

I WAS DREAMING of fireflies.

Sometimes, faraway in the place I called home, I might fall asleep on my balcony. Only nine o'clock, I might have had a drink or two or three and watched the darkness fall until the river was black and the forest was black and even the sky was a whirl of blackness... and I might fall asleep on my balcony, in my easy chair, and slop the drink into my lap.

And then wake up. And see the trees alight with fireflies. Hundreds of them, or thousands. The forest of Borneo a spangle of silvery lights, and their reflection in the river... a marvel... and for me, who would set my alarm for five in the morning, time to climb out of my armchair and stumble indoors to bed.

Now I was dreaming of fireflies, in my bed in my room in Chalke House in Lincolnshire, England. But when I woke with a start I saw nothing. The space around me was utterly black. Not a single glow in a slumbering forest, not a gleam in a mighty, mysterious river.

Nothing. Wide awake, I got out of the bed. I had to, I had an urge to look and look and find a vestige of my dream...

And when I peered out of the window I saw it. A light in the darkness, as if a tiny piece of my dream had escaped and found its way into the real, waking world...

There was a light in the trees.

I opened my window wide. The night was cool and fresh after my stupor of sleep. The trees moved in a lovely breeze. The foliage stirred. And a light flickered, beyond the pond, in the darkness of the woodland.

Was it real, or a part of my dream? Was it real, or one of the fireflies I'd been dreaming, burned onto my eyeballs and still there, although I was awake?

I closed my eyes and rubbed their lids. I opened them again and saw the trees stirring. I felt the cool breath of a spring night on my face and on my neck.

But the light was gone. Nothing. No starlight above me, not a glimmer of moonlight on the surface of the pond.

I slipped back into bed and dreamed of nothing.

Chapter Nine

WE WERE ALL a bit quiet at breakfast the following morning. Juliet looked wanly at me over a mug of coffee, blew on it and sipped and then smiled with a frothy moustache.

'How do you do it?' she said, with a husky, hung-over voice. 'I mean, how do you drink gin like that and then get up at five o'clock in the morning?'

'I have an alarm call,' I answered. My voice was a bit throaty too. 'The mosque. At five o'clock... it feels like the dead of night and I feel like death, and this guy is wailing from a bloody great loudspeaker a couple of hundred yards from my house...'

I grimaced at her, deliberately dunking my mouth deep into my coffee to imitate her moustache. 'But no, really, I don't drink like that in the week. I guess I was showing off last night, trying to look like an old Borneo hand...'

Unusually early, Lawrence was there too. He pulled a face, a snarly sneer with his upper lip, listening to me and his mother exchanging our morning-after banter. We were in cahoots, me and Juliet... he must've thought we'd been drinking and talking and spilling all sorts of beans while he was upstairs alone in his tower. He narrowed his eyes at his mother, as if, by doing so, he might burrow his brain into hers and find out what precious secrets she'd divulged to this latest incomer. That was why he'd got up and come down so early, in his t-shirt and shorts, because he knew we'd been up late together and he wanted to intercept any more indiscretions. But she just fluttered her eyelashes at him and then mock-rubbed at her temples, signifying that she was an adult with an alcohol-induced headache and he was excluded from the aftermath, because he was a boy and he should mind his own business.

He was miffed. Good. I winked at Juliet and she winked back.

He noticed. I think she meant him to notice and tease him, because he was in a funk of jealousy over her cosiness with me. He made a big play of nonchalance, busying himself with the toaster, and, to try and jolly him out of it, she leaned over and touched his downy arm. 'Hey, isn't it about time you changed into another shirt?' she said. 'How long are you going to live in this thing, day and night? What've you got stuck on the back?'

He wriggled away from her touch, but not before she'd picked off two or three tiny green burrs. 'Where've you been? You've got lots of these stuck on you...'

He shrugged. His face darkened, and he pretended to be preoccupied with poking a knife deep inside the toaster to dig out a smouldering crust. With his other hand he started scratching at the bare skin of his neck. He had a new rash of nettle blebs there.

'I couldn't sleep,' he said. 'I woke up in the middle of the night and went outside. I'd had that dream again. I thought Dad was back. I went outside and down the garden 'cos I thought he was back.'

'Silly boy,' she said very softly. A shadow had crossed her face too, the same one which had darkened his. She stood up and behind him and wrapped her arms around his waist. 'You and your dreams, you big bony silly boy...' She pressed her mouth between his shoulder blades. 'Phew, you're a bit whiffy, aren't you? Throw this old thing into the wash and run upstairs and get a shower. You'll feel a lot better and you and Christopher can spend some time together.'

'What about the birds, Lawrence? The swifts?' I said. 'We can get a good look at them from your tower, with your binoculars. You must have a bird book or something in the house, we can read up about them and...'

'I got a better idea,' he interrupted. 'But we might get a bit dirty. So I'll keep this shirt on a bit longer. For this morning, at least. Hey, Mr Chris, are you any good at climbing?'

Juliet tried to dissuade him, but she couldn't. She wheedled at him to go upstairs and get changed and spend some cool, calm, quality time with me... He ignored her.

She carried on trying to dissuade him, as we followed him meekly out of the French windows and into the woodland. But he hardly seemed to hear her, as he strode ahead. He was wresting the initiative back from her. She had had her time with me and told me who-knows-what family secrets and rumours and tittle-tattle, lubricated by wine and gin and snuggled into the sofa all night, and now, on a brightening summer's morning at the beginning of June, he was in charge and we were going to do what he wanted to do, never mind the so-called grown-ups who were fuzzy and fuddled and hung-over.

We came to the foot of the Scots pine.

First of all we appraised the car. It was impossible not to. Shabby and neglected, a hulking ton-weight of rust and blistered wood and wormy leather, it was still amazing: a Daimler hearse, in a Lincolnshire woodland. It wouldn't matter how often you strolled down there, on a frosty winter's afternoon or a moonlit midsummer's night, it would always be something to happen on, an extraordinary thing to behold.

So we paused and cocked our heads at the car. We couldn't help it. With its showering of twigs and moss, and the smash in the glass as though it had had a wonderful adventure with gangsters and shotguns, the mighty machine was a picture. For a moment I thought – and I was sure Juliet was thinking and hoping too – it might be such a distraction, such an anomaly in the scheme of things which might or might not happen that morning, that Lawrence's idea might be forgotten.

To prolong the moment, and to postpone what the boy was wanting to do, I skirted the car and had a closer look. I kicked at the tyres. I rubbed at the rust on the radiator grille. And, my hand going instinctively to the handle of the driver's door, I saw that it was ajar.

'Funny,' I said, opening the door wide. 'I'm sure I closed it properly. Leave it open and the courtesy light stays on and the battery goes flat...'

Sure enough, no light. No soft green light from the little bulb in the headlining of the car. I felt under the front seat, where I'd left the ignition key, slotted it in and turned it and heard the reassuring tick of the fuel pump priming. But then, when I pressed the starter button there was nothing but a click.

'It's dead. Not going anywhere.'

Juliet and Lawrence stood and watched, as I tried again. Futile, the second and third attempts. I was puzzled and annoyed. Puzzled, because I was certain I'd shut the door the other day, when I'd started the car and warmed it up and then switched off. Annoyed, because the presence of my father was so strong that I could hear him chuntering... I'd had the car a couple of weeks and already neglected its maintenance. Juliet folded her arms across her chest and frowned. The boy met my eyes without blinking, for one second. Then he looked away, and his hand went to his neck and he rubbed at the place where the nettles had swiped him in the night.

I let the door swing shut on its own weight. I went round to the back, muttering, 'Jump leads, my father's got everything in here, I'm sure there'll be jump leads...' I opened the door to the yawning space which had been his workshop and living-room and bedroom, clambered in and reached across the box of newspapers for the toolbox. When I lifted the lid, the leads uncoiled and sprang out, a black snake and a red one, as if they'd been waiting for me in the darkness. I was saying over my shoulder, 'Is it possible to get your car down here, Juliet, and try to get this poor old thing started?' and at the same time the snakes reminded me of how Lawrence had recoiled from the newspapers when he'd first peered into the car.

I climbed out of the hearse. My eyes fell on the headlines at the top of the pile: a football match, a hat-trick in a cup final or something. I did a double-take and read the headline again.

Before I could turn my thoughts into words, Lawrence butted in. 'So are we up for this?' My jumble of suspicions – the light I'd seen in the night, the boy's off-hand remark about his sleeplessness, the car door ajar, and now the papers rearranged – my suspicions stayed jumbled. They were real, as real as the sting of a nettle... but they needed an itch to create a visible rash, needed a scratch to form the clear white blebs. Before I could ask Lawrence why he'd been in the car in the night, he'd said with an exaggerated boldness, 'So, are we up for this? Can't you hear them? Let's get up there!'

It was no good Juliet trying again to dissuade her son. High in the sky, above and around the very top of the Scots pine, the swifts were screaming. The boy wanted to climb to the tree-house, and he wanted me to go with him. He wanted the upper-hand, he wanted to exert some kind of authority over me, to give me the option of feebly declining the challenge or letting him take me where his dare-devil father had been, to the summit of the tallest tree in the woodland. The other day, in his room, I'd somehow diminished him, by overruling him on his own territory. So now he said, with a crowing self-confidence, 'Mum, listen. He's a teacher, he wants to teach me about the swifts. So what's best? Sitting in my bedroom with a bird-book, reading and looking at the pictures and peeping out of the window with our binoculars? Or climbing into the sky, to be with the swifts, to be where the swifts live? What's best?' And turning to me, claiming the moment by tugging the jump-leads out of my hand, he said, 'What's best, Mr Teacher? What do you think?'

He handed the jump-leads to his mother. 'Of course I'm up for it,' I said.

It was easy at first. Despite my muzzy head, I was still fit from all my running and cycling on hot tropical afternoons. Lawrence swarmed up and up the tree and I followed, more slowly and deliberately. He was lighter, sinewy-strong, and he moved so easily through the dry black branches that he seemed to be dancing. I paused for breath and looked down. Juliet seemed a long way away, her face turned up, her mouth open and her eyes anxious. Beside her, the bulk of the car was a huge rounded boulder, dropped by a prehistoric glacier. I blew on my hands, which were burning from the coarseness of the bark, and I continued to climb.

And my legs were shaking. I wasn't afraid, exposed like a rock-climber on a slabby cliff; I was comfortable with the height because the darkness around me was like a cage, through which I couldn't fall even if I lost my grip and slipped. But the pressure of notching my feet into smaller and smaller spaces as the branches thinned out had started my legs quivering. I pulled myself up with my arms and saw Lawrence up there, already adjusting his frame onto the spars of the tree-house.

At last I clambered on board beside him... on board, because the tree-house was nothing more than the pieces of an old wooden pallet which had somehow been manhandled up and lashed onto the flimsy topmost branches... it felt like the debris of a shipwreck, a makeshift raft adrift on an ocean. I lugged myself onto it. I closed my eyes and hung on, to calm the thudding in my chest, and was alarmed when I opened my eyes again to see the vastness of the sky and feel the tree swaying.

'You did alright.' Lawrence was grinning at me. He was sitting cross-legged, quite at ease in his eyrie. I crouched beside him, and he must have seen my knuckles whiten as I gripped the knotted ropes which barely held the structure together. A little bit begrudgingly, he admitted, 'You did alright, I didn't think you'd make it...' and, his idea of fun, he shook the thing with all his strength so that it creaked and groaned.

The swifts. We were in their world. There were scores of them, and the sky was full of their screaming. They hurtled around us. They were black, like chips of jet, and they were breath-taking... the agility of their swerving, the rush and flicker of their wings, as though the air gave no resistance but was a vacuum through which they sped like fragments of pure energy.

'A good idea?' the boy said. 'Ever given a lesson in a classroom like this before?'

'It's marvellous...' I managed to say, 'and the birds are marvellous...' I found some more breath, despite the frailty of the bits and pieces I was hanging onto and the yawning space around me. 'I've got a colony of them, swiftlets, maybe a hundred of them nesting under my house in Borneo... and there are millions, or maybe hundreds of thousands, in the limestone caves in the jungle...'

He was looking sideways at me. 'I was joking,' he said. 'I didn't mean you had to start doing a lesson up here.'

'Devil birds...' I went on perversely. 'There's a lot of spooky folklore about them... because they're black, I suppose, and because they scream like mad, and because they fly so fast and so high and never seem to rest... in the old days people weren't sure where they roosted, and they made up stories that the swifts could sleep and fly at the same time, and mate and fly at the same time, or else they...'

The tree was swaying more and more. I squeezed my eyes shut again, opened them narrowly and saw through my lashes that we were higher than the boy's tower. I rolled my head the other way and saw nothing but sky as far as a foam of cloud which might have been the North Sea horizon. I felt my stomach lurch and a bubble of nausea in my throat. Fighting it, swallowing it, determined to keep up a pretence of confidence, I heard myself muttering, 'Tiny feet, almost nothing feet... their Latin name "apodidae" meaning "footless"... that's the family name of the swifts and swiftlets...'

Enough. I gingerly edged off the pallet and grappled with the tree again, to try and start climbing down. The boy was watching me, unwittingly impressed by a teacher so determined to impart his dried-up pellets of knowledge. With a show of youthful bravado, he stood up, just as I was slithering down, and he flapped his arms at the birds which dashed around his head. There seemed to be more of them, they mobbed him as if he were a trespasser in their space. Preoccupied with my own safety, finding it harder to climb down than it had been climbing up, I glimpsed him towering above me: an alien in the sky-world of the swifts, a lanky teenage boy in shorts and a smelly t-shirt. A bird banged into his face, and he swiped at it as though it were a wasp. For a second, by sheer chance he caught it in his fist, but then it squirmed out and away and tried to regain its control of the air... but one of its wings was damaged and it tumbled past me, down and down through the branches of the Scots pine, disappearing somewhere far below.

'Be careful, Lawrence!' I called to him. 'Get down! Come on, I'm going down now...'

Yes, it was harder. I couldn't see my feet in the gloom. Time and again I lodged a foot between branch and trunk, and then my weight would either crunch my toes or the branch would sickeningly creak. Slowly, painfully, with the boy huffing impatiently just above my head, I got halfway down and paused. Daring as an ape, he skirted past me, and the smell of his stale shirt and adolescent sweat was strong in my nostrils. He swung easily downwards. My sickness had gone, it had been the movement of the treetop, like the swell of a lazy ocean, which had moved my stomach... but my hands were burning and my legs were jumping. Closer and closer to the ground, I glanced down to see the humped outline of the car and hear Juliet and Lawrence in a heated exchange. Just then, when she called up to me, 'Are you alright, Christopher?' and I called down, 'Yes,' my left foot was jammed against the trunk with all my weight excruciatingly on it. I tried to shift some of the pressure to my other foot...

The branch I was holding snapped off. The one under my foot snapped off. For a split-second, there was a blissful relief from the pain... and then I was falling.

My fall was slowed by one crunching impact after another, until I landed in a wreckage of branches and twigs and showering needles.

Juliet knelt to me. I couldn't speak. 'Oh my god, are you alright?' she was asking again, and I was nodding and heaving for breath. I was fine, I was fine, I wanted to tell her, because the boy was looming over me with a wolfish smile and his Adam's apple bobbing, and he was chuckling a lot of hilarious nonsense about the wild man of Borneo and orang-utans and...

I wasn't completely fine. At first I'd felt nothing, because of the shock of my crash-landing. But when I tried to sit up, there was a dazzle, a blaze of white light in my head.

I cried out, a high, almost animal yelp. The pain rippled through my chest and into my brain.

THEY GOT ME up to the house. Lawrence tugged me upright, arranged my arm across his shoulder, and I hopped agonisingly beside him, through the woodland.

Every hop was a torture. I'd turned an ankle... annoying, niggling... but it was the hurt in my chest which made me bite my lips and cry out again. Juliet said I'd cracked a rib; she'd heard, from other people who'd done it, that it was the most painful injury you could sustain. I didn't need her to tell me. I could hardly breathe. The pain made me retch, and the pain of retching was worse.

A bizarre procession, through the dappled sunlight of a lovely June morning...

Me and the boy, conjoined, a wheezing, stumbling three-legged creature. A few paces behind us, a little light-footed woman, a kind of sprite or a faery huntress. And leading the way, the orange cat. It had emerged from the undergrowth as we'd started our journey from the Scots pine. Perfectly uninterested in what the ridiculous humans were doing, it had seen something much more fascinating. It had pounced on the disabled swift... pressed it firmly into the long grass and then caught it in its jaws. Now, with the bird in its mouth, the long black wings fluttering feebly, the cat was wonderfully exotic... a miniature tiger with a magnificent moustache.

So Lawrence lugged me to the house and lowered me onto the sofa. He couldn't wait to get away. He affected concern for his stricken tutor, but it wasn't very convincing. I was going to snarl at him about the car and whether he'd been in it... but he did his shifty sloping-off, again. I saw him grab the cat and prise the bird from its fangs; the swift was still alive, the terrified creature, and the boy cupped it in his hands and disappeared upstairs. I was going to growl at Juliet, that I'd arrived intact at Chalke House a fortnight ago and now I'd got a car with a shattered windscreen and a flat battery and myself excruciatingly crippled... but she was ministering to me, plumping me into a pile of cushions. I lay back and sipped the air. I watched the quick, nimble movements of her fingers and saw the anxiety on her face.

'I'm so sorry, Christopher, I'm so sorry...' she was whispering. The sibilance reminded me of the way her voice had altered the previous evening, when we'd shared this very sofa and swigged the gin together. 'I'm so sorry, so sorry...' and although it was only mid-morning, I thought how good it might be to share a stiff drink right now with this dizzy, fragile woman. 'I tried to put him off, you heard me trying to put him off, it was such a silly idea to go up the tree, but he's so selfish and stubborn and a show-off...' She was holding my hands in hers. She had dust in her lashes and pine needles in her hair and twiggy smudges on her face. 'Like his father, just like his father, just selfish and stubborn and showing-off...'

'Did he go into my car last night?' My voice was feeble.

The question stopped her dead. She said, 'What?' although she'd heard what I'd said.

'I saw a light in the trees. I got up and looked out of the window, I saw a light in the trees and thought I was dreaming or it was fireflies or something...' She let go of my hands. She was staring at me. I managed to wheeze a few more words. 'I mean, what was he doing? What was the idea? To open the door and leave on the light and run down the battery so that...'

'So that what?' She pulled away from me and blinked, a bit too theatrically. 'So your car couldn't start and you'd be stuck here and couldn't get away? Do you really think he'd do that to keep you here?'

'Or was he looking for something? What? What was he looking for?'

She stood up very suddenly. She did the squirrel thing, smearing the moss and dust into her face with the backs of her hands. 'I know you don't know him,' she said. 'How could you, after just a few days here? Lawrence has dreams, he dreams of his father... and they're more than just dreams, they're a kind of unreality he's created to help him forget the madness of his real world...' Her eyes brimmed with tears. 'I'm sorry, Christopher, I'm sorry you've blundered into all this... and now this has happened and...'

She spun away, out of the room.

I lay back and stared at the ceiling. In my fall, my foot had caught in the branches and wrenched my ankle skew-whiff. Much worse, I might've cracked a rib. I lay as still as I could, breathing as shallowly as possible, and wondered at what the woman had said, the muddle of messages I'd got from her. Did she want me to stay and befriend her son, or was she sorry I'd come and she wanted me to go away? Was she angry with me, was I angry with her, were we angry with each other? The boy too, his moody sulky brooding, his explosion of anger, the glowering darkness in his manner... hard to explain, but it was more threatening than teenage truculence.

I shifted my weight on the sofa, I suddenly felt as though the mounded cushions were a quagmire into which I was sinking... but when I moved, the pain in my chest dazzled in my brain. I clenched my teeth, relaxed and sank back... and when the pain stopped, my head cleared and I realised there were two things I really, pragmatically, needed to do.

I extricated myself from the sofa, as desperate as a Dickensian convict drowning in a salt-marsh... no, not that bad, but I needed to get out and hobble through those French windows and into the wildness of the garden again. Because I was bursting to piss.

Despite the pain, I had to reach the nearest nettle-bed and piss... the morning coffees and the residual bellyful of gin. I stumbled to the undergrowth and unzipped and the relief was so good it almost made me forget the muddle in my head and the bruising fall from the tree. The spray was a glorious rainbow. The steam was pungent, as rank as the *macaque* in my Borneo garden. The droplets were jewels on the hairy leaves of the nettles. I pissed for a minute, maybe more. Eyes closed, nostrils flaring, emptying my thoughts.

And then the other thing. Never mind the conundrum of whether I should stay or not. I wasn't going anywhere until I could jump-start the hearse or charge the flattened battery. Juliet had said there was a car at the back of the house. Hissing through my teeth, shaping obscenities on my lips, I went to look for it.

There it was, in a stand of holly. An ancient holly wood. The trees were centuries old. The boles were scarred like the limbs of a battle-weary warrior. An armoury of leaves enclosed and shadowed a car, swaddled in a mouldy green-brown tarpaulin.

It didn't look promising. Juliet had said she didn't go out much, indeed as seldom as possible. From the mossy-damp cover and the enveloping, almost submarine darkness, I guessed that, whatever it was, the car hadn't been started for weeks.

I undid a knot of nylon rope under the back bumper and peeled the cover off the boot. Metallic-silver paintwork, the BMW logo... of course, she'd been a pilot's wife, she was a pilot's widow, of course she'd have something swish.

I peeled a bit more. The rear window was steamed up. Its careful covering with the tarpaulin wasn't doing the car much good... it needed some air on it and in it, it needed starting and running and a snarly run into the sunshine.

I slithered off the whole of the tarpaulin, stood back and appraised the car.

Blood. A miscarriage. A horrid mess of red. There was a swirl of it on the roof and smeared down the windscreen, and the bonnet was a thick, congealed flow of deep, gleaming red paint. It was daubed on the roof, applied with ugly strokes of a big brush. On the bonnet, it had been poured straight from a tin or a bucket, luscious liquid runnels, dried into spools and whorls like lava from a volcano.

I tried the driver's door. Locked. It was gloomy in the holly wood and so I leaned closer, to rest my weight and steady my breathing, and to see the extraordinary vandalism more closely.

On the roof... letters? Was it a word? I strained on tip-toe to try and make it out. Something like a big E and then... and then a voice behind me. Juliet's voice.

'Eye. I think that's what it says. Like, an eye for an eye. That's why we don't go out.'

Not at all elfin, she was a wounded and embittered woman. She pushed past me. 'I told you not to bother with the car,' she snapped, and she started to tug the tarpaulin back on again. 'I don't cover it because I want to keep it nice. I cover it because it isn't nice. I'm ashamed of it and I can't go out in it, I'm ashamed to take it somewhere and get it fixed...' She was struggling with the heavy material. 'Help me. No, don't help me, you're hurt and you shouldn't have come round here and...'

'Who did it?' I asked her. 'What does it mean?' A thought sprang into my head and out of my mouth before I could stop it. 'Was it Lawrence?'

She just stared at me. Thinking she was pausing before an outburst of anger at what I'd suggested, I added quickly, 'I'm sorry, no, it's so ugly I'm sure he wouldn't do that. But who? Why?'

She surprised me by smiling. But it was a twisted sneer of a smile. It was cruel and sad, and it carried the threat of something sarcastic that she was going to say.

'Ugly? That's funny. I mean, it's funny you saying he wouldn't do it because it's ugly.'

Her shoulders started to shake. She was laughing and crying at the same time. She touched the crude letters, the word daubed red onto silver. Through a mumble of tears, she said, 'He can do ugly. This is nothing, this is nothing but a bit of paint on a stupid...'

She yanked with all her strength on the tarpaulin, and the effort stopped her crying. She covered the car. No longer a lean machine with a cryptic message botched onto it; just a mound of mottled green and brown moss, under a prickle of holly. When it was done, she took an enormous, quivering breath, smeared her hands up and down the front of her shirt and dabbed at her eyes. She sniffed and sniffed and, like a child, she wiped her nose on her sleeve.

'Alright, let me help you now,' she said. 'Hold onto me, please, I want you to. And let me hold onto you. Please, I want to.'

She slipped an arm around my waist and I slipped my arm around hers. She seemed even tinier, with her body scrunched against mine. I didn't feel I could lean any of my weight on her. But I was hurt, and she was hurting, and we helped one another around to the front of the house.

JULIET REARRANGED ME onto the sofa. I submitted to her. The cushions sucked me down again and somehow seemed to be absorbing the pain from my chest. She brought me a glass of water and a couple of paracetamol. When I closed my eyes and slipped into a shallow sleep, I dreamed of the swiftlets back home in Borneo.

THE MIDDLE OF the night, before the earliest cries of the mosque. Pitch darkness in my bedroom. Something had disturbed me, and I'd stared at the ceiling wondering why I'd woken. Then

I'd realised that the power was off. No overhead fan. I was hot. I was naked, flat on my back, I'd pushed back the single sheet I usually slept under. The slowing and stopping of the fan had woken me. The stillness. The silence. The fuggy heat of a tropical night.

This was all in my dream, a dream of something that happened frequently out there: a power-cut in the night. I felt for the torch I kept at my bedside, flicked it on, got off the bed and padded through the living-room, opened the door and went down the stairs to the black empty space beneath the house.

The swiftlets erupted from their nests as I flashed the torch ahead of me. Hundreds of them. They'd stuck their flimsy cups of grass and saliva into every corner of the stilts and the beams which supported the house. Now, aroused from their roosting and confused by the wavering light, they spun off their nests and dashed madly around me.

I was naked. I felt the birds fluttering at my body. They were screaming, a hundred or two or three hundred blinded and bewildered birds, battering around my head, beating at the focus of light. Trying to ignore them, trying not to react by swatting at them with my free hand, I pressed onwards through the whirling mob...

Found the aluminium stepladder. Propped it against the wall. Aimed the torch up into the high corner and wobbled up the ladder to the fuse-cupboard.

It had happened in reality... and now, in my dream, it happened again. One of the birds slammed so hard into the torch that the light went out. For a second, as befuddled by the sudden darkness as they'd been bedazzled by the torch, the birds seemed to cling and stick onto me. I felt them all over my clammy hot skin; their mole-furry feathers between my legs, their spindly-sharp wings under my arms, and scratting with their tiny claws at my face. I slipped off the ladder and crashed onto the ground.

The pain unmanned me. I heard myself squeal like a piglet. At the very same moment, as if my squeal had woken him, the man in the mosque began his dismal, dreary droning. I lay still. I didn't dare move. The swiftlets fell calm and returned to their nests. The sky lightened, imperceptibly at first, and then quickly, until the silhouettes of the coconut palms and banana in my compound took shape. When at last I tried to sit up, I squealed again...

So SHRILL THAT I woke myself up. And found myself lying, in exquisite agony, on a muddle of cushions in the living-room in Chalke House.

I gritted my teeth. I tried not to breathe too hard. I squinted into the light from the surrounding woodland. Something fell past the window. Like a rag, or an old glove... the boy must've dropped it from the balcony of his tower.

Hearing his footsteps clattering downstairs, I closed my eyes and pretended to be asleep. I felt the wind of his body as he burst through the room and past me and into the garden. And his mother. She'd heard the boy and followed to see what he was up to. I kept my eyes shut, but I knew she'd paused and bent close to me because I caught the scent of coffee from her mouth, and then she was gone.

Intrigued, I forced myself to sit up. The cushions were a trap from which I struggled to escape. A quick exchange of voices... I looked out in time to see the boy bending into the long grasses, searching for whatever it was he'd lost from high in the tower. I guessed that it was the swift he'd launched into space. Yes, he plucked it out of the grass, a bent and broken thing he was showing to his mother for a few moments before he folded it and pushed it inside his shirt. And then he was remonstrating with her, leaning over and jutting his jaw into her face, his voice unnecessarily loud... that he'd fixed it, he could fix it, he was good at fixing things. I would have hurried out to intervene, but every breath I took was like a blade in my side.

What happened next was oddly balletic. I mean, it was mannered, a scene from an absurd, modernistic play. The boy stopped his bullying. It just stopped as though a switch had been thrown. He stood, transfixed by something, entranced by something... yes, it sounds quaint and otherworldly, but he was enthralled. For a long moment he stared over his mother's head, and she stared up at him; it was, yes, like some kind of tableau, their movements slowed to nothing. He was holding his breath. And then he opened his mouth and inhaled, tasting the air with his lips and his tongue. His nostrils flared. He was scenting the air, like a dog.

When he moved, it was with a curious, graceful momentum. An expression of intense rapture on his face, he glided away from her, lost in a trance. He crossed the tousled lawn and dived straight into the nearest, densest nettle-bed. With a whoop of excitement, he thrust his hands and bare arms and his face into the stinging leaves. When he turned and looked back at his mother, he was blotched and reddened, a rash of welts, and his face was alive with a visionary joy.

'I did it! It worked! Mum, I did it!'

He tore off his shirt and threw it away. Holding the swift in one hand, he turned again into the nettles and deliberately swiped their hairy leaves across his chest and his neck. He grasped them and snuffled them with his nose. He inhaled the pungency of piss, he smeared the droplets which sparkled and splashed on his skin.

'I fixed the bird and I made it fly again... and I made a wish and it worked! He's back! Dad's come back!'

His mother cried out to him, her face contorted with a fear of his madness. She was paralysed, unable to cross the lawn either to confront or comfort him. 'It didn't fly, it didn't! He won't come back, he can't!'

But her voice was too feeble for him to hear.

Chapter Ten

ODD TO THINK how differently the rest of that summer might have turned out if I hadn't pissed into the nettles. Or, on the other hand, if I'd spoken out from my bed of pain, as they'd both come harum-scarum back into the living-room, and I'd scotched his fantasy by saying, 'No, Lawrence, it was me, it was me, I pissed into the nettles...'

But I had, and I didn't. I pretended to be waking from an agonised sleep, that I'd heard a bit of a ruction outside but didn't know what on earth was going on. I pretended I was surprised to see the woman so shaken and bleary with tears and the half-naked boy in a state of garbling euphoria. I was going to say, 'It was me...' but I didn't. Why not? A ridiculous sense of embarrassment, that I'd done such a thing in a stranger's garden? A reluctance to affront the fragile woman? The fear that I might further enflame the volatile boy? Whatever the reason, something constrained me from uttering a few simple, explanatory words. And a minute later, as they passed noisily through the living-room and disappeared, still wrangling in tremendous excitement, the moment to speak out had passed.

More moments passed. The day passed.

From time to time, Juliet and the boy came into the living-room to offer me or to show me things. The woman brought more water and paracetamol, and at midday a messy omelette and an untidy salad; tea in the afternoon and a little table strewn with out-of-date country-living magazines; as the light was fading, she did one of her lightweight gin and tonics, and then another which I persuaded her to make Borneo-style; and later, when the room was dark, with a hawk-moth butting and blundering at the lamp in the corner, she brought me a ham sandwich. But she hardly stopped to talk. She flitted, almost as flittery as the moth. All through the day, since the manic morning of tree-climbing and falling, the revelation of the car, the boy in ecstasy in the nettles, she'd thoroughly avoided talking to me. She'd come and gone and looked after me, but clearly she didn't want to be ensnared in more than a polite, perfunctory conversation. I'd thought that the second gin might have loosened her up... but, although the one she gave me was so strong I could see its oily-blue swirls when I held it to the lamplight, I think she'd made hers weaker again. She didn't want any difficult questions, about her, or her husband, or the car or the boy. So I didn't ask any.

What did the boy bring me? Three things.

In the morning, not long after I'd been well and truly abandoned into the depths of the sofa and he'd gone whooping up into his tower, he came down to show me something he'd fixed. It was the model of the Phantom he'd smashed in a fit of rage, when I'd trespassed onto the taboo of his colour-blindness. He'd made a splendid job of it. It was meticulously repaired. Every detail looked perfect. All his own work. He seemed, in his swaggering, self-satisfied manner, as proud of the fact that he'd smashed the plane as the care he'd taken in mending it, as though it was his prerogative, it was in his power to destroy and then rebuild. I dutifully admired his handiwork. I could see his clumsy fingerprint-smudges in the glue he'd used, but I didn't point them out.

In the afternoon he came down again. He'd changed into another shirt and a pair of jeans, no doubt encouraged by his mother, but he hadn't showered. I could still smell the urine on his skin. For a bizarre millisecond I thought it was the moment to tell him, to blurt out that the piss he was wearing like an expensive cologne was mine. I didn't. He'd brought me something else he'd fixed. Yes, it was the swift. He proffered it to me in his cupped hands, as though he'd mined some extraordinarily precious metals, fused them into an alloy the world had never seen before, and worked it into a miraculous piece of art...

It was indeed miraculous, but none of the miracle was of the boy's creation. A tiny broken creature, just about alive, it lay panting on his open palms... no, not panting, because that word implies a force, a rhythm, an energy. The bird was, I thought, taking its last breaths. Utterly feeble, it was unutterably beautiful. So dark and mysterious; a fragment of life so far away from me, so distant from the boy, that it might have been an alien from another galaxy. Lawrence was proud of what he'd done: he'd mended the broken wing by super-gluing a piece of plastic onto it.

I started to say to him, 'Look, Lawrence, you can't just glue everything, you can't just break things and glue them together again...' But he was cock-a-hoop. It would live. He had rescued it from the jaws of the orange cat, he had sallied it from his tower on a risky but necessary test-flight, and now he had repaired it. It would live.

I braced myself the third time he came in. But it was a truly delicate and lovely thing he'd made. 'I did this at school,' he said, and he knelt by the sofa, where I was still lying and breathing gingerly. He cleared away the magazines from the table and unrolled a piece of material. On it there was a representation I recognised immediately: the Scots pine, seen from his tower, silhouetted against a velvet-blue night-sky with a huge silvery moon, its outline reflected in the deep black pond. 'Batik,' he said. 'I did it in the art room at school. It was the only thing I liked doing there. You know batik? You do the design, you boil up the wax, you...'

Yes, I knew batik. The students in my school did it. Hot wax, boiling wax in a precarious pot. I was saying, 'This is great, Lawrence, the design and the vision and the execution...'

He smiled at that last word, as if I'd hit a nerve, as if, by accident, I'd pinged a harmonic and a forgotten note was humming in his brain... and just then, before he could respond to the genuine compliment I'd paid him, his mother had come in. She did an odder thing than the accidental note I'd struck. Seeing what Lawrence was showing me, she hurried forward. She snatched the batik off the table. She crumpled it up in a careless bundle, as though it was nothing more than an old newspaper. And, 'For heaven's sake, Lawrence!' she spat at him, 'what do you think you're doing? Don't you think? Don't you think?'

And the two of them went out of the room again, in a caterwauling confusion. Leaving me confused.

It was just one of the things I didn't mention to Juliet... later in the evening and into the night, when we were sipping our gin and eating our sandwiches, watching the hawk-moth butting and blundering in the lamp-lit corner.

I COULDN'T SLEEP. I'd been too long on the sofa, all day dozing off and waking in pain, dozing through the afternoon. Juliet, when she was ready for bed, insisted that I stayed where I was. She didn't think it was a good idea for me to hike up to my own room, she thought I'd cracked a rib and going upstairs would be bad for me. She was very firm about it. She brought me a toothbrush and towel and let me go as far as the bathroom just off the hallway before making sure I was plopped onto the sofa again.

I lay awake and listened to the wind in the trees. It started as a whisper, became louder and busier, until all the woodland was stirring and swaying. I manoeuvred myself up and onto my feet and went outside, into a roiling commotion.

I was glad. The days and nights before, in the little lost world of Chalke House, had been so still and quiet. Not now. There was no sleep in the trees that night, no restive dreams, no cobwebby corners or shadowy secrets. The beech and the chestnut and the oak and the hornbeam, slumbering deep in the wolds, had had enough of the stillness. Now they thrust their heads up and out into the big skies of Lincolnshire... to taste a bigger night, to smell some cooler air and even a tang of salt from the distant sea...

There was a huge full moon. And despite the growing storm, a clear sky. A single silvery-black cloud, like a ship which had broken her moorings, was dangerously adrift.

Barefoot, only in my shorts and a shirt, I moved away from the house. It was marvellous to be among the trees as they shook and shuddered overhead. When I turned and looked back at the house, it was bright in the moonlight. Every feature of the tower and its battlements was etched into the sky. And then, when the cloud crossed the moon, a ripple of darkness passed over the house and was gone again... a living thing which had emerged from the forest, a slithering creature of the night.

I paused by the pond. The water was strangely still. The moon was reflected in it, every blemish and pock, beautifully imperfect.

The woodland roared around me. I went down to the car. The Scots pine bristled and creaked and groaned, but the car was unmoved. It was a rock, a ton of glacial granite. It had endured millennia of grinding through a river of ice, so a summer storm was nothing but a bit of noise. I opened the back of the car, climbed in and pulled the door shut. Just as the rain began.

My own space again. The cosy warmth and the smells. And better for my bruised body, to lie flat on my back on the firmness of my father's couch, instead of wallowing on the sofa. Yes, it was better, I could feel my spine and my ribs settling. I lay still and heard the first droplets of rain which found a way through the dense branches of the pine. There was a rumble of thunder... and suddenly, with a whoosh like an express train hurtling through a station, a mighty downpour which thrummed on the roof of the car.

It brought with it a rattle of twigs. More than twigs, sometimes the thud of a bigger branch which the storm had loosened. I lay back and enjoyed it. I day-dreamed of a night I'd spent with my father, when I was little and he was a lithe, lanky man, and we'd parked in an orchard in Kent, the apples dropping from the trees and thumping on the roof of the Daimler. Amazing, now, to be lying in exactly this place, in this space, and hearing this sound. And then, such a flurry of rain and wind that the whole car shook. I day-dreamed of a night I'd spent with my father, when I was a teenager and he was a work-weary man, and we'd stopped in a field in Wales... and woken with a yell when the car was shaking as though a giant was turning it over. Only a cow, a big black and white cow scratching her backside on the back-side of the hearse.

The wind was wild. The rain was heavier still. It came drenching through the trees, as though I'd camped under a waterfall. But the old car was weatherproof. It was warm inside. I wasn't going to sleep, so I reached into my father's tool-box and felt for his torch.

A soft yellow beam, a circle of light on the velvety head-lining of the hearse. Again and again, it was me in this special space, where I'd spent so many days and nights of my youth. I made myself comfortable on the camp-bed with my father's blanket, although a spasm of pain shot through my ribs when I moved too quickly, and I reached for the box of old newspapers.

Not so old. My father had been working, or at least running the car and using it as a den, almost to the time he'd had his stroke. The torchlight was gentle on a blare of headlines: the triumphs and disasters of sportsmen and celebrities, their spectacular goals and shabby scandals. The beam faded, I shook the torch until it rallied a bit, and I dug deeper into the box. The paper I pulled out at random was last year's, although somehow it had found itself near the bottom. The torchlight blinked, there was a second of darkness. I shook it harder, and the yellowy light flickered on a headline. Words jumped off the page. Atrocity. Blinded. Batik.

The torch went off. At the same moment, the back door of the hearse flew open.

The storm blasted in. Somebody – a brawling impact of arms and legs – tumbled in, and the wind slammed the door shut again.

She was utterly breathless... sorry, sorry... and utterly drenched. She fell onto me in the pitchy dark. I felt her bare arms and legs and the splash of her hair, a shock of cold from a thin sodden shirt, and as she untangled herself... sorry, sorry... her breath was hot on my face.

We recoiled from one another. I was hurt. An elbow or a knee had caught me square in the chest. Hissing with the pain, I hunched in one corner of the space and drew up my legs. I sensed the woman in the further corner, doing the same, withdrawing as far from me as she could. But the space was small. It steamed up, with the heat of her wet body and wet clothes. I could hear her shivering.

'The storm woke me,' she said at last, in a thin little voice. 'I came downstairs and you weren't there... I looked out and saw the light in your car...'

I paused before answering. There were bewildering words in my head, left behind when the torch had failed. I said, 'I couldn't sleep. I came outside and down here. I was listening to the wind and the rain and reading last year's news...'

I heard her moving towards me. 'Help me, will you?' she whispered. 'I can't... I'm cold and it's so wet it's sticking to me...'

I reached for her in the darkness. I pulled her shirt up and over her head. I took off my own shirt so she could dry herself with it, and then we lay together on the narrow bed, under my father's old blanket.

Chapter Eleven

IN THE FIRST light of dawn, I was aware of her leaving. She slid away from me, thinking I was asleep, and I watched her wriggling into her shirt and working out how to undo and push open the heavy door at the back of the hearse. Probably she'd never tried to get out of a hearse before. But she managed it, she pushed with all her weight and slipped outside, and I heard her quick soft footsteps in the wet grass as she hurried away.

It was the first time I'd seen her, that night. From the startling, explosive moment when she'd burst inside, until her furtive exit, it had been as dark as the grave. Really, not a glimmer of anything: the same blackness that the Daimler's long-ago passengers had seen, screwed into their coffins and wafted to the cemetery or the flames of the crematorium.

Juliet had made love to me, first of all with an almost animal urgency, and then again and again, with a lingering tenderness. Dark... more than dark... only the light of our imagination inside our heads.

No. Twice, or maybe three times, there'd been a faraway flicker of lightning as the storm roared over and around us, and I'd seen her looming above me; a ghostly shape, her silvery skin, the gleam of her eyes or her mouth. And then the darkness again.

She wouldn't let me move. She bit my ear and her breath was hot, she told me I was wounded I was hurt I mustn't move... she bit my lip and her mouth was hot, she told me I was hurt I was wounded I mustn't move. I lay back and submitted to her healing. And I felt that she needed me.

But no, she didn't need me. In that impenetrable darkness, it wasn't me she wanted. She whispered a name. Once, in a glimmer of lightning, she shouted a name. Not mine. All the time she was on me and I was in her, she was with someone else.

In the first light of dawn I watched her leaving. I watched the wriggle of her body. I heard her, an elf, tip-toe through the dew.

I WAITED UNTIL the light was better, before I reached for the newspapers. And then I hesitated. I was afraid of what I was going to read. I lay and waited longer than I needed to. And still I waited. I'd seen enough, before the torch went out, to make me sick of what I might read. And so I hid under the blanket. I pulled it over my head and closed my eyes. I smelled my body and I smelled the woman's body on mine.

At last I threw off the blanket and sat up. I rummaged among the newspapers. I read this, I read that, I crumpled them up and tossed them aside... I uncrumpled and re-read them, I screwed them into tighter and angrier fistfuls and flung them into a blizzard of paper. But the story I'd glimpsed in the night wasn't there.

A FEELING OF apprehension, almost a nausea in my stomach... I went slowly up the garden, barefoot, in my shirt and shorts, and wondered what we would talk about, what Juliet Lundy and I would say to one another when I appeared in the kitchen. Coffee and toast would be good. But it couldn't be as simple as that, after yesterday and last night.

Nothing was simple. I was bursting, and it should have been the easiest thing, without thinking for a fraction of a second, to pause beneath a tree on a beautiful summer's morning and piss into the long grass. But where? The woodland was cleansed by the tremendous rains in the night. The oak and beech had had a work-out and a spring-clean, they'd shaken down a flutter of leaves and a litter of twigs and the whole world was sparkling fresh. So it wasn't that easy, after the almost religious experience the boy had had in the nettles near the house, to just stop and do it.

Ridiculous. The ridiculousness of it made me stop and huff. Back home, at night, after a few beers on my balcony, I just strolled down to the river... dangerous and exhilarating, to stand in the dense shadows of *nippah*, to stare into a gruesome tangle of mangrove roots, to piss for a long long minute and think of the crocodiles lurking nearby. Every few months a man or a child would be taken and drowned and eaten, not uncommon in the Baram river. But I was literally careless, the beer and just being in Borneo were a great source of bravado.

Now, in a Lincolnshire garden, it was complicated. I was reluctant to piss in case I conjured the spirit of a lost airman, whose body was nibbled and gluey at the bottom of the North Sea.

I pushed through the reed bed and pissed into the pond. So I left no trace, and there were no crocs to worry about. Only, far out in the middle, there was a slow, oily-green swirl on the surface, as though something big and old was moving in the darkness.

Juliet was in the kitchen. She was wearing a faded, pale-blue cotton blouse and faded denim jeans. Her hair was still wet from the shower. She turned towards me, from where she was standing by the kettle, and we looked at one another for a silent moment until we both said, 'Hi,' at exactly the same time. She smiled at the chiming of our voices, a small smile, fragile with the hope that I would smile too. When I didn't, she said, 'Coffee? Toast?' as if everything might be as simple as that.

She gestured me to sit at the kitchen table. Strong coffee and home-made bread with butter and thick-cut marmalade. She remained standing, leaning against the counter where she'd boiled the kettle. When she bit into her toast, the butter ran onto her chin and she did a tiny squirmy giggle as she dabbed it with the back of her hand. 'I'm so hungry,' she said, 'something's made me so hungry.' And I was hungry too. The nervousness in my stomach was still there, and another undeniable, disconcerting feeling which made my mouth go dry. I'd looked at her before, of course I had. In my first days at Chalke House I'd glanced at her throat and her neck and, in an oblique, abstracted way, imagined the small of her back. But now that I'd held her and touched her and tasted her and knew that I might do so again, something jumped inside me at the thought of it. Unsettling too, as I remembered how utterly invisible she'd been, in the coffin-darkness of the hearse.

'Batik?' The word sprang into my head. I said it without pausing to think.

She stared at me over the rim of her coffee cup. She gulped and licked her lips and set the cup down on the counter.

'A funny coincidence,' I said. 'Lawrence showed me what he'd done in school, and I was going to tell him I'd seen the kids in Borneo doing it too. And then, last night, I was reading those old newspapers in my Dad's car and there it was. The word, I mean. A bit unusual. Batik.'

She didn't say anything. She raised her eyebrows and tried to smile, to show a polite interest in what I was saying. And then, giving up, she folded her arms across her chest and narrowed her eyes, as though daring me to go on.

So I did. 'Lawrence was showing me his batik and I thought it was good. But you didn't seem so keen. I mean, like you didn't want him to show it to me. Why's that?'

There was a timely distraction. We both glanced down at a gentle commotion on the floor.

Gentle, commotion. The words wouldn't usually work together, unless the agent concerned was a cat, whose speciality was a combination of stealth and violence. It was the orange cat, again, which had wrangled a pigeon bigger than itself into the tower bedroom, which had ambushed the grounded swift and borne it home for the boy to experiment on. Now, as if to defuse a difficult moment between its mistress and a nosey newcomer, the cat had overturned a laundry basket and was dragging Juliet's wet shirt across the floor, the one she'd worn when she came to the hearse.

'Bad puss...' she hissed at it. She flapped with a tea-towel. The cat feinted from the blow and retreated under the table. One of its claws was snagged in the shirt, it couldn't have let go if it tried, so it skulked in the shelter of the table legs and under my chair. When I bent and picked up the shirt and unhooked the cat's claw from it, the animal swiped at my hand, a raking pass which didn't break the skin, and at the same time, something else which must've been stuck inside the shirt dropped out.

An odd sock? A handkerchief? The cat sprang onto it. It was a crumpled ball of newspaper.

A perfect toy for the killer cat, something to menace and maul, to swat this way and that across the kitchen floor and chase and pounce on again. Each time Juliet bent to pick it up, the cat was too quick. It got there first and batted the ball of paper out of her reach.

It could've looked like a game... a lissom woman and her tigerish pet playing in a sun-filled country kitchen. Until Juliet, lunging hopelessly for the third time where the cat had been, slung the tea-towel at it and said with tremendous force, 'Fuck you, you fucking cat!'

The ball of paper skidded to a halt against my bare foot and I bent to pick it up.

'Give it to me,' she said. She crossed the room and held out her hand, as if she were a schoolteacher and I were a naughty boy. 'Give it to me.'

'No,' I said.

I was starting to unfold the paper onto the table when Lawrence came in.

Chapter Twelve

LAWRENCE LUNDY. MY father had had trouble saying the words. Because of his stroke, he'd blurred them oddly in his mouth. He'd heard the name somewhere before, but it wouldn't come back to him.

And then at last it had. 'Bad boy, bad boy...' His face had twisted into a grimace of revulsion.

Lawrence and Juliet Lundy stood over me, on either side of the table. They could both see what I'd got in front of me and knew what it was, they'd both tried to prevent me from seeing it. Now they stopped short of physically wresting the paper from me.

'You would've found out sooner or later.' It was the woman who spoke first. 'To tell the truth, we were both surprised you hadn't heard about it already. Of course I would've told you. We only thought to keep it back for a while because we weren't sure you'd stay very long anyway.' She said all this without looking at me, looking at her son as though the words would filter through him and then reach me. She glanced down at the paper. 'Go ahead. And then me or Lawrence will try and make some sense out of it.'

Lawrence had a sickly smile on his face. As usual he'd appeared in the kitchen unwashed and smelling of his bed. He must have thought I looked unusually tousled, unshaven and unshowered, in my bed-shirt and shorts. He wouldn't know that I'd slept in the car and had just wandered in from the garden. In the same way that I got a waft of his sleepy body, he was inhaling the scent from me. Something in the smell of my shirt, my hair, something on my skin... as he watched me trying to open up the sheet of paper, he was leaning closer and more overpoweringly, invading my space.

And sipping the air. Tasting it. When I glanced up and saw that odd little smile, I caught a glimpse of that ecstasy he'd experienced in the nettle-bed. It was a gleam of almost transcendental joy. A shiver ran through me. I saw him catch his mother's eye and he mouthed the words at her, thinking I was too preoccupied to notice.

'He's here, Dad is here!'

My smell. The fragrance of his mother's body, on me. And I could hardly say, *No, Lawrence, it's me, it's me you can smell, not the ghost of your father. He isn't here, it's a sunny summer's morning in your kitchen at home, there's toast and marmalade and just you and me and your Mum and your pesky cat. No ghosts, alright? The smell is me, because me and your Mum had sex last night in the back of my car. Me, not your father!*

I couldn't really say that. He was gleaming and glowing and towering over me, sniffing the air like a bloodhound.

They watched me trying to undo the newspaper. It was difficult because it was wet. She'd grabbed it and squashed it into her shirt as she left the hearse, and in the kitchen she must have forgotten and slung the shirt into the laundry basket with the paper inside it. I prised it very gently open, like an archaeologist teasing the secrets from a manuscript discovered in a shipwreck.

The *Lincoln Gazette*. Last October. Lawrence's face, a mug-shot, nearly all of the front page of the paper. A zombie face. A shock of black hair, heavy black eyebrows, empty black eyes. His mouth a scar. Beneath the photo, simply the name. He looked dead. Hanged or drowned.

BOY BLINDED BY BOILING WAX. ATROCITY IN SCHOOL BATIK LESSON.

Lawrence Lundy, a student at Alford Secondary School, was taken into police custody yesterday afternoon and charged

with assault. Lundy, 15, held two younger boys captive in the
school's art room and poured (continued on page 2)

I tried to turn the page over, but it had already started to stick
to the table. Sodden, it was breaking up. I may have spilled
some marmalade, some butter or a slick of coffee... whatever
it was, the paper was sticking and shearing, and when I tried
to tear it off, the newsprint was a ghostly inverted reflection of
its original self, back to front and...

boiling wax onto their faces. Police were on the scene to
rescue the boys and they were taken to St Mary's Hospital.
One of the boys, Toby Carroll, 12, was discharged the same
evening. Simon Winton, 13, is still in hospital. There are fears
he might...

Lawrence leaned over my shoulder. He clawed the paper off
the table. It shredded under his nails. 'The photo's terrible,' he
said. 'I was nervous. The story's alright, the facts are kind of
alright, but...'
He clawed again and again at the table. His nails made a
horrid grating noise. It reminded me of how the orange cat
had batted the ball of newspaper backwards and forwards
around the kitchen and then its desultory, instinctive swipe
at my hand. I leaned back in my chair and let him do it. He
scrunched the paper into a tighter and tinier ball, like a child
making the cruellest snowball of grit and compacted ice... and
perversely, because it had taken some doing and an unexpected
fuck you to get it from the cat, he tossed it onto the floor...
where the animal pounced, smote it out of the room with a
top-spin forehand and disappeared into the garden.
'I'll tell you what happened,' Lawrence said.

IT'S A PISSY *tuesday morning. we drive to school and it's still*
dark because it's like october and it feels like we're burrowing
deeper and deeper into a miserable long winter. it's raining.

leaves blowing everywhere, they're falling off the trees and blowing everywhere and the road and pavements are kind of black and shiny.

mum drops me at school. tuesday is crap, school is crap full stop, but tuesday's the worst. the morning's maths and english, lord of the fucking flies again with mr ramsay just reading it to us in his plummy reading-aloud voice. death by boredom. tuna sandwich in the canteen and then it's art club in the afternoon. which is good. I mean it's all crap but art club is the only time in the week when my head isn't just banging with boredom.

art club with mr bray. he smells, his clothes and his hair smell of cigarettes and his fingers are yellowy with nicotine. drink too, on his breath, even in the mornings, I guess it's from lots of beer or whisky or something the night before.

but he's an artist. I mean, really. I've seen his stuff. I don't know why he's a teacher, like ramsay and all the others who are just so crap and ordinary and boring. he plays music in his art room too.

so it's tuesday afternoon. there's bray and me and two other kids in the art room. it's pissing down outside and already getting dark, only three or half-past, and the tree outside is scratching on the window. bray says it's a quince or something, he says it's rare maybe the only one in the county. I don't care what it is, but I kind of like the scratchy sound, the rhythm of it and the rain. bray's got some jazz on, piano and bass and drums, says it's errol garner. I like it. and we're doing batik. so the room's warm and fuggy and nice, with a big pan of wax heating up on the gas ring in the corner.

someone comes in. a girl. a woman, I guess. annoying, it spoils the private art club thing. bray says she's a student from lincoln university doing her teaching practice and wants to watch the club. she's thin and white with thin ratty hair, smells of some kind of cream for spots. a wash-out, I can tell straight off. trying to be nice. pathetic. she's been in the room two minutes and I want her to piss off.

*worse, she's doing a project. she's got a lot of big books
and stuff and bray says she's going to do some tests on us. so
I'm starting to feel scratchy because it's spoilt the mood and
the music, and even the quince on the window is annoying
scratchy instead of part of the music and rain and a nice dark
afternoon...*

*bray goes out. I guess he thinks he can slip out for a coffee or
a drink or something because the student's there.*

*she calls me over, I have to leave what I'm doing, even though
the pan of wax is boiling bubbling and I want to paint it onto
my material, and she sits me down with her at bray's table.*

*big heavy books she's got. she turns the pages and there are
lots of dots and spots and different colours. she asks me what
I can see, any shapes or numbers or letters in the dots. some
of them are clear. some of them a bit vague, I'm not sure.
and pages where there's nothing, nothing but kind of washed-
out pastel colours with no shapes or letters or numbers or
anything.*

*she's looking at me funny sideways. asks me to try some of
the pages again. and she's writing stuff in her little exercise
book. One of the other kids, a little twat called carroll, that's
his surname, he's a boy called carroll, wanders over and he's
looking over my shoulder and he kind of snorts each time I say
there's nothing. I turn round and tell him to fuck off.*

*the student-girl-woman goes red. the other twat called
winton comes over. I can feel him there behind me and I can
hear him sniggering, so I turn round again and tell him to fuck
off too.*

*student's very red. not blushing, but blotchy. thin sea-weedy
hair and a big spot on her chin and blotchy. she stares at me
so I stare at her and she looks scared. she pushes weedy bits
of hair behind her ear and she writes in her book. her ear's red
too. I want to tell her to fuck off.*

*when I stand up and walk away, she calls after me, like
trying to be nice and friendly but her voice shaking because
she's nervous and weak and frightened of me. she's saying stuff*

like don't worry it's quite common, it's mostly boys, reds and greens and browns the commonest type... and she's wittering on and her voice is scratchy and grating and she's saying stuff like they call it colour-blindness but it's nothing serious and won't make any difference you just see things differently and...

I walk back towards her and put my face right up to hers and whisper look I don't want to hear this so fuck off will you

so she does. she scurries out of the room like she's going to piss herself, with her big magic books and her secret little note book, a spotty little student-witch with her silly spells.

I can't remember the rest of it so clearly. I remember rubbing my eyes a lot. rubbing them because... I don't know I'm mad because she said about blindness it makes me feel angry for my eyes, for being blind, not really blind but... I mean she can see stuff I can't see, and the twats carroll and winton are sniggering because I can't see stuff they can see and there's something wrong with me and

angry. angry with the student doing her experiment on me for her fucking project... angry with the other kids. I go to the door and lock it.

I jab carroll in the stomach. that's all it takes. he falls onto the floor like he's choking, like he can't breathe. I shove winton so hard he goes down too. he isn't sniggering anymore. like he's crying, frightened because I locked the door.

got a feeling, a kind of calm feeling. know what I'm going to do. don't need to think. suddenly it's nice again. art club, a dark rainy cosy october afternoon.

erroll garner. quince. batik. and the wax is boiling.

someone's banging on the door, someone's shouting outside...
I get the wax off the gas ring, carry it across to the kids.
white faces. big eyes. big eyes better than mine.
not fair. so I pour the wax.

Chapter Thirteen

I SPENT A long time in the shower. I ran the water as cold as I could get it and stood there in my shirt and shorts. And then I peeled them off and soaped myself from head to toe and examined my body.

The bruises on my ribs were changing colour: yellows and browns and darkening blotches of purple at the different points of impact with the branches of the Scots pine. I soaped and rinsed and massaged gingerly with my fingertips, and I wondered what the boy might make of the varying shades.

Colours and shapes... whatever he might see in the bruises which were altering as my body adjusted to the pain, that afternoon in the school artroom had been life-changing for him. A few thoughtless words had blighted his prospects of emulating the father he hero-worshipped, his boyish dreams had been shattered, he'd been grounded. A trivial thing, for a teenage boy to be colour-blind, not uncommon or noteworthy, unless it simply, unalterably, thwarted everything.

Life-changing for one of the other boys too. So Juliet had told me, when Lawrence had finished his horribly casual drawling of what he'd done and he'd loafed into the garden. She'd closed the story with a pithy footnote: one of the boys had been permanently blinded by the wax.

'So now you know,' she'd said. 'I didn't take him out of school because he's colour-blind. He was kept in a kind of detention-centre and they ran all sorts of psychiatric tests on him. I was here on my own and it was awful. Whenever I went to the village or into town I had people staring at me and even calling me in the street. And someone did that paint-job on my car, I don't know who, maybe the boy's mother or father or someone...'

She'd crossed the room towards me. I thought she was going to touch me or hold me, or she wanted to be touched or held by me, but she went past and looked out of the door to see where Lawrence had gone.

We'd both looked out. He was outside with the cat. He'd confiscated the newspaper from it. It had torn the ball open, and bits of the newsprint were scattered on the grass, like the feathers of a bird it had killed. Now, belying its prowess as a hunter, it was rolling on its back and letting the boy tickle its furry white belly. The boy, having lulled the cat into an almost hypnotic state, straightened up and wandered down the garden, where he tossed the ball high into the air and watched it splash into the middle of the pond.

'You smell of us.' Juliet had turned to me at last. Her hands went to my waist and I winced in anticipation of her touching my ribs. Hiding her face close to my chest, she'd said, 'You smell of us. Go and get showered and then do what you want. You could pack up your stuff and get out of here. It's a thirty-minute walk to the top of the lane and there's a bus every hour.' She lifted her face and looked up at me. 'But I want you to stay. And I think, in his odd, perverse sort of way, Lawrence wants you to stay as well.'

I wasn't so sure about that. And I wasn't sure what was happening with me and Juliet. My body, a foolish man's body, seemed to know. Despite the coldness of the shower, it reacted unequivocally when I thought of our love-making in the hearse.

So what did I do? Get the bus back to Grimsby? I put on my favourite t-shirt, the one I used for my late-afternoon runs into the jungle, worn and washed seven days a week for years. It had faded to grey, but the print on it was still clear: *Sarawak, Borneo,* with a representation of a hornbill surrounded by the scroll-work typical of the ethnic Iban. And I went upstairs to the tower.

The boy had showered too. Indeed his room was more fragrant, or less pungent than usual. He'd sprayed something around, an air-freshener or a cologne. He'd opened the windows on all four sides, and the very sky, with all the scents of the woodland and the summer itself, was breezing in. The model planes were whirling and clacking overhead, engaged in an endless dog-fight, and the boy and his cat were sprawled on the bed. He didn't seem at all surprised that I'd come in. He had some books open in front of him, and, as though I'd been there all the time and we'd been engaged in a conversation, he was saying, 'Yes, the footless birds, the Latin name for swifts and swiftlets is *apodidae,* meaning footless... because their feet are so small and feeble and almost nothing at all...'

He turned and looked at me as I stood in the doorway. 'And what was it you were saying about devil-birds and some kind of spooky folklore? I like the idea that they're so specialised for flying that their feet have shrivelled. I mean, like the planes my Dad flies, they're so awesome in flight that any other kind of unnecessary stuff's been designed out of them.'

I hesitated in the doorway. He waved me closer to look at the books he'd spread onto the bed. 'They're my Dad's,' he said. 'I thought I'd dig them out. I think there are more somewhere, under Mum and Dad's bed or something.'

I hesitated for another second, and then I sat on the bed. I could've turned and walked out. A bus every hour. But I sat on the bed, and I heard myself windily speaking, as though it was someone else's voice in the blustering room... 'devil-birds, yes, because they're so dark and mysterious and screaming like crazy, hurtling and swerving and never stopping... and legends about the swifts, mating in mid-air and sleeping in mid-air... and when it gets dark and the swifts go quiet and disappear, they vanish into ponds and lakes and they stay there all night, deep in the mud at the bottom...'

The boy had almost stopped breathing. He was sipping the air and holding it in his chest and letting it seep out again. My voice took up again, windswept, weaving in the clack and clatter of the planes on the ceiling. '...or they go to the moon, look hard and you'll see the moon is shaded and blotched with patches of grey... enormous flocks of swifts, clinging with their tiny feet and roosting all night...'

Thoughtful, he reached under his pillow and pulled something out. It was the piece in batik he'd brought to show me the other day. The Scots pine, the bright moon, the dark pond.

He stared at it and pursed his lips. 'Funny, I did this,' he said very softly, almost wistfully, 'I did this in the art club with Mr Bray last year, before... before it all happened. And now you're here and we're talking about it and I never thought... I mean I'd never really noticed the swifts before, I'd never really seen them. But look, look what I did... I've even done the little grey shadows, the swifts roosting on the moon...'

Indeed he had. It was beautifully executed. We examined it closely. 'And now you'll always see them,' I said, 'you'll see them and marvel at them until it's time for them to go away at the end of the summer.'

'Maybe they won't go away,' he said. 'Do the things you like always have to go away?'

He folded the batik and pushed it under his pillow again. He did it with a childish gesture which was odd in such a rangy, manly boy: he had a downy face, hairy legs with great muscular calves like a cyclist's, an Adam's apple like a golf-ball in his throat, but he kept the picture he'd done in art club under his pillow, like a comforter.

He noticed me watching him. 'I made it for my Dad,' he said, with a shrug and a mocking smile. 'I keep it here for when he comes back. The big tree, because he built the tree-house so I could go up there and watch for him coming back from his missions... the pond, because he told me stuff about it since I was little, about the monster pike and stuff... and the moon, well, it just looks good, and now it's good because I got the swifts on it and it...'

He shrugged again. The self-deprecating smile. He was almost charming.

No. Monstrously, he was wooing me. I couldn't help staring at him, with a kind of dreadful fascination. Fascination for a boy who, less than an hour ago, had described in a weary nonchalant voice an atrocity he'd committed. And a feeling of dread in the pit of my stomach. A dread of whatever ugliness he might still be capable of.

No, Lawrence Lundy was not charming. Enthralling? I didn't want to be in thrall to his fake little smile, to the complicated trap I was slithering into. Captivating, like the pitcher plants in my Borneo garden – slippery, inescapable, carnivorous.

I met his eyes. His eyes met mine. And a strange thing happened. In a breezy, sunlit room, on a morning in June, an ice-cold shiver ran down my spine. I was afraid.

SARAWAK, BORNEO... MAGICAL words. When I'd made the decision to stay a bit longer at Chalke House and go upstairs to the boy in his tower, I'd deliberately put on the t-shirt as a kind of visual aid, a conversation piece, the sort of thing educationalists had started calling 'realia' – anything a teacher might take into a lesson, other than books, to interest his students. Sure enough, when the smile slipped off Lawrence's face and he noticed the shirt, he read the words aloud. They hung in the cool English air of his bedroom, as mysterious as the human skulls I'd seen hanging in the smoke-blackened rafters of the longhouses on the Baram river.

I told him more about my life out there, that many of my students were Iban from the *kampongs* in the rainforest, whose tradition of head-hunting had persisted until fairly recent times. There were stories that, when north Borneo had been occupied by the Japanese in World War II, the Iban had been encouraged to take the heads of enemy soldiers who strayed too deep into the jungle. I'd been invited to my students' homes for the annual festival of *gawai*, to stay the night and drink their brain-damaging *tuak*, and, eventually collapsing onto the bamboo floors of the longhouse, I'd drifted into a nightmarish sleep with the cobwebby skulls dangling over my head...

It wasn't difficult to regale the boy. Man-eating crocodiles, the scorpion in my bathroom, the cobra in my backyard. The folklore of the indigenous people, their tales of witchcraft and superstition. The veneer of Islam – the cry of the mosque in the darkness before dawn, in the glare of the day, in the golden light of the evening and again at night, as though the drone of repetition might smother all pre-existing thought.

'And what's this, the bird?' he asked.

'Hornbill. It's a symbol of Borneo, so typically a part of the island, like the orang-utan or the proboscis monkeys, that it's always used on tourist brochures and souvenirs and things. For me, they're a real part of my life out there. Every afternoon, at about five o'clock, I get a flock of them coming up river, I've counted more than fifty sometimes. They pause in my compound, they crash into one of my trees and rest for a while and then they carry on upstream, on their way to roosting somewhere in the forest.'

'And the pattern? What's all this?'

He took me by surprise. Not the question, about the Iban scrollwork on my shirt, but the way he jabbed at it with a bony finger and caught me hard in the ribs.

'Hey, watch out...' I gasped and jumped away from him.

He mouthed a word which could have been *sorry*, hard to tell because his lips were curled into a smirky sneer. And then he managed to say, 'Sorry, I forgot,' as I stood away from his bed and tried to ease the pain by pressing the flat of my hand onto the bruises. 'Sorry, let me see ..'

I warily allowed him to examine the discolouring skin, as I'd imagined him doing when I was in the shower. This time there were no cryptic signs to be discovered, it wasn't a challenge which might undo all the dreams he'd held so precious. He said to me, 'I can see all the colours, you know. A lot of people, even the so-called experts who examined me, they think that if you're colour-blind you see everything in black and white. It's not like that at all. Look...' And with the tip of the finger he'd jabbed me with, he touched the bruises with exquisite gentleness and whispered, 'Orange... a kind of yellowy... this is red going to purple...' and seemed to relish the words in his mouth like charms or spells.

He got most of the colours right. Yes, he could see them and identify them and even roll the words on his tongue with a thrill of pleasure. He could enjoy them as much as I could, as much as the boys in the art club could until he'd splashed boiling wax into their eyes. But he got some of the colours wrong. Enough to spoil everything.

The wind dropped. The model planes stopped knocking together and there was a stillness in the trees in the woodland. It was so sudden that a new sound crept into the room. It was coming from under the bed, yes, like a creeping or a creaking, or a scratching. I cocked my head at it. The boy saw me listening, and his voice was unnecessarily loud when he butted into the quietness, 'you were saying about the swiftlets in Sarawak...' and he was poking his finger at my shirt again, dangerously close to my bruises, 'you said you've got a flock of them under your house, and...'

'What's that noise?'

'I couldn't find much in the books about them,' he went on, 'but you said you'd got lots at home in Borneo, and thousands of them, or was it millions? in the caves nearby...'

I hushed him sharply, and he stopped. I said, 'Listen, you've got a mouse or something under your bed, Lawrence. It'd better watch out for your killer cat. Shall I take a look?'

He didn't move. He seemed resigned to let me nose around, as if he couldn't be bothered with what I might find or he was just humouring me. I knelt down and peered into the shadows: dust and cobwebs, and the empty cardboard boxes in which the model planes had been packed. I thought that a mouse or a rat or even a squirrel might skitter past me, as I pushed some of the boxes gently aside, but there was no movement, only that sound: a scratch and a flutter. A bad smell. And when I laid my palm flat on one of the boxes, a feeble vibration.

I slid the box out. A Phantom. I opened it and the swift was lying in a pool of droppings. At first, stunned by the light, it was perfectly still. It wasn't even breathing. I thought that the shock of my opening the box might have killed it. But then it shuddered... hardly alive, it quivered its long black wings like a dying butterfly, in an effort to unstick its matted feathers from the glue of its own mess.

'What are you doing, Lawrence?' I said softly. 'Why have you done this?'

I glanced around at him. He was agitated; he was sitting on the edge of his bed with both his hands inside his shirt, scratching with his nails as hard as he could, at his chest, his arms, his neck, at the blebs of the nettle stings.

'I want to keep it,' he said. 'You let the other one go, the one that came into my room. I want to keep this one. I caught it in the sky, at the top of the tree. I saved it from the cat. I mended it and tried to make it fly again. It still can't, but I'm keeping it and maybe it'll fly one day...'

'It'll never fly again. This poor little thing will never fly again, Lawrence. For heaven's sake, look what you've done to it!'

He'd removed the plastic strut which he'd stuck onto its broken wing, but the feathers were botched with the glue he'd used. As I lifted it out of the box, it scrabbled at my hands with its pathetic, vestigial feet. It rowed at the air with all the strength left in its wings. It blinked its eyes, but they were blobbed with mucus and the yellow-white mutes it had squirted into the darkness and smeared around.

'It's going to die, Lawrence. It is dying, inside this shitty coffin. For heaven's sake, can't you smell it?'

'Give it to me.' He stopped scratching himself, reached forward and flicked the bird off my hands, back into the box. 'Give it to me. Of course I can smell it. Why do you think I've sprayed around?'

He took the box from me, closed the lid and slid it back under the bed. End of lesson.

Chapter Fourteen

I WOKE SO suddenly that I heard myself yelp. I didn't know where I was. I was in a bed in a dark room, startled from sleep by a beam of light on the window.

For a few moments I was at home, in my stilted house in Borneo. I listened for the mosque. Not a sound. It must be too early, only two or three o'clock in the middle of the night. The room felt big and empty around me, a shadowy space, it was my room in my home, and outside the window lay a slumbering forest and a huge whispering river.

A light. The wandering beam of a torch. Someone was out there, in my garden. I froze and listened, for an intruder trying my door or scaling the stilts to reach my window. I sat up and swung my legs out of bed... and the reality of the room came back to me, because someone was in my bed and stirring and waking and mumbling.

'What is it? Who?' She sat up and reached for me in the darkness. 'Are you there?'

She was naked in my bed in my room. She'd come to me at midnight, as she'd come to the car in a torrential storm – a woodland elf, invisible but sweetly tangible. And after she'd made love to me, we'd slept so profoundly that my dreams of Borneo and Lincolnshire were entwined.

Now the dreams were gone. We were both starkly awake. Her first touch on my back froze too, when she noticed the light. We held our breath and listened, heard nothing, as a round yellow beam stroked this way and that across the front of the house and faded away.

We went to the window and looked out. The boy was outside on the grass. He was a pale figure in nothing but shorts, a torch in one hand and something else, his binoculars on a loop around his neck. As he moved beneath the trees, his body washed by the moonlight and then hidden in shadow, he would pause as though lost in thought, and then turn again to the house and play the torchlight on it.

We instinctively flinched from it. As the beam slid towards us, Juliet took my arm and pulled me away from the window. We waited and we watched as the light fell into the room. For a moment it bathed the narrow, rumpled bed, and then it moved on and the room was dark again.

'What's he doing?' she whispered. I felt her body on mine as she pressed me back to the window. 'What's he looking for?'

One more raking pass across the house, too quick for us to avoid it, and the torchlight flicked off. Strangely, it made it easier for us to see the boy. There was a big moon, dimly shrouded in clouds which seemed to cling around it like cobwebs. It gave a gentle, silvery-grey light, and the boy's body was lean and lithe as he went through the woodland and down to the pond. There he stopped, and he peered with intense fascination at the surface of the water. No movement, not a bubble or a ripple disturbed the glassy darkness. He did a strange thing: he dipped to the ground and put down the torch, he straightened up and clapped his hands once, and a second and a third time. It echoed, sudden and alien in the softness of the summer's night. When he stopped clapping and the only sound was the stirring of the branches all around him, he waved his arms slowly, dreamily, at the pond, as if he might catch the attention of some torpid creature and awaken it.

'He's looking for the birds,' I said.

He bent again, and I thought he might pick up the torch to flash it across the water. But no, he started pulling clumps of weed and grass and tossing them onto the surface. They landed like thistledown. Looking for anything larger and heavier to throw, he drifted into a huge black shadow beneath an oak tree and emerged with an armful of twigs and sticks. He tossed them into the air. For a few moments, the surface of the water splattered and splashed. But then it was still again.

The boy stood as still as stone, and he stared across the pond.

At last he bent and reached for the torch. Deliberately, with a solemn purpose, so that the glimmer of the pond might not distract him, he strode back into the shadow of the oak and he braced himself, his body like a strong white fork set into the earth, to aim the binoculars at the moon. He stayed like that, a statue of a young god, for a minute and another minute, long enough for me and Juliet to look away from him and see what he was seeing.

The cobwebby moon. Fogged with cloud, as though the night had breathed on it and then forgotten to polish it clean.

The boy swung the binoculars away from his face. Thinking that the dampness of the woodland was on his lenses, he breathed on them and rubbed them on the hem of his shorts. Again and again he huffed on the lenses and wiped them, and he aimed at the moon. No, no good. Far beyond his reach, a negligible cloud was thwarting his vision.

'The birds?' The woman's voice was very small. It trembled with fear. 'What do you mean, the birds?'

'The swifts. He can't find where they're roosting. He's looked around the house, under the eaves and the battlements of his tower, but they aren't there. I've looked too and I don't know, and now he's...'

'Now he's what? What are you talking about? I mean, the pond? The moon? What's he doing?'

We turned from the window and she tipped her anxious face up to mine. I hesitated. Our bodies were inches apart, but there was a silence between us. I tried to speak, but I couldn't find words for the foolishness I'd told the boy, the stories of ignorance and superstition. Not then, as we stood naked in the darkness of my bedroom. I couldn't tell her why her son was transfixed by the moon, like a medieval lunatic. And when we glanced outside again, the boy was gone.

'Where is he?' Fear in her voice. 'Is he coming inside?'

I heard his footsteps as he padded through the living-room and into the hallway. Heard him pause down there. It was so quiet, as the two of us strangled our breath and strained to listen, that I thought I could hear the boy's breathing as he came up the stairs. Juliet made for the door, and in a moment of panic she flitted across the landing into her own room.

Her door was wide open. Mine too. I heard a flurry as she dived into her bed. I crossed to my bed and slipped under the sheet, just as the boy reached the landing and stopped.

Yes, I could hear his breathing. And I could smell him. I knew, although my eyes were tightly closed and I was pretending to be asleep, that he'd come into my room and was leaning over my bed and his face was only an inch from mine. I could smell his breath. He was so close I could hear him licking his lips. I could smell the woodland on his body, the grasses he'd torn up, the bosky fragrance of the branches he'd held against his skin. I thought of surprising him by flicking my eyes open and shouting into his face, for no reason except to show him I was as awake and sentient as he was... but then I sensed him moving away and out of my door.

I let him go. When I heard him cross the landing and go into his parents' room, I took a breath and followed.

I stood in the shadows and watched him. Something about his movements... I'd sensed something different when he was outside, a sleepy kind of stealth, almost a slow-motion in his actions. Not the torpor of the swifts, which they could achieve when at last they rested from their manic hurtling, but the rhythm of his breathing and every step he took was slower, as though he were moving in water or some kind of dream. He stood over his mother and stared at her.

He was huge, nude, a towering man. He bent to her, as I'd felt him bend to me, and he put his mouth so close to hers I thought he might kiss her. No, he was smelling her. He was tasting her in long, greedy inhalations. His face touched her hair, I saw her hair move in his breath. He smelled her skin, where her shoulder was out of the sheets, and his tongue flickered out and he licked her.

He padded across to the wardrobe, opened it and pressed his face into the clothes hanging there... his father's shirts and trousers, his RAF uniform. Moving to the dressing table, he picked up a bottle of after-shave, sniffed it and put it down. He picked up a hairbrush, a man's, and he teased at the bristles until he'd extracted a spool of hair. He put down the brush, rolled the hair into a ball in the palm of his hand, sniffed it as though it were a rare and precious drug, and then he blew it away into the darkness.

And then he crossed to his mother's bed again. I felt a swooping in my stomach: fear of what he might do.

He knelt on the floor. He slid under the bed. He slid so far that only his legs stuck out, and he was rummaging for something, feeling for something, searching...

Quite bizarre.

Me, a teacher from Borneo, stark naked in a house in the Lincolnshire wolds.

My father, gaga in Grimsby.

A woman, who'd been fucking me like a ferret barely an hour ago, paralysed by fear and flashing me a terrified look through slitted eyes.

Her son, a gangly youth with a record of horrible violence and an inclination to believe in ghosts, under her bed with his legs sticking out.

The boy emerged. He came out with a book. He stood up and blew the dust off it. It was one of his father's bird books.

He opened it there and then, standing tall and lean by his mother's bed. He flicked on the torch, riffled the pages and played the yellow beam onto them. They threw fluttering shadows on the ceiling, like images from the first magical moments of motion pictures. And, 'Where, where, where...?' the boy whispered through dry, dusty lips.

It was then I realised... I realised why his movements outside, by the unresponsive pond and under the foggy, ineffable moon, had seemed so slow. He was asleep. He'd been asleep all the time.

I knew, because he came out of his mother's bedroom and past me without a glance in my direction, although I'd made a clumsy, belated effort to withdraw from the landing. He paused, yes he paused for a moment and tasted the air. He inhaled and pursed his lips like a sommelier, and he felt at the empty space where I'd been standing, as though somebody was still there.

With the faintest smile on his mouth, he disappeared up the narrow little staircase to his tower.

Chapter Fifteen

'SO THIS IS where you are. I wondered where you'd gone.'
Juliet's voice surprised me. I turned round. She was standing
in the late afternoon sun, dappled in green, a denizen of the
forest clothed in a glimmer of holly. She threw her arm up to
her face, because something was dazzling her. 'And I can't find
Lawrence. I thought maybe you'd gone out together. Do you
know where he is? What are you doing?'

I'd been down to the hearse for some of my father's tools
and then around to the back of the house. As surreptitiously
as possible, I'd taken the mouldy tarpaulin off her car. First
of all, I'd managed to open the driver's door and ping the
bonnet-release catch. I'd heaved up the bonnet and with some
difficulty I'd removed the battery.

My mind had been a muddle of thoughts. About the woman
and me... I marvelled at myself and the kind of person I must
be, because in all my several relationships with girls and
women since my teens, I'd never once been the pursuer, they'd
always come to me, to my room, to my bed and slipped into
it. About my ribs, which I'd thought were getting better, and
the discomfort was easing... until I wrestled the battery out the
car, and the weight of it sent such a stabbing pain through my
body that I yelped and nearly dropped the wretched lump onto
the ground. The dense cover of holly, bristling darkly behind
the house, had given me a sense of privacy, a retreat from the
woman and the boy and whatever he was up to. I thought I
knew what Lawrence was doing: he was looking for the place
where the swifts might roost at night. Why, I wasn't sure,
but it seemed a harmless enough project to occupy him, and

even his loony rambles in the garden were hardly worrisome, compared with the damage he'd done in the real world.

That was the way my mind was muddling, when I'd hidden myself in the holly wood and pulled the tarpaulin off the car. But then the real world had jumped out. Eye – an eye for an eye – daubed in blood.

I winced at the ugliness of it, and all the hatred that had gone into it. When I touched the red paint and felt the thickness of it, the way it had pooled and set, I could feel the anger. The mother of a blinded boy had lifted a full, heavy bucket and tipped it, pouring out her pain and bitterness. That was reality. Lawrence Lundy mooching in the garden was... well, nothing, he was just a mooching teenager, indulging a mood.

The bonnet was still wide open, a glaring slab of red. Juliet threw up her arm to shield her eyes from it.

I was holding the battery. The deadly weight of it was stretching my arms and tugging my ribs. I said feebly, 'I want to start up the Daimler. It doesn't mean I'm running away or anything. It's my Dad's car and the battery's flat and so I owe it to him to try and fix it.'

'I hear you,' she said. 'But I can't see...' She strode past me, reached to the bonnet and pulled it shut. There was a tremendous clang, probably the loudest noise the valley had heard since the glacier was grinding it out. It echoed through the trees. A volley of wood-pigeons erupted into the sky.

In the silence that followed, Juliet appraised the damage to her car as though it had just happened, as though she'd never seen it before. I mean, I watched her and I could imagine how she'd first discovered it, returning to the car with her shopping, on a bright autumn day in a busy high street or a town centre car-park. She stared, she stared longer, she looked closely and she cocked her head at the horridness of it. And then? What did she do? She did what anyone, even the burliest, bravest man would have done... sensing a murderous anger in the air, she glanced around with fear in her eyes, in case the person who had done it was still there.

I felt a surge of compassion for her. She was only a little green elf. The prickliness of the holly gleamed on her. She was so small, so alone, so wounded, so afraid. Looking at her and the way she flinched from the shadows, I was suddenly so moved that I dropped the battery with a thud and took her into my arms.

'There's no one here, there's no one here...' I was whispering into her hair, ' and no one's going to hurt you... it's all over and it's horrible but it's all over now... I'm going to stay and there's just you and me and Lawrence and we're all safe and no one's going to hurt us and...'

She was shuddering against me. I held her very tightly, her face buried in my chest.

A curious and very wonderful thing happened. The wood pigeons clattered into the holly trees around us. We could hear them settling into the dense foliage, adjusting themselves into the armoury of spikes... and when she sniffed and wiped her nose on my shoulder and we both looked up to watch them, they were as plump and smug as choirboys preening in a vestry. As though the huge metallic clang had never happened and their life was as orderly as ever before, they started to coo.

The wood-pigeon coo – the softest, sleepiest sound the world had ever heard. I felt her body relax against mine. She was boneless. The shuddering didn't stop, but I realised she wasn't crying anymore or frightened. She was giggling. The cotton-wool cooing was as marvellous as morphine. Everything was alright. How could it not be, with the fat, silly pigeons cooing so cosily over our heads?

'All I want,' she said eventually, spluttering with laughter, 'all I want... all I want is to blubber onto your shirt, listen to these birds in the trees, and know that Lawrence is safe. That's all I want, to know he's safe.' She looked up at me, and her face was streaky with tears, like a child awakening from a nightmare. 'Stay with us and we'll all feel safer.'

* * *

So. It was a bit ironic, after that injunction, to be stumbling through the woodland with the battery bumping against my ribs, to try and start the car which might facilitate my leaving. But that was what we did. We covered her car with the tarpaulin, we dragged the mouldy green stuff across it, and it was no longer the 'ultimate driving machine' but a mouldering heap – disfigured, disembowelled, an animal which had died in the forest and would soon be fetid with fungi. I carried the battery. Juliet walked beside me.

Before we got to the hearse, we found the boy. There was a crash of breaking glass. A whoop, like a head-hunter or a baboon. Another smash of glass.

And the boy emerged from a dense green shadow into a shaft of sunlight, like an end-of-the-pier comedian bursting on-stage. 'I found them! I think I found them! Come and look!'

Blood. He shook his head and spattered us with blood. He was a grinning goof, in the same old t-shirt and shorts, with a fresh, big gash somewhere in his hair. I felt it splash onto my face and saw it on his mother's. I dropped the battery. Before we could smear at the blood, he took hold of Juliet's wrist in one hand and my wrist in the other and tugged us with him... and he was so strong, so hot and young and sinewy, that we could do no more than simply stumble behind him.

He dragged us through a barricade of nettles and bramble, through a forest of elder and cow-parsley. He'd flattened them already on his way through, and in doing so he'd crushed the stalks into a sappy fume – heady, the green essence of summer. Some broken bricks underfoot, where a surprised toad sprang away from our clumsy tread... and we were into the derelict greenhouse I'd first spotted when I'd arrived at Chalke House.

'I looked in the books!' he was saying with great excitement. He still had us by the wrists, and his grip was harsh. 'One of Dad's books, I got it out last night, from under Mum's bed when she was fast asleep... nowadays they never nest in natural places, I mean they always use barns or houses or old factories or churches or whatever, you know, man-made buildings to nest in... and here they are, in the greenhouse!'

'But what've you done, Lawrence? Your head... let me see...'

He let go of our wrists and bent towards her. Blood was welling from his scalp. Again, unnecessarily, he shook his head, with a kind of gruesome friskiness... and as a haze of it blurred into my eyes, I had a vision of a puppy I'd rescued from a monitor lizard in my garden, and its nose and mouth had been lashed by the lizard's tail and it was licking at my face with a mixture of panic and joy and gratitude. 'I was climbing the vine, I grabbed one of the old beams and the glass broke and... don't worry Mum I'm alright I'm alright...'

His mother was trying to inspect the wound, but he grappled her off him. The blood ran off his brow and down his nose and into his mouth. He grinned, and his teeth were red. 'Come and see, let me show you...'

The old greenhouse was a marvellous place. As big as a squash court, it was a grand structure of sagging beams and mossy glass, leaning wearily against an overgrown cliff. Difficult to tell, at first glance, if the ancient, serpentine vine which had torn up the brickwork of the floor and was feeling into every corner and space of the building with long, muscular tendrils... hard to say if the vine was pulling the greenhouse down or holding it up. Whatever else had been cultivated there, flowers or fruits or vegetables for the residents of Chalke House, had been overwhelmed by the flora of an English woodland. Yes, it was a fragrant wilderness, and nothing wrong with that.

And all along the overhead rafters, the nests of the swifts. Dozens or scores of them. Not at all spectacular to look at – little cups of stuff stuck here and there, clumsy little cups that primary school kids might botch up with papier-mâché for an enthusiastic teacher – except that the boy was brimming with the joy of their discovery. He was spouting at his mother through his horrid red bubbly lips, all sorts of garbled facts he'd got from his father's book from under her bed... about the swifts gathering their nest material in mid-air, catching straws and feathers and dust in flight and sticking it all to the rafters with their own saliva... all true and extraordinarily wonderful, except that I was watching him with a kind of morbid fascination, the fascination I'd felt when I'd been nude and afraid in the shadows and his mother had been naked and fearful in her bed and he'd been licking her.

I looked at his teeth. The blood on them. His lips and the mucous blood on his tongue. His eyes were wild as he enthused like an eccentric professor, about the swifts and their mad, relentless flight. Now and then, as he waved his arms at the rafters, where after all there were no birds but only their gobbets of saliva and grass and other regurgitated fluids, a new gush of blood would burst out of his hair and dribble into his eyebrows. And I wanted to get out.

'I'm going to come down here this evening, I'm going to stay down here and wait and watch them coming to roost! Look up there, that's where I climbed up, there's lots of holes in the glass, where the glass is broken... that's where they come in!'

I edged away from him. I passed my hands across my brows and nose and chin and felt the smear of his blood. He was enthusing to his mother, looming over her and quite unaware of my leaving. She shrank beneath him, quivering like a shrew he'd discovered in a damp corner of the greenhouse, amazed by his sheer size and power. So full of himself and his own strange purpose, he'd blanked out everything but this burgeoning project. He didn't notice as I moved out of his range, but Juliet was overwhelmed.

It was a relief to be alone in the woodland. The boy's hectoring voice faded as I picked up the car battery and walked through the trees. It was about six o'clock, or later, one of the longest days of the year. It would be light until ten, cool and light: blissfully refreshing for me, after the unchanging years in the tropics, where the months were no different except for the roaring rains of monsoon. No seasons, and every evening at half past six, when the mosque was calling the faithful to the *maghrib* prayers, there was dusk and nightfall, from daylight to darkness, in a matter of fifteen minutes.

A long, English summer's evening, holier than a perfunctory prayer-time.

I came to the hearse at the foot of the Scots pine. I looked into the dark foliage and I could see the trail of my fall, the branches bent and broken by my clumsy impact. Higher still, the spars of the tree-house, the pieces of a wooden pallet which Lawrence's father had manhandled up there and lashed together, so that his son could have access to his world, his infinite sky-world, where he hurtled god-like in his mighty machine. Where the swifts were hurtling and screaming, splinters of god in their own infinity.

Lawrence had been there, but only as far as the crude platform his father had made for him. He would never go higher. He might stretch his hands to the blue, he might barely touch it. He might imagine the further, higher world of his father's flight, and the flight of the swifts. It would be a dream of flying, and no more.

I felt sorry for the boy, and for the boy he'd damaged, and I'd been moved by the depth of his mother's hurt. But I'd never forgotten the reason for my returning to England, more important than my entanglement in the Lundy family at Chalke House. My father. And here was his car, which had rolled into the shadow of the pine and been scarred even as its wheels had stopped turning. Now the grasses were growing higher and higher around it. Neglected, it would be swallowed by the woodland, absorbed into this hidden valley, it would disappear without trace unless it got moving again. Me too.

'Hey, you and me, we gotta look out for ourselves,' I said to the car. 'No one in the world knows where we are or where we've gone. If we get too comfy here, we ain't goin' nowhere...'

The Daimler didn't reply. It just eyed me with its huge round headlamps, as doleful and rheumy as a bloodhound. I opened the driver's door, slid inside and pinged the bonnet-release catch. Again, the warm, earthy smell in the car was an instant hit on my memories – the feel of the leather and the carpets and the touch of my father's hands on the wheel. With a renewed energy I got out and heaved open the bonnet, and the pain in my ribs was good, I was alive and it hurt and I had my own purpose in life, beyond the cobwebby entrapment of the Lundys. A minute later, wielding the tools which my father's fingers had worn smooth over decades of use and meticulous maintenance, I'd disconnected the battery from the monstrous engine, lifted it out and connected the battery from Juliet's BMW.

I stood back and admired my handiwork. A new heart, transplanted from a young athlete into a wheezing pensioner.

Juliet was there. I'd been aware of her presence for a while, I heard her come closer and I knew she was watching me. Like me, she'd smudged the blood on her face, rubbed it smooth into her complexion. But there were clotted streaks of it in her hair.

She said, 'I've sent Lawrence indoors. He's alright, just a cut on his head, I told him to jump into the shower and get it clean.' She frowned and added, 'Is this going to work?' just as I was settling into the hearse again. 'I mean, I haven't started my car for weeks. The last time I tried it was as dead as a dodo.'

'Thanks,' I said. 'Now you tell me.'

I turned the key in the ignition. The petrol pump ticked. I pressed the starter. Nothing. I pressed again. Not a groan or a murmur.

'I just thought... I don't know what I was thinking.' She flapped at her hair with both hands, at some imaginary wasp. 'I wasn't thinking anything. When I found you with my car and the bonnet up and I was upset and...'

I pressed the starter again. Not a thing. 'Juliet,' I said, 'we walked down the garden together, with me lugging the battery, and so you knew what I was going to try and do, and you didn't say anything. I don't get it.'

She shrugged. 'There's nothing to get,' she said. 'I'm sorry. I can understand you wanting to start the car, it doesn't make sense not to, whether you're trying to get out of here or not. But I was upset, I've told you that's why I keep my own car covered up and hidden away, so that Lawrence can't see it... and I was anxious because I didn't know where he was.' She shrugged again. 'I'm sorry, that's it. There's nothing to get.'

'Alright,' I said, 'never mind. There's always tomorrow. We can phone, and someone will come.' I saw her glum face, and something else too, a look in her eyes. She was hurt, but behind the fear in her demeanour I could sense the stubborn resilience of a wounded creature. Yes, she was bloodied and cornered, but she would defend her corner with a furious strength.

I tried to make her smile. 'Hey, don't worry, I'll phone and someone will come. This is England, not Borneo. There are no crocodiles in the pond, no head-hunters lurking in the jungle. In any case, look at you and me, all smeared with blood... if a party of head-hunters bumped into us now, they'd run a mile.'

But she didn't smile. 'No one will come,' she said, in such a cold, flat voice that I shivered at the chill in it. She turned and walked back to the house.

Chapter Sixteen

AND SO IT seemed that the two of them, Juliet and Lawrence Lundy, had, in their different ways, recovered the spirit of the missing airman. Her husband, his father – they'd found him again.

Easier, first of all, to talk about Juliet. She fucked me inexhaustibly. She came to me in the night, she came to me in the daytime, in the first light of dawn and in the long afternoons, at dusk when the night was swaddling the valley and suffocating the house and us... yes, suffocating us, in a summery darkness. Was it the hottest summer in living memory? Memory, what was it, but a jumble of sensations: blurry snapshots, snatches of songs, dusty smells and fading perfume? Dreams and flashbacks. Who remembered anything? Who cared? Days and nights and maybe weeks went by, and Juliet Lundy was all the scent in my nostrils, all the taste on my tongue, all the sweetness and sweat on my fingertips. Memory, what was it? She was emptying my brain and re-filling it with herself.

She called his name. She would rock and rock on top of me, and her eyes were elsewhere. She was on me, I was in her, but she would swivel her head and stare around the room as though he had just come in, as though he was standing there and watching us, as though he had tiptoed close and his breath was hot on the back of her neck, hot in her hair, hot in the small of her back as she rocked on top of me.

In me, on me, she had repossessed her husband. Ironic, that the release she achieved when she collapsed on my chest and I could feel her very bones dissolve and all her fears and nightmares and memories of ugliness fall away from her... ironic that her release was won by her having me.

And the boy? It was a wonder – no credit to me, but sheer chance or serendipity – that the swifts had re-connected him so sweetly with his lost father. The first encounter was a miraculous accident, when the bird had swerved into his room and fought among the dangling model planes and fallen onto his bed: a gift from the gods, a fragment of god, flung into his tormented world. It had fired his imagination, although I'd exerted myself over him and set it free. The second encounter, when, trespassing on their airy space, he'd batted at the swifts so precariously on his sky-platform, and for a moment he'd clutched at one of them and held it and it had wriggled free... after a tumbling descent through the sooty branches of the pine, after a nightmare in the jaws of a cat, it was festering in a box under the boy's bed, buried alive in a coffin of pitch-blackness and its own oily mutes.

And now the greenhouse. Throughout the summer, indeed for all the summers of Lawrence's life and long before he was born, it had been the roosting place of the swifts of Chalke House. For decades they'd squeezed through crannies and cracks in the collapsing timbers, they'd found holes where the panes of glass had broken, and they'd enjoyed a warm, safe, fusty darkness: a perfect sanctuary for them, to build their nests and feed their chicks and rest their sickle wings after hours and hours of non-stop flight.

'What on earth is he doing down there? Will you go down and look, please, Christopher?'

Gin was not salving her. It was a balmy night in July. The French windows were wide open, it was ten or eleven o'clock or maybe later, and we were nestled in the cushions of her sofa. A hummingbird hawk-moth was whirring around the lamp-lit living-room, the most delicious and perfect piece of a midsummer's midnight. It nuzzled into the curtains, clung for a second and shed a whisper of dust from its velvety wings, and then nuzzled its way out again.

A tawny owl was calling, somewhere in the woodland. I heard the yelp of a fox.

Gin was salving me. The moth and the owl and the fox and the gin. For a magical moment, the moth came bumbling into my face. I swept it away as gently as I could, because it snagged in my hair. It dropped into my empty glass. It fizzled in the pool of ice, and the sound of its humming-bird energy was loud until I tipped it onto the carpet ... where it shivered itself dry, achieved a clumsy lift-off, butted its way around the dim, dozy room and out of the open window.

'Go and see, will you, Christopher? I hope he's alright...'

'We know what he's doing, Juliet, the same as last night and the night before and so on. And we know he's alright.' Nevertheless, I extracted myself from the sofa, put down my empty glass and made for the window. 'Are you coming?' I turned and asked her. She said no, she wasn't, she might go upstairs and watch from the boy's tower.

He was in the greenhouse. I found my way into it, even through the deep shadows of the trees and the dense undergrowth, because I could see the light of his torch. I pushed a way through the darkness. In the overhead branches of a horse chestnut, the owl fluttered away from my passing. No sound of the fox, although the scent of it was strong in my nostrils.

'Hey, Lawrence...' I didn't want to blunder in and startle him, in his communion with the swifts. For the past week he'd gone down to the greenhouse at dusk, with his torch, with the sandwiches and flask of soup his mother had insisted on plying him with, to watch the swifts coming in to roost.

'Hey Lawrence, are you there?' I knew he was somewhere, I could see his torch propped into a clump of nettles and beaming into the rafters.

A spectacle... not on the scale of the swiftlets' caves at Mulu or Niah in Sarawak, where, every twilight, every day of the year, for thousands of years and long before any human had ever seen them, a million birds funnelled into the caverns in a vast black spiralling cloud. And at the same time, defying the probability of myriad aerial collisions, a million bats came out. Swifts and bats, in their hundreds of thousands, the birds going in and the bats coming out... and dashing among them, a hawk, snatching randomly here and there with its talons.

A spectacle, not on the scale of prehistoric Borneo, but lovely in Lincolnshire.

As the light faded on the wooded valley of Chalke House, the swifts came into the greenhouse. Hundreds of them. And the boy would crouch inside, waiting, listening, and when the birds came in through the broken panes with a rush and a rustle of their wonderful wings, he was ready with his torch.

'Lawrence?' No reply. 'Are you there, Lawrence?'

I felt my way gingerly over the uneven brickwork underfoot, felt the bristle of nettles on my hands and arms as I pushed my way in. There was his torch. I saw, in the yellowy light which spilled from it, his packet of sandwiches untouched and the unopened flask. No boy, although the place in the cow-parsley where he would crouch and hide was flattened to the shape of his body.

I'd watched the spectacle with him. Crepuscular, gloaming, twilight... the words were lovely, and in England on a midsummer's night the reality was lovely too. Just as the light was fading, to be lying in a bower of elder and bramble, with the shrew and the toad and a shiver of moths... to lie back and watch the darkness of dusk through the mossy windows of a derelict greenhouse... no sound until the swifts came furtling, hustling and snuggling in. And then to catch them, to hold them, to play them in the beam of the torch.

This time, no boy. 'Lawrence? Where are you?'

The birds were in. I could hear them in the spaces above me. Their black velvet-furry bodies. Their mole-furriness. The rafters above me were rustling and whispering, alive with the roosting of the swifts. They were clinging to their gobbets of nests. They were snuggling together, folding their wings after all the hours of flying, steadying their breath after lungfuls of screaming, fidgeting away the last of their frenetic energy until they might sleep. To achieve a release, a torpor. I could hear them. I could smell their dust, and the breath of their whiskery mouths.

But no boy. 'Oh shit, what are you doing, Lawrence, are you there?' Not sure why, I felt sick in my stomach.

His torch was pointing where the rafters were crawling with birds. I moved to the torch and picked it up and waved its beam around me. 'Lawrence? Are you there? Oh shit Lawrence where are you?'

He was up there, hanging. I shook the torch, its feeble yellow beam.

Juliet would be watching from the tower. We'd watched from there together, and it was lovely to stand on the boy's battlements and see the greenhouse down in the woods, to see the torchlight sweeping this way and that and know what the boy was doing, that he was safe and cosseted in his faery-world of the birds and the moles and the voles and the moths... safe, albeit in his own otherworld, his abstract unreality. We'd watched together, myself uncomfortably disinterested, Juliet sick with worry for the boy, but feeling that, at least for the time being, he was safe from harm or from self-harm.

It was our secret, private *son-et-lumiere*. The light was the rhythmic movement of the torch inside the derelict building, soft on the mossy panes and sparkling where the panes were broken. And the sound – the fox and the owl, and sometimes, unnecessarily beautiful, the song of a blackbird in the dead of night.

I looked up. He was hanging. 'Oh shit no Lawrence what...?'

For a terrible second, my stomach lurched. Worse than nausea. Fear in my bowels, loosening them.

He was at the top of the vine, where it had snaked the length of the building and was prising open the very timbers of the roof. His face was turned up, away from me, and his body was dangling.

'Lawrence... what the fuck...?'

The torchlight faded from yellow to a wash of pale-silver. For another second, as I craned my head so hard my neck was aching, all I could make out was his bare legs swinging in mid-air, the bare skin of his belly where his t-shirt rode up, and the whiteness of his throat, stretched.

Fuck! I banged the torch into the palm of my hand *fuck* it was bright again. His face swivelled down to me.

'Hey Chris, this is amazing... can you get up here? And bring the torch?'

So I scrambled, somehow, up the vine. It would have been easy, but my ribs seemed to grind together with every tug of my arms on the sinuous branches. I couldn't speak when I made it close to the rafters. Lawrence's face hung close to mine. With the sinewy athleticism of youth, he swung from beam to beam like a lemur. Yes, he'd been hanging, from his fingertips, as he communed with the rustling, roosting swifts.

I clung to the vine. He steadied himself next to me, took the torch from me and stroked its beam fondly among the birds. They were crawling around his head, he nuzzled his face among them. He was lit with a strange glow of joy. His eyes were wild, he gleamed with sweat, his smile was wet. His lips and his chin gleamed with saliva, and wisps of feathers and dust had stuck there.

'My birds...' he was murmuring, although his voice was lost in the furry friction of their bodies. 'My birds, my sky, my space...'

The sibilance was a part of the rustling. For me, the words had no meaning, they were a whisper from the secret shadows of his mind – a puzzle, a poem, a prayer?

I slithered down the vine. He was still up there as I slipped away and out of the greenhouse. My head was troubled by what I'd seen, and tormented by what I'd thought I'd seen.

Not all of the swifts were in the greenhouse with Lawrence Lundy. As I moved through the midnight garden, I paused and looked up at the moon; a gleam of white satin, dappled with grey, where millions of swifts from all over the world were clinging with their tiny, negligible feet. Again I paused, and I heard a swirl and a splash... where a few stragglers, too exhausted to fly to the moon, were seeking their rest in the deep dark mud of the pond.

Juliet was already downstairs in the living-room as I entered through the French windows. 'I was watching the light and it looked lovely,' she said. 'Is Lawrence alright?'

Although her voice was bright, she looked so brittle that the slightest jarring word might break her into little pieces. She had no idea what I'd seen down there, or the horror I'd imagined. She was trying to look nonchalant, but she came towards me with a terrible pleading in her eyes. To make sure she got the answer she wanted, she pressed me with the two things she thought might soothe me.

A big, swirly gin and tonic... she touched my cheek with the glass, an icy kiss. And she moved her body against mine. I hesitated for a moment and answered. 'Yes, he's alright.'

Chapter Seventeen

WHEN I AWOKE the following morning the house was unusually quiet. It felt empty, as though I were the only human being alive and breathing in it. Outside my window the trees were still. The birdsong seemed faint and faraway. The world was muffled in a cotton-wool silence.

Juliet hadn't come to me in the night. After our drink together, we'd stood outside and watched the torchlight flickering far down the garden, inside the neglected greenhouse. It was probably one o'clock in the morning. She was worried because it was so late and suggested we might go and tell Lawrence to give it a rest and come in; but I'd tried to comfort her by saying he would stop when he'd had enough and get himself to bed. The truth was, I thought she was too fragile to see him as I'd seen him, like a person possessed in some kind of horror movie, crawling on the ceiling with a spittle of regurgitated insects stuck around his mouth. But just then, as we'd been dithering about what to do, the torchlight had clicked off. The pale figure of the boy was moving through the trees and towards the house. Good. We'd slipped indoors before he reached us. Before he came in through the French windows, we were up on the landing, she'd gone into her bedroom and I'd gone into mine.

No, Juliet didn't come to my room that night. I'd heard the boy moving around downstairs, closing the windows and switching off the lamp, and then he'd come softly upstairs and continued up to his tower. I must have fallen asleep, so tired that I hadn't washed or brushed my teeth or even taken off my shirt and pants. Sometime later, I'd woken with a start, and with a dry mouth and a stirring of desire in my belly. The woman was standing at my door. She was perfectly still, and the cast of the moon showed her nakedness beneath a thin white slip. She seemed to be watching me, perhaps thinking I was still asleep. And when I licked my lips and whispered, 'Juliet... are you coming, Juliet?' she was gone. I heard the creak of her footsteps as she went upstairs to the tower.

A breathless morning. I got out of bed, crossed the landing and looked into her room. The bed was empty. I tiptoed upstairs so gently that a mouse might've made more sound on the ancient floorboards, and the powdering of chalk-dust as it puthered around me. At the top, the door was ajar and I peered inside.

A sweetly slumbering room. Windows wide open on a summer's morning. The squadron of model planes hung motionless. The orange cat was asleep on the foot of the bed. Juliet and Lawrence were sleeping too, her hair fluttering in his breath, like fairy-tale children in an enchanted castle.

The cat stirred and stretched, arching so hard that it quivered the bed. I moved down the stairs and heard behind me the mumbles and movement of awakening.

Yes, the whole house was comfortably dusty, every inch of everything touched with dust as soft as talcum, but the phone in the living-room looked as though it hadn't been used for weeks or months. It was furry with cobwebs, and the chalk was a whisper of whiteness on it, as though a wizard had sworn it to silence. Even when I blew on it, and then puffed as hard as I could, the dust stayed stubbornly where it was. I picked up the receiver and held it to my ear. The phone was dead.

No mystery. It hadn't been cut off in some gothic thunderstorm. The wires hadn't been sliced by an axe-murderer. Someone had simply pulled the plug out of the socket. So I pushed it back in, expecting nothing more than the purr of the dialling-tone in my ear.

A blink of orange lights. And a voice. A message on the speaker-phone.

A horrid voice, snarling and ranting. A guttural torrent of words. A woman, barely human... *you fucking bitch and your mad fucking bastard boy you can fucking rot in hell the both of you and if you ever come out of your fucking madhouse I'll tear your fucking eyes out you fucking bitch and your mad...*

I tried to stop it. It was loud and ugly and unstoppable. I jabbed randomly at the blinking lights – *fucking eyes out you fucking bitch and your fucking bastard son* – but then there was a flurry of bare feet and a couple of bare arms shoved me out of the way, and Juliet was yanking at the plug... *I'll fucking tear your fucking eyes out you mad fucking bitch...* until she pulled it out of the socket again.

She stood over me, panting, white with anger. 'What are you playing at? Why can't you just...? I mean, the car, the phone, why can't you just...'

'Just what?' I tried to be calm, in the face of her glaring and blustering. 'Hey, Juliet, I'm sorry I'm just trying the phone alright? I checked out your car because someone flattened the battery on mine... hey it doesn't matter that you just watched and said nothing while I lugged your battery down there and you knew all the time it was dead, but, hey, I'm sorry, now I'm just trying the phone to try and...'

'Try and what? Try and what?' She took a very deep breath and stood away from me. 'I'm sorry, no I'm sorry, of course you want to...' She moved to the French windows, opened them and gulped at the morning air to calm herself down. 'I'm sorry, I was in the kitchen, I heard the voice, I only heard it once before and I pulled out the phone and I've been too frightened to use it ever since.'

I crossed to her and folded my arms around her. She was trembling, as though she might quiver herself to death. Leveret. For a split-second I recalled, so vividly that the name came to me, a churchyard in Sixpenny Handley, my Dad working, and me surprising a buzzard amongst the overgrown gravestones... how clumsily it flapped away, how I picked up the leveret it had had in its talons, and how it was trembling, as though its little heart would burst. I held her close. I could smell the boy's body on her, his breath in her hair. 'Hey Juliet, it's alright... I heard it, I heard it by accident and it's horrible... I understand why you're afraid, why you're so upset...'

She clung to me. My hands went to a favourite place, the sweet hollow in the small of her back, and I pressed her even closer. For a mad moment I thought of taking her, manfully carrying her, to the cool grasses of the woodland or even the rough, dry blankets in the back of the hearse.

But we heard the boy on the stairs. I let her go, she let me go.

'Maybe we don't need the phone,' I said, before he came into the room. 'Is it far to the village? Is there a shop? I mean, I'll take a walk and get bread and milk and stuff.' I lifted her face to mine, made mine as theatrically portentous as I could, and added, 'More important than food, we need gin.'

Chapter Eighteen

NO GIN. I got port.

'Any port in a storm,' I said, and it wasn't very funny except that we'd nearly emptied the first bottle and we were ready to giggle at anything.

It was late again, dark, so it must have been after ten o'clock, and we were sunk into that sofa, the most ensnaring, all-consuming, carnivorous pitcher plant of all sofas. Lawrence had, to give him the credit he deserved, cooked us the sausages I'd brought back. He'd burnt them, yes, but then he'd squashed them between slices of white bread and smothered them with ketchup so we'd had to admit, a bit begrudgingly because they looked such a messy burnt-offering, that they tasted delicious. Another slosh of port, and the sausage sandwiches could've been *Cordon Bleu* from the Savoy.

I'd tried to make my account of the day's expedition as light as possible. I told her how, after striding out of the driveway of Chalke House, I'd laboured up the wooded hillside for what seemed like an interminable hour, my ribs twingeing with every step. I'd spouted to Juliet, as we rolled the port in our mouths and snuggled deeper into the cushions, that the walk was nothing really, nothing compared to the slog to the summit of Mount Kinabalu in Sabah or the trek through the Bario Highlands of Sarawak and the breathtaking scramble to the pinnacles at Mulu... except that the climb up a gently dappled Lincolnshire lane had almost knocked me out, and every breath I'd taken was a lancing pain in my chest.

At last I'd emerged into the fresh open sunlight of the wolds, the first time I'd felt it on my face since the day I'd arrived at

Chalke House and rolled the Daimler into the shadow of the Scots pine. Another half hour and I'd come to a village. With a shop. And it made – I was saying to Juliet, and I saw how the port had smudged her lips and her teeth and her tongue was a darker pink like some kind of luscious sea anemone – it made some of the seediest *kampongs* along the Baram river look rather salubrious. That was the word I used, and I tried it again because it rolled very nicely on my own, undoubtedly pink and luscious tongue. Not a salubrious village.

There was some kind of garage or workshop, next to a duckpond. It was a muddle of sheds, collapsed together in the kind of accretion achieved by submerged shipwrecks: rusting corrugated-iron colonised by masses of parasitic growth, in this case, a plague of purple fireweed. I shouted hello, and a man appeared. He was so oily and squat that it was impossible to approximate his age more accurately than to say he might have been thirty or seventy, clad in a filthy string vest and brown corduroy trousers held up by a length of rope. He was hawking into a rag and then wiping his hands with it. He'd emerged from beneath an indeterminate car from a not-so-bygone age – a Hillman or a Humber, not-so-long-ago defunct but utterly nondescript except to the saddest of enthusiasts.

I was going to ask him if he might 'come out' to Chalke House and get the Daimler started, but it looked to me, from the way he swiped at his hands with the rag and swatted at his mouth with it, that surfacing from under the Hillman-Humber thing was about as far as he might ever come. And in any case, an ancient, spavined, one-eyed bullmastiff was lumbering along beside him and growling, so I smiled and waved and retreated hurriedly.

The village? A clutter of post-war pre-fab bungalows. The shop? I described it to Juliet. I didn't suppose she'd ever been there, she would have swished by in the silver BMW and onwards to the supermarket in Alford. The shop had many shelves, most of them empty. Gin? The little girl behind the counter, looking after 'business' for her Daddy who'd gone out, didn't know what it was. She had toilet rolls. She had processed cheese. She had a bit of bacon and the sausages in the freezer. And port, from South Africa. I'd bundled it all into the rucksack I'd brought with me and come clanking out of the shop, the bottles digging uncomfortably into my spine.

Juliet had found my account quite picturesque. Alright, so I'd embellished the garage and the shop a little bit, the mechanic and his dog, and the bareness of the shelves in the shop, which compared unfavourably with the wondrous accumulation of bits and pieces to be found in even the shabbiest *kedai* in the *kampongs* of Marudi. I poured us another glass of the cooking-port. Lawrence had gone up to his tower, deciding to give the roosting swifts a rest from his intrusion with the torch. There was a wind in the woodland, a rustling commotion, so we cosied together for a downpour like the one which had thundered on the roof of the hearse the first time she'd come to me.

Any port in a storm. But the storm had not come. The wind grew stronger and there was a rumble of faraway thunder. But no rain. The leaves of the broad-leaved trees turned this way and that and the branches groaned. No rain.

I didn't tell her about the bus...

As I'd been leaving the village and frankly not relishing the long walk back with the heavy rucksack, I'd stopped at a roadside bench to rearrange the bottles and stuff so they wouldn't dig into me.

I didn't think much of the village: no pub, no school, no church, it was nothing like the picture-postcard villages I'd seen with my father in the south and west of England, in the Lakes and in Wales. But the air was good. It felt good to be in the air. Apart from a straggle of wind-blown hawthorn around the pond, there were no trees, and the hedge at the side of the road had been layered into a dense gnarly scrub. Nothing until the horizon, in any direction. Only sky. I was in it, and it felt good.

So I'd unpacked the rucksack onto the bench, taking my time, salving the pain in my chest before setting off. I heard a vehicle approaching and hadn't bothered to turn and look, until it noisily slowed and stopped right next to me.

It was a little country bus. There was a hiss and the door opened. No one got out. The bus was idling and rumbling and throwing out a fume of blue diesel smoke. I straightened up and peered in and realised it was waiting for me. Indeed, collapsed into the hedgerow there was an iron post with a sign and a timetable attached to it.

'Are you getting in?' a voice said. 'This is a bus stop.'

The driver, a very fat woman trussed up in a council uniform, leaned across her steering-wheel to see what I was doing. She narrowed her eyes at the bottles on the bench. For a fanciful moment, I thought she'd taken me for an old-fashioned tramp, a knight of the road.

'No, thank you, no I'm not,' I said, and then, as an automatic after-thought, 'where are you going?'

'It says on the front. Grimsby.'

The word seemed to hang in the air. I could taste the salt in it, in the air and in the word. I could hear gulls in it, in the air and in the word. Whether she sensed my hesitation or saw a shadow of indecision on my face, the woman squinted at me and then she turned and stared through her windscreen, at the long empty road ahead of her, at the absence of anything but sky.

'Where are you going then, if you aren't going to Grimsby?' she said. 'There's nowhere else.'

Nowhere else. Nowhere else but Grimsby.

I could have changed my mind and got on board. For a blinding moment I could have climbed on the bus with my rucksack and never come back. I think I turned and moved to stuff the provisions into the rucksack. Yes, I started to shove in the cheese and bacon and sausage, the bottles of port... until I slowed down and stopped and thought of minor details, like the Daimler, and my passport, and other reasons why I couldn't leave for good. Minor details. Juliet. The boy.

'Thank you,' I said to the woman. 'Not today. I'm staying around here.'

She was nosy. There was no one on the bus, she had time to be nosy and no other passengers pressing her to drive on. 'Around here? Where?'

Nowhere else. As though this was wilderness and Grimsby the promised land. I gestured vaguely down the road behind her, where the lane fell away and vanished into the valley. 'Down there,' I said. 'I'm staying at Chalke House. It's down in the woods.'

Her face froze. Her lips whitened. A grenade of anger detonated inside her. If she hadn't been strait-jacketed into her bus-driver's uniform, she would have launched herself out of her seat. Instead. she crunched the bus into gear. And just before she pressed the button to hiss the door shut, she hissed at me, 'Whoever the fuck you are you can tell the mad fucking bitch and her mad fucking boy they can both fucking rot in hell and...'

The bus lurched away. A plume of stinking black smoke billowed from it. It plunged and stalled and plunged, like a buffalo with a pride of bloody-faced lions clawing at its haunches. I watched it go. It made the air horrible. It made the clean salty air horrible, and even the sky.

I sat on the bench and waited, until I thought that the smoke of the bus and the woman's words had faded.

The smoke faded. A minute or two after the bus had gone, the Lincolnshire wolds were as sweet as ever before, as sweet as the long-ago days when never a bus or an indeterminate Humber or Hillman had exhausted its fumes into the enormous air. But the woman's words did not fade. All of their poisonous hatred stayed in my ears, in my mind, as I packed the bag and walked painfully, slowly, down and down through the woods... towards the nowhere else... towards Chalke House.

MIDNIGHT. A DRY wind through dense, dry branches. Juliet had listened to my carefully edited account of the expedition to the village. I'd heard my own voice slurring with the port on my tongue, and sometimes my words were lost in the movement of the leaves. Midnight. The room was dark and still and her eyes were drooping. I wanted to be in bed with her. As a post-script, to compare my quest for gin with its Borneo equivalent, I was embroidering the end of the story. 'A flying coffin... the quickest way to get to Miri, the nearest place to get supplies of alcohol and...'

Her eyes flicked open. Her body stiffened. She stared into my face, as though she'd never seen me before and I was an intruder in her house, and then she was looking over my shoulder, into the shadows of the room.

'Juliet? What did I say? Are you alright?'

'Sssh.' She was holding her breath. She was staring towards the doorway behind me. Holding her breath. No, her nostrils were flaring, her lips opened, and she was testing the air like a dog. She stared past me, every muscle in her body tensed. 'Lawrence? Lawrence, is that you?'

His voice was quiet but very clear. 'Who else could it be?'

I turned to see him come in. He'd been standing in the darkness of the hallway, I couldn't tell how long he'd been there and listening. Inhaling deeply, Juliet said, 'Lawrence, have you been...? I wish you wouldn't, you know it upsets me.' At the same time, as he loomed close and tall and bony, I could smell an after-shave which wafted in all the space around us.

He ignored her. He said to me, 'I've been listening to your story. About the village up there, and the people in it. That's why we don't go.'

He remained standing, a gangly, awkward figure in nothing but a pair of underpants. It was uncomfortable, for me and his mother, because we were sunk into the sofa and our faces were level with his knees and he was an enormous man-boy, big and hairy and yet only a gawky boy who'd blundered into the grown-ups' world... difficult to explain, but he was simply too big to be so naked with us, in his little boy's pants. If only he'd sat down on another armchair or even knelt on the floor... but he filled the space with the body of a man and the gracelessness of a boy, with his teenage odour and the waft of his father's cologne. And he was holding something. A box.

'What were you saying just then?' he said. 'About a coffin? What's a flying coffin?'

'It's just a nickname,' I said, 'for the speedboat which goes up and down the river, from Marudi to Miri on the coast of the South China Sea. It's long and very streamlined, kind of tubular, like a jet plane on the water. It goes really fast. It takes about thirty or forty passengers, you sit in rows like in a plane, and it feels a bit closed in, kind of claustrophobic, as you look out of the little portholes and see the riverbank zooming by.'

Juliet was listening too, but she was looking at her great near-nude son as though she could hardly believe such an ogre could be hers. The box he was holding, it had once held the pieces of the model Phantom he'd built.

'The flying coffin?' I went on. 'Well, from time to time there's an accident. The boat's whizzing along and it hits a log. The Baram river is full of logs, logging is the main business upstream and there are some hefty bits of driftwood half-submerged in the water. So the boat hits a log, it turns over and sinks, with everyone inside it. No one gets out.'

He didn't say anything. He was cradling the box to his stomach.

'Is that the bird?' I said. 'What are you doing with it?'

He opened the box and held it towards my face. It didn't smell bad, although the swift had been dead for days. The mutes which had dried and caked and powdered around it gave only a whiff of animal fustiness. And the bird, so small, so thin, no more than a mummy... there was nothing much left of its marvellous little body to make an odour of any kind. If, soon after the swift had died, a bluebottle had come into the box to take a look, it had gone away without bothering to leave an egg and a squirm of maggots.

He shrugged and put the lid back on. 'I tried to keep it alive,' he said. 'I caught some insects and put them into the box, but it wouldn't eat anything. I didn't want to tip it outside for the cat to find. I wanted to keep it. So I just kept it. It's dead now.' He held the box to his face and sniffed it. 'It doesn't smell of much. I thought it was going to, that's why I squirted a bit of Dad's stuff on it...'

'Put it outside.' It was Juliet, trying to sound assertive without unsettling him. 'Just leave it in the long grass, and it'll be gone by morning.'

'No,' he said. He smiled at me, the nicest and warmest smile he'd bestowed on me since I'd been there. 'I was going to take it to the greenhouse, so it could be with the others, I was going to climb up the vine to the nests and put it somewhere. But you gave me a better idea...'

'Lawrence, where are you...?' his mother began. But he'd crossed the room and was out of the French windows before we could heave ourselves out of the sofa.

The storm, the storm we'd been so casually invoking. It started with a skirling in the beechwood, like a jazz drummer teasing the skins with his brushes. And then there was a broiling of wind in the branches. And no sooner had the boy stepped out of the house, but there was a magnesium flare of lightning and a clap of thunder which rocked the house.

Still no rain. Me and Juliet, we stood outside, expecting a torrent. We didn't follow the boy, we didn't need to. In the flutter and blaze of light, we could see him as clearly as if he were spotlit on-stage.

He went down to the pond. Like some kind of boy-god, born of the storm in all his nakedness, he took the bird out of the box and floated it onto the water.

It drifted away from him. A Viking funeral, a body launched into the underworld or the hallowed halls of Valhalla? A corpse relinquished to the sacred waters of the Ganges? Whatever the boy was thinking, in the half-baked notions of his teenage mind, he slid the swift towards the middle of the pond.

It rocked there, very gently. There was a long, holy moment. And then, two things happened. The rain started, a sweet summer downpour. And the bird disappeared, to join its brothers roosting in the muddy bottom... a swirling commotion of the water, which sucked it down and gone.

Chapter Nineteen

ENTRAPMENT. I'D EXPERIENCED it in Borneo. The institutionalised entrapment of mosque, school, alcohol.

Possession. The never-changing of seasons. Mosque, school, alcohol.

Another *orang putih* had said to me... when she'd come to stay for the weekend and was so pissed I'd had to grab her, just in time, from swaying off my balcony into the mangrove swamp, and I'd steered her to the toilet where she'd sat down and fallen fast asleep... she'd said, when I'd shaken her awake and helped her off the toilet and collapsed her onto my sofa... 'It's rehab, me and you Christopher and all the other ex-pats... why did we come out here? Running from something, hiding from something? Borneo is rehab...'

Borneo. A blur of days and nights, and weeks and months and years. I'd gone out with a two-year contract, thinking it would be more than enough for me to live cheaply and save some money and see something of south-east Asia. I was still there six years later. What happened to the time? There were no seasons, so what difference did it make if you rolled out of bed, hung-over, and sloped into school on a morning in February or May or October? No difference, it sounded and smelled and looked the same, every day. The mosque was mumbling in the darkness before dawn, it was muttering in school from six-thirty to seven-thirty, there were prayers and Koranic verses from the loudspeakers in every corridor and every classroom and even in the canteen nearly all the time. And then the call to prayer at twelve-thirty, at three in the afternoon and at six-thirty and at seven. After that, in the gathering darkness, every evening and much louder on a Thursday evening, there was chanting and reciting from the tower of the mosque, for an hour or two or three...

Every day. Relentless. Repetitive. The same. The same. The same. The fucking same.

Borneo. A magical word, like a word from a dream... a blurry, repetitive dream, in a long, hot night. The timelessness of sleep, punctuated by odd, mismatching, uncomfortable images.

My first day in school, I'd walked into the principal's office and he'd waved me to sit down while he scanned my letter of introduction. He was a fierce-looking man, an Iban with a scowly moustache pasted onto his mouth, and behind him, through the window behind his desk, such a rain-lashed morning that the palm trees were thrashing as though they would snap. I was nervous and excited, I was in the tropics, in a rainstorm on the edge of the rainforest. But what did he say to me? What were the first words I heard in my employment as an English teacher in magical, mysterious Borneo?

'Sut dach'i y bore ma?' He'd looked up at me and grinned and asked me how I was this morning... in Welsh. He'd done his Master's degree in Aberystwyth, and thought I'd be impressed.

My head-of-department, the most urbane of men, had a degree from Loughborough and a Master's from York. Looking glum one day, he told me he'd been to a funeral at the weekend. His three-year-old niece had been killed. By a falling coconut.

The school cleaner, whom I befriended and teased as she swabbed the corridors with a fragrant mop, was recently widowed. With her husband, an official in a government department, she'd travelled to Venice and Rome and Florence, but now she was a cleaner, since he'd been half-eaten by a crocodile somewhere upstream.

Things didn't match. The dream was a warm, friendly blur, but it was shot through with jarring, unfriendly images.

We would have a school assembly, all fifteen-hundred boys and girls and a hundred teachers gathered for a pep-talk from the principal. One morning, it was the turn of the discipline-teacher to rant about the scourge of drugs, the danger of un-Islamic substances smuggled into the country from the dangerous world beyond. He'd brought a unit of young policemen with him. To warn the impressionable teenagers of what might happen if they got mixed up with the infidels who were threatening the health of the nation, the policemen propped up a lifelike, life-size dummy of a man and thrashed it so hard with a rattan cane that the hall echoed with the thwack of it and a pall of dust rose into the slowly-swirling overhead fans.

But, at the back of the room, I noticed a group of teachers unimpressed by the display. They were huddled over something more interesting in the local newspaper: a full-page photograph of a python, so bloated it was unable to move and surrounded by sight-seers... protruding from its mouth, the feet and legs of a girl it had swallowed.

Marudi, Sarawak, Borneo. I got into my routine. It was a kind of hypnosis, so comfortable and all-enveloping that it might have been torpor. School, my goofy boys and the loveliest funniest girls. My colleagues, the meticulous Chinese with their staccato voices ringing from the classrooms, the diffident Malays whispering *insha'allah* to excuse their institutionalised procrastination. School, and a sleep in the afternoon, and then a bicycle ride through the *kampongs*, where the dogs snapped and snarled at my wheels and the kids called out 'Hello Mr Chris' as I went wobbling by. Home for a shower, the noodles I cooked. And alcohol.

Alcohol on my balcony. Alcohol, with the river slithering by, and who-knows-what-else slithering in the mangroves which tangled in the stilts of my house. The python? Replete with another child it had smothered and crushed and swallowed whole? The crocodile? Which took dogs and pigs and sometimes, on an especially bountiful day, a fisherman who'd leaned carelessly into the water?

I didn't care. I'd perfected my gin *stengah*. With the supplies I'd got from Miri, on a hurtling ride to the city and back in the flying coffin, and with ice from the nearby *kedai* (ice was *ayer batu*, 'water stone'), I would settle on my balcony and relish my nightly three or four or five thirst-quenching drinks. More than thirst-quenching, they would sink me so deeply and blurrily into my easy-chair that the forest was a spangle of fireflies, the sky a sparkle of stars.

Much later, too late, off to bed... stark naked under the fan, more or less comatose and too pissed to be troubled by mosquitoes. A few hours of snoring, sweaty sleep, and the next day would start all over again – my alarm call at five o'clock, the muttering of the mosque and me cursing and rolling off the bed and under the shower, for another morning in school.

February? May? August? October? No difference. The mosque and the hangover were always the same. The same. The same. The fucking same.

Possession. It was a kind of madness. It was surreal, a very nice trap. I knew every sound and smell. I knew every ant and spider and *chick-chak* in my bathroom. I liked my colleagues, some of them liked me. I'd learnt the long, complicated names of all my students. I knew enough Malay to make them laugh and to rub shoulders with shopkeepers in the town, with the people in the *kampongs*, with people whose grandparents had been head-hunters. So who cared what day it was, or which month? The very language was unfussed by the importance of time. The verbs had no tenses. Why would you need them? In the present tense you'd say 'I go'. In the past you'd say 'I go' and toss in the word 'yesterday'. To express the future, you'd say 'I go' and throw in the word 'tomorrow'.

Time... nothing but a gentle collision of yesterday and today and tomorrow. Its passing was marked by mosque and school and gin. Simple.

Possession. Sometimes the students were possessed. It happened now and then, frequently enough to be unremarkable. Without any warning, in the middle of a lesson, a girl would start moaning, and then shouting, and then screaming and pulling off her *tudong*. The other girls would start too, and it might spread from classroom to classroom until all the girls and even a few of the women teachers were screaming. They called it 'hysteria'. The male teachers, led by the Islamic Religious Knowledge department, would quell it with barking cries over the Tannoy and prayers at full-blast. Prayers... they always worked, loud and long and dinning, to drive out the evil spirits which had crept out of the jungle and into the school.

At first I found it terrifying. I saw how frightened the boys were, big beefy boys who quailed at the sight and sound of hundreds of girls possessed, and I was surprised how frightened I was too. They would pray, to protect themselves from evil. I wouldn't, although I was unnerved. One day it had started in my own classroom. Asked to do some English lit, I'd gone to the shabby, dilapidated school-library to dig out a story and come out with a collection by Guy de Maupassant. We were 'doing' a story: Maupassant, in English lit, in Borneo. It was very hot. A black rain cloud was rolling towards the school, fast and huge as a tidal wave. Just outside my window, a bulldozer was chewing at the trees, revving noisily and belching smoke and breaking them down, one after another, in a rude and ugly assault on the forest. The hysteria started in my lesson. Just as the crash of the rainstorm hit the roof, a sweet little girl called Dayangku Siti Hafizah Qurr'atul binti Hj. Mohammad Alimin fell off her chair and started crying. Despite, or because of, my attempts to comfort her, she got louder and louder. Within moments, nearly every female in the building was wailing.

It didn't last long. When it was all over, thanks to the over-layering of male voices praying through the loudspeakers, a boy told me that a spirit from the trees collapsed by the bulldozer had come into our lesson and possessed Siti. That evening I had an extra big, extra swirly drink on my balcony, to settle my nerves and keep the spirits of the forest at bay.

Allah akbar. Gordons is great. I heard it from the mosque five times a day and I celebrated it in the evenings. I didn't know if the gin was keeping me sane or driving me mad. Rehab? After a year or six in Borneo, I wasn't sure if I was running from something or I was sliding headlong into a trap I'd never escape.

I remember talking to one of my students, a girl called Fatin. We were practising for her oral exam and I was asking the usual questions about her family and friends and hobbies and hopes for the future. She told me her father was the *muezzin* at the mosque. In my imagination, I pictured the stern, sanctimonious man whose voice woke me and needled me every day, and I looked at her earnest, perfect little face. She had the smoothest brown skin, the most perfect teeth and the biggest brownest eyes a caricaturist could draw... except that she was real, a living human being swaddled in her crisp white *tudong*. Trying to tie the question into the kind of format she could expect in her forthcoming exam, I asked her what she might want to do in the future. Mischievously I asked her, could a girl ever be the *muezzin* in the mosque in Marudi?

With the greatest seriousness, she answered, no. If ever a girl or a woman did the call to prayer, the world would end.

The world would end. At least that would be something. It might awaken me. At least for a millisecond, in whatever cacophonous, tumultuous moment the end of the world might occur, I could awaken from my dream of swiftlets and fireflies, from the mumble of meaningless prayers, from the mosque and school and alcohol the same and the same and the same and the fucking same...

AND NOW? AND now, I'd flown seven thousand miles to England. From the sweet, seductive pitcher-plant entrapment of Borneo, to the Lincolnshire wolds.

Same difference. The days and weeks of June and July and August blurred dreamily together. What did we do, the three of us, me and Juliet Lundy and Lawrence Lundy? Was it real, or part of my dream? Were they real, this woman and her boy, or had I conjured them, in my fumey, sweaty sleep?

I tried, one morning, to call my father. I remember trying to re-connect with the reality of my returning to England. While Juliet was changing the bed upstairs and the boy was in his tower, I went into the living-room and plugged the phone into its socket. A cheery nurse picked up, in Grimsby. I could hear a radio playing a pop song in the background, and then, when she turned it off because she couldn't hear what I was saying, I could hear the seagulls. She said sorry, no, Mr Beal was resting comfortably in his room, but he wouldn't be able to talk on the phone. He was quite alright, but his speech was... she tried to think of an acceptable euphemism... his speech was compromised. Mr Beal was alright in himself, he was eating and sleeping, he had the television and the daily newspaper, but he couldn't speak. Come and visit him anytime, she said, he would no doubt be very happy to see me.

I thanked her. I listened to the gulls for another second, long enough for me to imagine my father at the open window of his little room, the salty air and the fustiness of his own smell, before she rang off.

A brief encounter with the outside world. Yes, it was still out there, somewhere, not so far away. But when I pulled the plug of the telephone out of its socket so that Juliet wouldn't know I'd made a call, the sense of isolation was so intense that I could hear the falling of dust around me and feel the weight of it on my shoulders.

Another day... was it the next day or a week later?

I found myself wandering deep into the woodland and past the hearse and onwards to the end of the drive. I was going, for only the second time since I arrived, to set foot outside the limits of Chalke House. Not sure why, because my ribs were still aching and I had no intention of plodding up the lane and surfacing into the upper world, except maybe to gulp at the air like a drowning man whose clothes were utterly waterlogged... and there was Juliet, with the boy.

He was carrying a big, heavy cardboard box. She was carrying a smaller one. She was radiant, and her voice chimed among the trees as madly as the laughter of the yaffle. 'Hey, Christopher, where are you heading off to? Up to the village again? No need... we've got enough supplies of everything to keep us going for a month, maybe more.'

I turned and trooped back to the house, behind her. She wouldn't let me take the box. I could hear the clank of bottles, but she insisted she could manage. She'd made a call to the supermarket in Alford, she'd quoted her bank card number and they'd delivered her order to the end of the drive. She was bubbling with the success of such a simple *fait accompli*. There was a triumphant note in her voice. 'No need for any of us to go anywhere...' a bit out of breath as the box bumped against her chest as she walked, 'I heard you on the phone the other day and I guess your Dad's ok or else you would've said something... and now we've got food and drink... we've got gin!... So we're alright and the rest of the world can go hoot as far as I'm concerned... what d'you think?'

It didn't seem to matter what I thought. It was a rhetorical question.

Meekly, I followed her and the boy through the French windows and into the kitchen, where I was told to sit down and keep out of the way while they unpacked the groceries and re-organised them into different cupboards. They were in cahoots, the woodland elf and her ogre-son. I felt a deliberate sense of exclusion. I was, just then, as superfluous as if I'd never called from Lincoln railway station and never blundered into their life. And the satisfaction with which they stacked the shelves... they were so smug, as if the outside world were smitten by plague and yet they were safe, they would survive, some invisible benefactor had smuggled in the life-saving supplies and they would be alright.

*   *   *

No need to go anywhere. So what did we do?

I coupled with the woman. I engaged with the boy. But everything we did was tinged with a strange, desultory madness, as though we were simpletons... droll, harmless inmates of an asylum, with tasks assigned to fill our time between eating and drinking and sleeping.

Everything was pleasantly pointless. Even the sex.

Me and Juliet, we did it like children who'd discovered a new game, a game so marvellous that when we got the urge to play, we went at it in a frenzy which blanked out all the other games we'd played before. And then, when the game was over, we lost all interest in it. Like spoilt children, who could have whatever we wanted whenever we wanted it, we pushed the game aside, not bothering about its bits and pieces and who might tidy up afterwards.

In the daytime, we did it in the garden. Juliet on top, always, worried about my ribs, although the bruises had faded from black to purple to a kind of Tuscan ochre... concerned for my ribs, that was the reason she put into words. In the hearse, she pressed me down, her body forked on top of me, my father's blanket coarse beneath my back. Under the Scots pine, she forked me into the sweet dry needles. At night she came to my room. In the moonlight, she was a silvery nymph who'd slipped into the house from the shadows of the woodland and captured me, a trophy she might take back to her faery-world. Or a wild creature. She pinned me down, panting and staring fiercely around her, like a hawk on a feebly-fluttering thrush.

For those brief moments of uncontrollable ecstasy, she didn't seem to know or care who I was or where I'd come from. It was a kind of madness. In her head, she was making love to a man whose body was decomposing in the North Sea, a corpse, nibbled rotten, but more or less intact because it was encased in a helmet and flying-suit.

Yes, I engaged with Lawrence.

One day, nearly all of a pleasantly pointless summer's day, we worked on the hearse. I remember suggesting it to him at the breakfast table and he agreed with a shrug. In the morning, when the shade was cool and we could hear the swifts screaming around the remains of the tree-house, we opened the bonnet of the car and cleaned the engine. By no means an expert myself, I expounded the pedigree of the sooty machine – the same XK straight-six which powered the Jaguar saloons and sports-cars and even the legendary D-type which had won the Vingt-Quatre Heures du Mans. We checked the oil, extracting the dip-stick and wiping it clean. We checked the water in the radiator. We tested the tension in the fan-belt as though we knew what we were doing. And then, until Juliet called from the house that it was time for lunch, we salved the smooth surfaces of the engine and the black rubber hoses with oil, every mysterious bit whose name we didn't know.

It looked great, as though we were entering it for a classic-car competition. But all the time I was thinking, and no doubt the boy was thinking too, that the car wouldn't go, however great it looked. Quite incongruous beneath the bonnet, there was a flat battery from a modern German car. And the Daimler's own battery was flat too.

But we didn't stop. We worked with great seriousness, as reverent as priests with the body of a pharaoh, preparing it for some spurious afterlife. It was dead, the heart of it was dead. But thanks to our earnest ministrations, the corpse was fragrant and clean.

'How are you boys doing down there?' Juliet was amused. Also, she was pleased. She presided over the pâté and salad she'd spread out, some of the bounty she'd received from beyond the borders of her domain. She smiled on us, on her boys. She had us where she wanted us, safe and sound and no reason to go elsewhere.

In the afternoon, we opened the car itself and cleaned it out. I sprayed furniture polish on the sunburnt woodwork beneath the windscreen and around the dash. Lawrence buffed as though his life depended on it, and the whorls of walnut re-appeared like magic. I applied unction to the upholstery and Lawrence buffed until the leather was gleaming. We took everything out of the capacious, corpse-carrying compartment in the back, we swept and dusted. We discovered a system of runnels in the floor, and a hole with a plug in it under the driver's seat; and Lawrence, pretending great wisdom in such arcane matters, declared it was there to drain out blood and other bodily fluids which dripped from the caskets.

I wasn't so sure. But I didn't know, so I nodded and agreed with the possibility. And the macabre supposition was part of our business; our painstaking maintenance of a vehicle which didn't go, and in any case, was already close to its retirement as chicken-shed or tool-cupboard.

We didn't stop until the evening. For a few moments we'd thought about tackling the rust-pitted chrome of the classic, fluted radiator, and the chrome bumpers and headlamps. But no. We stood back and appraised the hulk looming in the woodland.

Yes, we'd been honouring my father, who was dribbling in an old people's home in Grimsby. But the futility of what we were doing dawned on me. I remember I blinked and stared at the car. I narrowed my eyes and looked and I saw what it was: a superannuated hearse, subsiding into the long grass on its slowly deflating tyres.

Lawrence and I glanced sideways at one another. No, we weren't going to polish the chrome. We walked back to the house. I didn't know what the boy was thinking, but for myself it was a mixture of satisfaction – that I'd engaged busily with him as I'd been hired to do – and dismay, an inescapable sense of the surreal.

STRANGE DAYS. WHAT else did we do? How did the dream-like days of summer unfold?

'Anyone for tennis?' The boy came down from his tower with a couple of badminton racquets and a battered shuttlecock.

It was a sweltering, airless afternoon. Me and Juliet and Lawrence, we carried our drinks of lemon barley water outside, to a flatter space of tousled grass beside the pond, and we took turns to swat the shuttlecock backwards and forwards until most of the feathers had been knocked off it. At last, when I'd smashed it far over Lawrence's head and into the nettles, he'd groped around and suddenly declared, 'Even better, this'll do nicely,' before turning towards me and hitting something high into the air.

Even as it floated down, spinning and twirling in a dazzle of sunlight, I could see it was a bird.

A fledgling blue tit. Dead, of course. Either he'd seen it dead or it had died the moment he'd smacked it with the racquet. In any case, my instinct was to step away and let it land.

But I surprised myself. He shouted, 'Go on, Chris, hit it!' And I did.

The woman was laughing. The boy was laughing. I heard myself laughing. And for a horrid, hilarious half-minute we played the best rally of the afternoon, popping the blue tit back and forth a dozen or twenty times.

It got smaller and smaller. At last it disintegrated in a puff of feathers. Still laughing, we collapsed onto the grass and drank our lemon barley water.

SO THE DAYS and the weeks went by. If I'd thought Borneo was a dream from which I would never wake up – where I'd been steam-rollered by the mosque, unmanned by the heat, lulled into niceness by the niceness of my students, slugged into unconsciousness by gin – then the summer at Chalke House was *sama sama*, as they said in Malay. Same difference. The same contagion of torpor. The dream was intoxicating.

Me and Lawrence, we discovered the garden of Chalke House. I stumbled on a bed of mint, so swallowed by fireweed that it had almost disappeared. Me and Lawrence, we scythed the fireweed and the mint was revealed, its perfume fresh and clean in the smuggy heat of July. It inspired us to look again, into the smothering wilderness, and find what men had planted, what previous owners of the house had done...

We found rosemary, we found lavender. There was a burgeoning stand of rhubarb, so strong that when we'd cut away the suffocating grasses we could hear its muscular, rubbery growth. Mint and rosemary and lavender and rhubarb... and horse radish, a superb and secret root, secreting its heat in a jungle of cow-parsley.

And lupins, a peppery miracle. My favourite from a childhood in my father's garden. Me and Lawrence, we found lupins, lost in the overgrown woodland of Chalke House.

And what did we do, not knowing or caring what day it was... in June or July or August or whatever?

We cut lupins by the armful and carried them into the house. Juliet put them in vases, in her shabby, seductive living-room. We drank gin. We had rosemary with the lamb they'd delivered from the outside world, we had horse radish with a succulent steak. We had rhubarb with the cream they'd smuggled in. We washed it down with wine from Chile or California.

And at midnight, when Lawrence had gone to bed, she would take me into the woodland, where the wren was ticking and the owl was calling, and roll me into the mint, for a dreamy herbal fucking.

Chapter Twenty

Virginia Woolf wrote, in one of her celebrated letters, 'Life is a dream. 'tis the waking that kills us.'

When does a dream become nightmare? What is the transitional moment, when the pleasant, random ridiculousness of a dream alters and shifts and is tinged with fear?

I could feel it happening at Chalke House. The woman – her laughter, which had seemed so blithe and fey, was jarring into the cackle of a woodpecker; her silvery body, which had come to me as a miraculous sprite, was pinning me down. The boy – his teenage gawkiness, as daft and clumsy as my boys in Borneo, was now imbued with a strange, nude, muscular strength.

And their collusion. The two of them. I'd had an inkling when I'd arrived that they were riven somehow, there was a rift I was required to heal. No, not now. No, longer: a month or six weeks or two months later. Whether it was me who'd achieved their reunion or some other energy afoot in the woodland, they were together again, and a force to be reckoned with. What did they want of me? Who did they want me to be? Who did they think I was?

'Poor baby... you just stay there and stay cool...'

She'd coaxed me, one lunchtime, into a second and then a third glass of wine I hadn't really wanted. It had been a hot, hot morning, and the three of us had been cutting the grass outside the French windows. Why? Because Lawrence had emerged from his communing with the swifts in the greenhouse with an ancient, rusty scythe he'd discovered, an antique trophy he wanted to try out, and in any case it was that kind of late summer morning when the air was heady with elder and you could hear the gorse-pods popping in the heat. A day to be bucolic. Stripped to the waist, me and the boy, spectated by the woman, we'd wielded the scythe this way and that and managed to flatten a lot of the grass with the blunt blade.

She'd disappeared into the house and made lunch. Dizzy with the sun on my head, aware of the sinewy leanness of the boy's body as it gleamed with sweat, I'd drooped into the shade of a horse chestnut until she called us indoors.

Noon. A green salad. And chilled white wine; the shock of it was so delicious, I'd gulped it like cordial. She topped me up, although I tried to stop her with my hand over my glass. The little hit of alcohol buzzed in my brain and awakened the blurry buzziness of the previous night's drinking. And I could feel the sun on my forehead, on the back of my neck. But the salad was good, and the olive oil from the world outside, all the better for the second glass of wine I'd tried to refuse. I saw her exchange a glance with her son, when, by a sleight of hand, she poured me a third.

Bucolic... alcoholic... we finished lunch, and the room was a heavenly haze. It seemed to purr, with a soft, humming kind of energy. Or maybe it was the hum in my head. 'Poor baby...' she was whispering as she pressed me gently, firmly into the cushions of the sofa. She wetted a napkin with water from the ice-bucket and laid it on my brow. It felt like a big, cool kiss. 'Poor baby, I guess in Borneo you don't go out in the midday sun, mad dogs and Englishmen and all that. Just stay there and stay cool.'

I slept. And the orange cat wasn't orange anymore. It was covered in blood.

It dashed into the room, through the open windows. A dream, it must have been, because in the real, waking world there were no cats which had once been big and bushy with orange stripes and then slick and dripping in blood. With a bubbling yowl, because the blood was in its mouth as well, it launched itself from the carpet and landed on my chest with a soggy thump. For a moment, its face was dribbling onto mine. Then it was off again and hurtling helter-skelter about the room, as though it was on fire and the blaze on its body was a torture.

I leapt up. Apart from the madness of the cat, the room looked real. My head was throbbing. I saw the remains of lunch on a tray on the floor, the bottle of wine up-ended in the ice-bucket. Unable to yowl anymore, its throat a gurgle of blood, the cat fled to the window again and out.

Asleep... I must have been. A blood-sodden cat? Bloody footprints around and around the carpets of a country living-room? The blood was on my face. I touched it with my fingers. It didn't smell like blood. I followed the trail outside, and through the muzziness of my sleeping brain I heard an agitation of voices.

The boy was braying, manly, stentorian. And Juliet... was she laughing or sobbing? 'Get down from there! Are you mad? You've killed it!'

I rounded the corner of the house, into the holly wood, where a drunken dream became nightmare.

Buckets of blood? Lawrence was covered in it. In his little boy's pants, he was kneeling on the roof of the car, which had been a sleek silver BMW for a fighter-pilot, his pretty wife and his wholesome son, before death and madness and blindness were visited on the Lundy family. Shouting, the boy was on the roof. He had a plastic bucket up there and he was sloshing a solution of soap and water everywhere and scrubbing at it with a brush. The red paint, which had been slopped on the car to avenge the child whom Lawrence had blinded, was now partially dissolved and smeared into a gory mess.

'Help me, Mum!' And she, Juliet Lundy, was botched with the blood as well, with the solution of paint and soap and some kind of turpentine the boy must have added to the mix. She was stripped to her bra and pants. Giggling, weeping? She reached up and took down the empty bucket from the boy. Then, with a huge effort which tautened the muscles of her stomach and lifted her breasts, she stretched up to him with another full bucket of soapy solution.

The red slush was everywhere. As they lathered and swabbed the car, as though it was a war-horse returned from battle, the horrid stuff slithered off in streams and swirls and pooled into the holly wood. The boy was slick with it. The woman was gleaming.

They saw the cat before they saw me. For some perverse reason, suicidally disorientated, it returned to the scene of its dousing. It blundered through the poisoned grasses, in such a panic for its life that it banged its face on the car door. So that the boy heard it and looked down and...

'No, Lawrence, please no not again please no!' his mother cried out.

Too late to stop him. With a savage grin on his face, he stood up tall on the roof of the car. He could have been naked, because his pants were as red and wet as the rest of his body, so he looked like a pantomime savage, or the real thing from a long-ago scene of blood-letting and sacrifice. The grin, and the whites of his eyes as they rolled in heathen ecstasy, were the only glimmers of whiteness on his body.

He yelled, 'Here puss, you come back for more?' and tipped the bucket.

The sheer weight of the liquid knocked the cat over. It lay in the puddle, quivering. I stumbled forward, they both looked up and saw me, and indeed it was Juliet who reached down and picked up the cat before I could get there.

Asleep? A dream? All three of us seemed to awaken at that moment.

Me first. I heard my own voice, my tongue furry with wine. 'What the fuck are you doing? Are you fucking crazy?'

And the woman. All but naked. Dripping red, a denizen of the wood who'd dropped from the trees all prickled and smeary with her own blood. She adjusted the mask of her face, from bewilderment at seeing me there, to her quick, elfin smile, and she opened her mouth to answer. 'Crazy? No, we...'

The boy. He jumped off the car and loomed over us. I was afraid. I felt the adrenaline of imminent violence flooding my arms. For a second he towered over me and every muscle in his face was horribly clenched. He glared at me, his eyes pale with rage, his teeth clenched so hard they might crack in his mouth. He didn't recognise me. I was a stranger intruding on the bizarre ritual he was performing. But then his muscles relaxed a little and he stepped back and he knew who I was – a busybody who'd blundered through a dream and trespassed into the terrible privacy of his nightmare. He bared his teeth. 'Fucking crazy? Yes, we are!'

And the cat. Just then, cradled in the woman's arms, it shook its head and sneezed. It opened its eyes and blinked, deciding it might not die after all. In any case, the second and cleaner bucketful it had just suffered had sluiced off most of the earlier, concentrated redness which the boy must've thrown over it. With an angry spluttering, it wriggled to the ground and shot away, disappearing around the corner of the house like a flame.

There was an awkward silence on us.

Mother and son, their bare feet squelched into the sodden grass. They looked awkwardly at each other's bodies. Me, I heard an echo of my blurted words, in my befuddled head, in the dense foliage of the woodland.

And then, 'We did your father's car, remember?' It was Lawrence who spoke. 'We cleaned it up, remember? Why did we do that? Do you know if he's still alive?'

His eyes were dead and cold. Strange, in such a boiling boy. When I didn't answer, my tongue too numb to make words, he looked over and past me and into the empty corner where the cat had vanished. He stared at the emptiness, and he smiled.

'So we're doing my Dad's car,' he said very softly. 'He's still around.'

* * *

THE THREE OF us showered together. Me and Juliet and the cat.

Leaving Lawrence outside, where, in a mood of bliss and rage, he resumed his lathering of the car, Juliet and I went into the house and upstairs. She picked up the cat on the way, which had been rubbing its body up and down the length of the sofa and leaving a rosy wet smear. Sleight of hand, a feminine magic, how did she do it, managing a blurry, befuddled me and her slippery self and the wriggling cat at the same time? With a shimmying side-step at the foot of the stairs, she was in and out of the kitchen, in and out of the fridge, and then somehow, summoning all her pixie spells, she had the three of us under the shower in less than a minute with a simultaneous pop of a bottle and a clink of glasses.

'Keep your clothes on.' Me, in my shirt and trousers, the cool water coursing over my head. She, still in her bra and pants, her body pink with the dissolving paint. The cat tried to escape, but she closed the bathroom door and it cowered in a corner while we drank our first glass of champagne. 'Keep your clothes on,' she whispered against the whispering of the water, 'he might scratch.' And I held the cat close while it wailed and fought and she soaped it and rinsed it and soaped it and rinsed it, until all its resistance was worn down and the redness was gone and the wretched beast was a shivering skinny drowned-rat. At last I dropped it gently down. It shook itself orange again.

We let it out. We drank champagne and we showered together.

'WHERE'S LAWRENCE? WHAT'S he doing?'

She didn't seem to hear me. 'Hair of the dog,' she said. 'And cat.'

We were drinking into the evening. For a change we'd carried a couple of chairs into the garden and watched the dusk and the twilight settling onto the trees. She said it was too smelly in the living-room, where the cat had rubbed itself and dried itself and licked itself back into a gorgeous bouffant cloud of fur; otherwise it seemed none the worse for its experience, its starring role in my afternoon nightmare. But the house was strong with that rank, dank odour of wet animal, so we sat outside, barefoot in a glorious gloaming, and surrendered deeper into the gentle embrace of alcohol.

By now it was very dark. The moon was invisible, hardly a glow of silver to show where it might have been hidden in cloud. No stars. Even the looming bulk of the woodland was lost in the blackness, part of a vast, infinite sky. We'd eaten earlier, bits and pieces of left-overs Juliet had got out of the fridge. Lawrence snatched and gobbled, wolfish as any teenage boy, and the hue of his skin, his face and his bony fingers, was still tinged with the blood of my waking dream. Juliet and I, we'd eaten quickly too, our appetites whetted by sex and champagne and the first two doses of gin, and then we'd come outside.

'Is he still in the tower?' I tried again. She hadn't heard me before, and we couldn't see each other at all. I heard her swallowing the last of another gin and tonic, sucking on a piece of ice, and I could smell on her the lotion we'd used for our long and leisurely showering. But I couldn't see her, I couldn't see anything. 'He was upstairs a while ago,' I said. 'I heard him on his battlements. I heard him coughing. Do you think he's alright?'

Her voice. Disembodied. 'Why shouldn't he be? What do you mean?'

I chose my words carefully. 'He wasn't really alright this afternoon, was he? I mean, was he alright?'

There was a longer pause. I heard her swirling her glass and drinking it down. She was choosing her words too.

'Of course he's not alright.' Her voice was soft and slurry, she had had plenty to drink and she had a piece of ice in her mouth. 'As you know, as you've gathered since you arrived here, he's got a... a preoccupation with his father, which you'd kind of expect, after what happened to him. And then... and

then the horrible business last winter. Sometimes he thinks...
I mean sometimes he imagines his father is still here, or he's
waiting on pins for him to come back at any moment... or...'

She stopped. We both held our breath and listened. It was
as though, because we were talking about the boy, we could
feel his presence, he'd crept close, invisible, and was listening
to what we were saying. I shuddered at the thought of it. I felt
him standing right behind me, holding his breath too, so close
he could lean down and breathe on the back of my neck or
curl his fingers around my throat. I listened for him, for any
movement, and my scalp prickled. He was somewhere nearby,
in the garden with us, or in the house. And yet the garden and
even the house were invisible.

'And me?' I said. I took a deeper breath and, emboldened by
the darkness and the alcohol, dared to ask the questions which
had been entangling themselves like cobwebs in the corners of
my brain. 'And me, who does he think I am? I mean, am I a
father-figure for him, does he see me as a kind of replacement
for the father he's lost, or another kind of intruder on the
empty space his father's left behind?'

She didn't say anything. I couldn't hear her breathing.

'Because...' I went on, trying to clarify my thoughts,
trying to make something of the cobwebby stuff in my head,
'because I'm getting mixed messages, aren't I? From Lawrence.
Sometimes we're alright together and I feel as though I'm
doing what you said you wanted me to do, to be a friend or a
brother, a companion, and I even imagine I'm a kind of half-
adequate stand-in for his father... at least for the summer, like
a man around the house, someone he can bond with and do
things with, even if it's only tinkering with the car or playing
a bit of badminton.'

Still no response, although I waited in the darkness for her
to take in what I was saying. I thought I heard the creak of her
chair as shifted her weight on it. But no voice.

'But then...' I took the chance to proffer the more worrying
side of the ideas I'd been weighing, 'but then, I've got to tell

you, Juliet... and you must've seen it too, like this afternoon when I interrupted your mad car-washing thing... sometimes he looks at me as though... well, as though he could kill me.'

The last two words came out, dull and blunt in the night air. I let them drop into the silence.

'I mean, what does he want from me? Is he glad I'm here, because his father has gone? Or does he hate me being here, because his father has gone?'

There was a long, long, longer silence. Nothing but silence. The cobwebs in my head fluttered. By speaking my mind I'd breathed on them and shifted the gathering dust. But now I felt them falling still again, as the vibration slowed and stopped.

In exasperation, as my words faded into nothing, apparently as airy as the skidding of the bats in the enveloping night, I said louder, 'Hey Juliet, are you there, are you listening? And what about you? What do you want me for? I mean, when we're drinking gin, when we're making love, is it me, or is it him?'

Nothing. Nothing.

At last I huffed into the void, started to try and stand up. 'I need another drink, I need some light, I need... not sure what the fuck I need...' I felt for her hand, felt for the chair beside me. 'Juliet, I'm going in and...'

She wasn't there. Her chair was empty.

I slumped down again. I waited, blind. How long had she been gone? Had she heard a word I'd said? I waited, thinking any moment the lamp would flick on in the living-room and a soft yellow glow would fall into the garden. It didn't happen.

I struggled up, felt for the French windows and stepped inside.

Coffin-blackness. Coffin-silence.

No. I could hear breathing. Someone was there.

The air moved around me. Something, someone, brushed past me. I heard a gasp, and there were fingers touching my face.

And three voices rang out, at the very same moment.

Mine. 'Juliet?'

Hers. 'Lawrence?'

His. 'Dad?'

And then we were fumbling together, groping to locate one another, to identify who and what...

The boy said, 'Dad? Are you...?' and his hands were clammy on my skin.

The woman, 'Who is it? Oh god please...' and I smelled the panic on her gin-breath.

My own voice, shaking with an unwonted fear. 'For fuck's sake, a light, for fuck's sake, can't you just...?'

There was a shattering crash, as one of them, or me, toppled the lamp in the corner. And the cat was somewhere. It spat and screeched and its fur was electric as it squirmed through the room and out.

'Dad?' The boy's breath was in my face. I shoved past, my bare feet crunching on broken glass, and found the doorway to the hall.

Fumbled for the switch. Turned the light on.

AN ONLOOKER, A fly on the wall, would've thought we were all mad.

Not that we were doing anything manic. We weren't doing anything at all. But in the way we stood and swayed and ogled one another, there was more than a whiff of insanity.

Whiff... the room was pungent with alcohol and wet cat and teenage boy. The overhead light was too bright. We blinked at one another, in a curious tableau, as though the three of us, inmates of a grim institution for the dangerously deranged, were humouring a drama teacher and doing some kind of batty theatre-therapy. Freeze. He, or more likely she, had told us to freeze whenever the light came on.

I was barefoot, with blood oozing between my toes. Giddy drunk, tousled and bleary, and staring fearfully around as if I was expecting somebody else to walk in through the open French windows. The woman was in a half-crouching, half-cringing position, her knees bent, her face screwed up and her arms over her head, as if expecting to be hit.

And the boy? As we unfolded our bodies from the assault of the light, it was the boy who radiated an aura of distraction.

Mad? Hard to say. He was more or less naked, in his bed shorts or some other tattered pants. With a pair of binoculars slung round his neck. Holding a badminton racquet. Mad? He wasn't himself. He was changing, he was changed.

'Lawrence? What on earth...?' His mother moved to touch him, but he flinched away.

The smell of him was strong. Something animal, a fume of some feathery dust seemed to rise from his bare skin. Dusty. Where he'd been gleaming with paint in the afternoon, now a film of the chalky powder which covered every surface of every room of the old house had clung to him. And hairy? I saw, we must both of us have seen, that he was hairier than before... an illusion of the sudden light?... but his hair was too long, the pelt of it fell across his brow and shadowed his eyes, it was shaggy on his ears and it formed a pointy tuft at the nape of his neck as though it would grow along his spine like a mane. And his face was more than downy. It showed in the glare of the overhead bulb. He'd never shaved, but now he needed to. He had a bluey-velvet nap on his cheeks and the first blurring of a moustache on his upper lip.

He was bent, like his mother, cringing from the light. He looked up at me through the fall of his hair and he opened his whiskery mouth. At the very same moment as his mother whispered again, 'My love, are you...?' and feinted at his head with a wary hand, he started to cough.

A dry cough. At first it was almost the sneezing of a cat.

But a terrible, rather horrible thing happened. He was gripped by a kind of convulsion, as though his body had been seized by a cruel, powerful hand which was squeezing the breath out of him. He coughed. Louder and louder, a dry retching. He dropped the racquet, doubled over with his hands on his kneecaps, and a relentless force bent him lower and lower until he fell to the floor. The binoculars swung from his neck, banged on his chest. He coughed. No, he couldn't, he tried to cough, but there was no more breath in him and I could see the bones of his ribs standing starkly out and every knob of his backbone.

The woman knelt – 'Oh my god do something!' – and wrapped her arms around him. I knelt too. I massaged hopelessly at his neck, where the sinews stood out like wires. 'Do something! Oh do something!' she was shouting, to the boy as much as to me.

There was a madness in the room, a piece of nightmare. It was in the boy. It was on us.

And suddenly, an explosion of energy from the boy's body repelled us from him and we stood away, powerless, as somehow, from somewhere, he'd found a pocket of air in his lungs which allowed him to cough once more.

A huge, howking cough, big enough to bring up all the contents of his stomach in one mighty eruption.

He didn't. He retched something onto the carpet and peered closely at it. And then he slowly stood up.

Nothing really. A blob of grey mucus, a congealed pellet which had lodged mercilessly in the back of his throat. But the sight of it, now that his fit was over, seemed to give him a curious satisfaction.

He swivelled his head to his mother and then to me. His eyes were wet. His smile was spooled with saliva. He tried to lick it from his downy lips, but it resisted his tongue. A sick, sticky smile.

He bent to the badminton racquet. He flipped up the pellet with it. And, before Juliet could try again to comfort him, he popped the pellet back into his mouth. He loped across the room and was gone, into the darkness of the woodland.

THE DARKNESS. THE night. A long night. A long tunnel of darkness. Such a blurring of nightmare and reality that it was impossible to tell which was which.

I tried to stop Juliet from pursuing her son into the garden, but I couldn't. And anyway, in an odd, selfish way, it was a relief to flee the glaring light of the living-room with its stink of booze and sweat and smeary furniture, from the broken glass and mysterious stickiness on the carpet, and melt into the sweetness of the night outside. Everything we did was hampered and thwarted, as though, in a limbo between wakefulness and the chaos of dream, our movements were slow and laboured. Or it was the drink? Or the adrenaline in our limbs? Or we were asleep?

Straight out of the French windows, with shards of glass in my feet, we blundered into the chairs we'd taken outside and fell headlong into the long grass. Together we rolled onto the lawn, and the chair I'd hit was a crunching pain on my ribs. We got up, bruised, panting, and stumbled away from the house, and immediately the blackness was impenetrable. Blindness – it was the same blindness which had surrounded us as we'd sat and watched the gathering twilight. And now, as we moved deeper into the woods, it was a reckless, haphazard descent into an invisible world.

I felt for her arm. She gripped my hand. There was a gleam of light, a sliver of starlight reflected from the hearse, and then a faint glow from the derelict greenhouse.

She dragged me towards it, knowing the way better than I did, careless of the nettles which were chest-high and even wafted their stinging leaves at my face.

'He's in here,' she hissed unnecessarily, and I tried again to stop her, to make her pause at least, or to pull her away.

'Juliet, no. I'll go in and see what he's...' I was panting. 'Juliet, you wait out here and I'll take a look and make sure he's...' In my stomach I was sick with a fear of what we would see, of what he might be doing. Because I knew. I knew. And I didn't want her to see.

But I couldn't stop her. She possessed the unstoppable strength of a mother fearful for the sanity of her child. I had such a stabbing in my ribs that every step made me gasp, and the broken bricks underfoot, they ground the splinters of glass deeper into my soles. I couldn't stop her.

We fell together into the greenhouse.

The boy, we couldn't see the boy. We couldn't hear him. He must have propped up his torch, it was beaming from somewhere at ground-level, from somewhere in a clump of brambles or the tangled roots of the vine; it was beaming up into the rafters and shattered panes of the ceiling. The swifts were in full panic. Hundreds of them – screeching with their tiny, tinny voices – were pell-mell in the confined space. The air above us and around our heads was alive with their dashing, hurtling, furry-feathery madness. A Bedlam of birds.

Lawrence... Lawrence?

He was up there, clinging with his toes and fingertips, where I'd discovered him once before: his outline blurred by the movement of the birds, a figure from an old black and white movie, flickering in the kaleidoscopic light.

Oh god. What was he?

A piece of myth? Some kind of bird-boy, a figment of legend or superstition? A boy who came out of the night, who emerged nude from the mud of the pond or dropped from the cloud-covered moon, who hung in the rafters festooned with the nests of the devil-birds and was a part of their mystic roosting. He was nude, dusky, his skin matted with their dust and down, his hair a sooty pelt, and oozing from his mouth a...

Yes. We stood and gaped up at him. His whiskery wide mouth. Oozing. His body heaved with the effort of retching, and – unless I was hallucinating and tunnelling deeper into nightmare – he sicked up a mess of saliva, which gleamed in the quivering torchlight before he smeared it onto the rafters with his tongue.

The birds... they were a frenzy of screaming, a sooty haboob, so dizzying and so loud I didn't notice that Juliet was no longer standing beside me.

Until I glanced down. She'd fainted onto the ground.

* * *

AT LAST THERE was a lull in the lunacy of that night.

No, not then, in the greenhouse... somehow, I got the woman out of there. Not sure how, like one of those cuts in a 1950s film, a swirling of the screen and a tag-line swimming into focus: *Later the same night*. There was a blurry commotion and a lot of pain. The trees were huge and black around me, and an enormous, elephantine roaring, either in their lofty branches or inside my head. Did I carry the woman on my shoulders or drag her bumping and bumping by the heels?

Not sure. But there was a lull – *Later the same night* – and for an hour or two it was almost sane.

I was in bed with her. In her bed, for the first time, the bed she'd shared with her husband. Somehow, to use that convenient word again, I'd got her up the stairs and toppled her like a sack of potatoes onto the rumpled sheets. I was exhausted – the pain in my ribs, the effort of manhandling the woman from inside the greenhouse and through the woods and into the house and upstairs, the discomfort of my wounded feet... And yet the pain itself was disconcertingly reassuring. Fuck, it was real. Every stab and twinge of it was a lurch back into a real world I'd felt slipping further and further away.

I think we slept. Not sure. Juliet awoke from her deadfaint long enough to realise she was on the bed with me, long enough to mew pathetically like a kitten while I undressed her and myself and we pulled the sheets over us. She smelled of the woodland, sappy and green, she smelled of the leaves and the grass and the earth. And gin. And fear.

I slipped off the bed and saw the orange glow of the light in the greenhouse, and when I slipped beside her again and held her close I whispered in her ear that everything would be alright, that the boy would be alright, that he would come to no harm while I was here and I would take care of them both... murmuring platitudes, sweet useless nothings, which lulled us both into a woozy, warm, welcoming sleep.

I think we slept. Impossible to tell.

Sleeping or waking, nightmare or reality? What was the difference? What did it matter? Whatever absurdities I dreamed – Welsh-speaking head-hunters, schoolgirls possessed by spirits of the forest, my indomitable father drooling in an old people's home – they slid seamlessly into the horrid oddness of that night.

Absurd... and horrid.

I dreamed of a madman. While I nestled in the limbs of a naked pixie-woman, naked with her in the wide expanse of her own bed for the first time, I dreamed of a medieval madman. No, not medieval, except in the long-ago, long-lost lunacy which gleamed from the grin on his face... because in one hand he was swishing a modern-day badminton racquet, and in the other he was swinging a hefty pair of black binoculars on a leather strap.

I dreamed of him. He was huge and nude. He loomed in my dream.

He wafted the racquet over my head, and it was furry with flies, they dripped off it and pattered on my head and face. In my dreaming, although I was wrapped in the arms of the pixie-girl and safe in her bed, I was afraid. Can you smell things in a dream? The madman smelled bad. He smelled of stagnant mud, a brackish slime. He leaned so close that even his shadow smelled bad. His mouth smelled bad, of sickliness and sick regurgitation. I was afraid, in my dreaming...

Not a dream. I blinked awake and Lawrence Lundy was standing over me.

I stared up at him. He smiled at me. A spool of saliva... a silvery thread of it, with a silvery blob on the end, drizzled from his lips and hung in mid-air, until the blob gathered enough weight in its mucous liquidity to drop into my mouth.

He moved across the room. He opened the wardrobe doors and nuzzled through the hanging clothes. This time he took them out. He took out his father's RAF jacket and trousers, the squadron-blue suit he might wear for special or ceremonial occasions, and he laid them carefully on the bed. For me? No, not for me, but on the end of his father's bed, for his father, who must be lying in this bed with his mother.

I held my breath and watched. It was beautiful, this ritual, the laying-out of his father's clothes, in its deference, its pathetic humility. He took his father's cologne and sprayed the clothes with it. Like a blessing.

Almost lovely, a part of the lull in the nightmare.

But then, as he moved around the foot of the bed and out of the room, I could sense a sudden anger in him. It was rank in his sweat, on his breath, on his naked teenage skin, and in his stale mouth. A terrible anger.

I followed him, fascinated and sick with fear of what he might do. He seemed to hum with anger, as though his bones would crack with the tension. I could hear him grinding his teeth. He moved quickly, with a fell purpose.

With three strides he was across the landing and into my room. He swung the binoculars from his neck, gripping the leather strap in his right hand. He hurtled them round and round like a sling... and with every ounce of strength in his body he smashed them onto my pillow.

Again. And again. With a greater, more terrible force each time. Until he was heaving with the exertion.

At last he stopped.

He let go of the binoculars and stared at them, embedded in the pillow. He exhaled a long, long, wheezing breath, until his shoulders relaxed and the tension was gone and his whole tormented being was deflated.

He turned and walked past me, oblivious of the reality of my presence, and he went silently up to his tower

Chapter Twenty-One

WE WERE HAVING breakfast in the kitchen. It was as though I'd just arrived and the world was a warm, sunlit heaven. It was all real.

Juliet had made eggs and bacon for the three of us, with coffee. She was putting on some toast and turning out the cupboards in search of honey. Me and Juliet and Lawrence, and the cat.

And outside, two wonderful things, two things so truly marvellous that the reality was almost unbearable.

First of all, through the open window of the kitchen there came a whiff of autumn.

Impossible to describe, it would be presumptuous to try: something lissom and sly in the way the leaves were turning, the dark green leaves of late summer. The tiniest shiver in them, and a restless shifting this way and that as though they knew, they could sense the coming of a time when the air would cool and the winds would rattle them off and down and tumbling to the ground below. A whiff, a scent and a shiver I hadn't had for all my years abroad. The changing of the seasons – it was late-August, and simply the idea of September, the loveliness of that word, the idea of September in England was more delicious than all the honey in Lincolnshire.

Juliet found the honey, an unopened jar of it, tucked in a corner of one of the cupboards. She'd entirely emptied the cupboard, she'd hoicked out everything, so the kitchen was a muddle of batteries, boxes of candles, rolls of sticky-tape and wrapping paper, soap and shoe-polish, and for some mysterious reason the elusive jar of honey had got pushed into the cupboard and hidden at the back. With a housewifely smile of triumph, she set it on the table. Lawrence tried to open it. He couldn't. He wrestled at it with all his manly stubbornness, refused to let me try, and eventually relinquished it to his mother, who stabbed at the lid with the point of a knife and effortlessly twisted it open.

'Brains,' she said, 'not brawn. It takes a woman to know these things.'

Small talk. A small triumph. Nice, yes. Nice and banal. We were three normal human beings, like a family, eating eggs and bacon, rummaging for a jar of honey and struggling to open it. The sun, a cooler, paler sun fell into the room, and it was alright for me to say, 'What a lovely morning!' It was alright to state the blindingly obvious, it felt so good to be back in a normal world.

The other thing? 'Listen,' I said, to engage the boy and his mother, 'do you hear it? You won't have, not since the springtime, and it's a sure sign that it's nearly the end of the summer. Listen... the robin.'

The most delicate, silvery song. A trickle of quicksilver. 'You'll hear him singing in the spring, when he's disputing territory and looking for a mate and nest-building, but then he'll stop. Not a peep, through June, July and into August. Listen, that's the robin singing, that's the sound of soon-September.'

We all listened. The cat listened. It had been lying asleep on the floor, away from the table and the movement of the humans' feet. But now, as if required to stir itself and pay attention, it opened its eyes and blinked around the kitchen. Like Juliet and Lawrence, it was still and quiet, and listening.

At the same moment, both Juliet and Lawrence cocked their heads slightly in the direction, not of the garden, but of the kitchen door and the hallway and the foot of the stairs. As if they'd heard something out there and they were waiting.

Not the robin. Something else. Somebody else.

The cat started purring. It got up and stretched, arching its back and shimmying all its fur into a huge orange halo. It moved to the door and stood there, purring loudly, and staring up the stairs. There was a creak of the floorboards, a flexing of the old house in the warmth of a summer's morning. Another creak. And the boy and his mother, perfectly synchronised, their eyes fixed on the doorway, turned their heads and followed something, or somebody who came in. No, actually a nothing, an utter invisibility, which didn't come into the kitchen and sit on the empty chair at the breakfast table.

The cat too. Purring like a sewing-machine, in a state of bliss, it folded its body as voluptuously as only a feline can, in and out of the legs of that chair, the empty chair, on which no one was sitting, an empty chair at which two people were staring with beatific smiles on their faces.

Nothing. I stared at the chair as well. Was it Banquo's fucking ghost or what? The cat sprang onto the chair and sprawled on its back with its legs wide apart, as though someone was stroking its tummy, nubbing its nipples...

Juliet and Lawrence turned their heads and smiled at each other. She, her eyes gleaming with incipient tears, reached for her son's hand and squeezed it. I was completely effaced. For them, I wasn't in the room. They were engrossed in one another and the phenomenon they, and the cat, had conjured.

'Excuse me...' I tried sarcasm, to hide my exasperation, to quell a qualm of fear I felt in my stomach. 'Excuse me, did we hear the robin singing? In the garden? The first one I've heard in six years?'

They blinked at the sound of my voice. I heard myself clawing at the reality I thought we'd had in the room, clutching for it, desperate for it, feeling it slipping away from me. They both looked at me, a flicker of puzzlement on their faces, as though they'd discovered a stranger sitting at their table and helping himself to their toast and honey, and I said, a bit louder, groping for the moments of sanity I thought we'd been sharing, 'The robin? The end of the summer? The days will get shorter and cooler and...' I sighted on the boy and aimed an idea at him, to try and wake him, to try and bring him back to the real world. 'And Lawrence, soon the swifts will be thinking of leaving, we'll go out one morning and find they've all gone.'

He stared at me. My voice, my words, seemed to jar on him. I saw, in his eyes and in the tensing of the muscles in his forearms, a warning glimmer of the anger he'd manifested before.

He controlled it. He looked at me through the fall of his hair. He simply said, 'No.'

I tried to smile at him. I wanted small talk. I wanted little, everyday conversation. 'What do you mean?'

'I mean no. The swifts won't go. They don't have to.'

I felt the smile falter on my face. I fixed it there, but I knew it was only a mask and he could see through it.

'Lawrence, I know, and you know, they'll fly away soon. They always do. And they'll come back next year, the very same birds will return to the very same nests. Their migration, it's one of the marvels of nature. Those tiny creatures, weighing no more than a couple of ounces, will set off and...'

'No, they don't have to,' he said. 'You don't know. You're a teacher, but there are things you don't know.'

Oh god. No, not oh god. Oh fuck. I felt myself encloaked in a dream. Was that a word: encloaked? The weight of it, the very darkness of it, was like a smothering cloak. All of the delicious, chilly end-of-summer, and the miraculous robin... smothered in his truculent teenage words.

In a maudlin millisecond I had a dream come back to me, in a nightmare or a blur of reality.

In my first month in Borneo, wet behind the ears and not a clue about how to live and eat and work and sleep there, I'd tacked up a mosquito-net over and around my bed, and clambered in, unwashed and sweaty with gin, and woke in the night with the net collapsed on top of me, enmeshing me, smothering me, suffocating me, so that I cried out loud and fought and fought to get out, while the sweat of the gin was on me and the mosquitoes whined in my ears and jabbed their bloodthirsty needles into my skin. A horrible trap I'd set for myself, and the more I struggled to get out and the louder I shouted the more I was enmeshed and ensnared and suffocating and...

Juliet intervened.

'Alright, Lawrence,' with a toss of her head and a furious blinking, like a child annoyed at being woken from a daydream. 'Lawrence, it's alright. Chris is a teacher, and he's travelled to a lot of places we've never been to and he knows a lot of things we don't know. That's why we asked him to come here.'

Her voice was bright, but as tinny-empty as the bell on a bicycle. It chimed in the air, and the boy swatted it away with his hands. 'More toast, more coffee?' She persisted, as he ducked his head and sniggered behind his hair. 'Or maybe you two men can help me tidy up a bit? Lawrence, can you put all this stuff back in the cupboard for me? Not the long-lost honey, of course.'

She twittered on. Like the song of the robin, wistful for the passing of summer, brave in the face of an imminent winter. She seemed determined, after her relapse into a dream-world, to emerge into an everyday day and live in it, at least for the moment. And so she delegated the chore to her troubled, troubling son, as deliberately humdrum as the soap and batteries and shoe-polish and candles he rearranged into the cupboard.

Possession? Why did you, Dayangku Siti Hafizah Qurr'atul binti Hj. Mohammad Alimin, why did you fall onto the floor and start crying?

You were always such a quiet and studious and serious girl. You sat at the front and blinked up at me from beneath your perfectly ironed *tudong*. You smiled at my *orang putih* jokes and you always did your homework. So why, when a bulldozer outside my classroom was chewing and gnawing at the forest, did the spirits of the fallen trees come whispering through the window and... and, well, why did the spirits of the forest possess you? Why did you tear off your *tudong* and start screaming so loudly, so madly, that a thousand other girls and boys and even teachers with degrees from Worcester and Gloucester and Brighton and York start screaming?

Possession? Like this boy? Lawrence Lundy, the mad? Sniggering mad... sniggering mad, with insects in his mouth.

I saw him. I saw him on the battlements of his tower. With his badminton racquet. Never mind fucking blue tits. I saw him, outside the windows of his tower, at night, swatting at the insects with his racquet, at the night bugs and cockchafers and moths until the racquet was encrusted with their gauzy and chitinous bodies, and then scraping them off and stuffing them into his mouth. I saw him. And I saw him, in the rafters of the old greenhouse, a mythical swift-boy, naked and dusty and drooling, a mythical boy from the pond, or from the moon, sicking up... sicking up a drool, a spittle... a mad boy.

Possessed? He possessed his father. The ghost of him. The invisibility of him. The presence of him. The nubbing the nipples of a cat of him.

And me? Afraid. Afraid for the boy, afraid of the boy? Afraid for Juliet, so fragile, so fey. She also, I saw it with my own eyes, she also saw... I saw her and the boy as they followed with their eyes, I saw with my own eyes, they saw someone come into the kitchen and sit at the table with the toast and the honey, and the cat came purring like a panther and jumped onto his lap...

His? How could I say his? Or think his? Unless, me too, I saw something? No. I didn't see anything, anyone.

But at night, I heard voices. I heard a voice in the tower. Someone was talking.

I AWOKE. I thought I awoke... and the woman was nude in the moonlight, beside me.

She was lovely. The moon cast her body in silver and grey and an indescribable blue – nothing like the sea or the sky, but an ineffable blue from the shadows of the moon and its light through the clouds and the trees and our open window. She was asleep, and she smelled of sleep and our love-making and herself, so it couldn't have been her voice I had heard. She was whispering; a tiny, faraway whisper, as she breathed, as she dreamed, which blew the fall of her hair across her lips. So it wasn't her voice I'd heard.

I slipped out of bed and onto the landing and listened. And I heard voices up in the tower.

I tiptoed up and up the stairs.

Pitch darkness. A narrowing space, as though I was burrowing my head and shoulders into a shrinking, suffocating nothingness, a kind of vacuum which might swallow and smother me. I controlled a panic of claustrophobia and trod to the top, where I took a huge breath and pushed open the door.

The boy's room was full of moonlight. Impossible, of course, but it seemed to fall into the tower from all four sides, filling the room with a powdery, chalk-dusty talcum of moonlight.

He was sitting on his bed. Lawrence, it was his voice I'd heard. He turned and smiled at me. He beckoned me in. He was naked, like a god. His hair was dense and purple-black, and his nakedness was slick with an iridescent slime.

A man was sitting on the bed with him. He was handsome and young and he was wearing his RAF suit. They had the pieces of a model aeroplane laid out on the bed between them, and a tube of glue, and they were making the model together.

They both looked up at me. They smiled.

When the boy smiled, a spittle oozed through his teeth. It was flecked with grey and black, the indigestible remains of the insects he'd swatted with his racquet and stuffed into his mouth.

When his father smiled, his teeth were brown and broken. Sea-water dribbled out, and then a gush of it, the contents of his bloated, submarine belly.

Oh god, oh fuck, I could smell it. You can smell things in dreams, the reeking rank viscosity of a drowned man. And I could feel it was hot, it splashed onto my bare bedroom feet.

Bedroom? I awoke. I think I awoke. And I was in bed with Juliet.

She was silvery nude and fast asleep beside me. I was naked too. The sheet had slipped off us, or maybe we had pushed it off because the night was so warm. I was suddenly wide awake, and the exposure of my own body in the moonlight was frightening.

I awoke and I was afraid. Because someone else had come into the room and was staring at me.

Yes you can smell in a dream you can smell the sweat of your fear from your own body, and you can smell the slimy sweat of a huge naked boy standing so close to you and looming so close that you can hear and smell his breathing...

He stared down at me for a long moment, and then he moved around the foot of the bed, past the dressing-table and to the wardrobe. As he had done before, he opened the wardrobe, felt among the hanging clothes and nuzzled his shaggy head into them.

But this time, something was different. The boy stepped back from the wardrobe and he smiled. He made a curious, beckoning gesture with both hands, as though inviting something or someone to come out. And then he waited.

The clothes on their hangers, they moved. They moved aside. And a man stepped out.

In his smart RAF uniform, dapper and self-assured, the boy's father came out and he looked around the moonlit room. I was lying naked on his bed, beside the naked body of his wife, but he didn't see me. He moved to the bed and looked down on the sleeping woman. He appraised her face and her body, and tears of joy seemed to shine in his eyes. But when he bent to kiss her, a bubble of rusty-brown water broke from his shattered teeth.

He straightened up and adjusted his uniform – on parade. He went to the dressing-table and sat in front of the mirror.

He smiled at himself, oblivious of the dead and decomposing ugliness of his mouth, and he took the brush from the table and brushed his hair with it. He set it down, satisfied with his dashing, jet-fighter-pilot good looks, and he sprayed himself with cologne.

He went back into the wardrobe. He pushed the clothes aside and slipped between them. The boy closed the door on him. The boy went out of the room and I heard him go up to his tower.

PREPOSITIONS ARE TRICKY. My students would say so. Small, inconspicuous little words, which look so unimportant, but which change the meaning of a sentence, change the meaning of everything.

In the morning Juliet made love to me. She made love on me. And then, she made love without me. She rolled off me and lay still, staring up at the ceiling and at the dressing-table and at the wardrobe door. And she made love to herself.

She'd woken me with a swift, slithering movement of her body, and she was straddling me, astride me, and making the most of my male, waking-up readiness. And there was something different in her, something akin to the change of the season. She'd been russet, she'd been tawny, she'd been the red squirrel or the marten, a marvellous forest creature, ever since she'd dropped from the pine like an elf on a gossamer thread. For me, exiled for years to the torrid tropical jungles and dreariness of the faraway mosque, she'd been the electric-blue shock of the jay and the flash of the yaffle in an old English woodland. I'd rubbed her and smelled her, the sweet fibrous earth and the fragrant mulch of the ancient trees.

Now she'd changed. How to describe her body? It was weathered, it was chapped. The raw wind from the north sea had somehow funnelled down from the wolds and pinched her. The season had changed her. Everything must change. The sallow greenness of summer, the sappiness and pith, was drying up. I could taste the change in her mouth. There was something metallic in her mouth; it tasted like blood. It was the taste of autumn.

I watched her and listened as she pleasured herself. And when she'd finished, with a sudden arching of her body and a dry croaking in the back of her throat, she'd asked me in a perfunctory, matter-of-fact way, 'Was he here last night? Did he come in? I wasn't sure if I heard him or I was just dreaming.'

I hesitated and answered. 'Lawrence? Yes, I think he...'

She'd thrown me a queer, sideways look and rolled off the bed and tiptoed to the dressing-table.

Naked, scented of me and then her own self-satisfaction, she looked very small, like a girl. She sat at the mirror. She puffed a cloud of cologne into the air and watched as the droplets caught the first of the morning light and then disappeared. She picked at a few hairs on the brush on the table and studied them minutely in her fingertips.

'Lawrence?' she said to her own reflection. 'No, I didn't mean Lawrence...'

Chapter Twenty-Two

I FOUND MYSELF doing a strange thing, later the same day, in the afternoon. I climbed the Scots pine to the very top and stood on the tree-house.

Why did I do that? In the morning I was in the garden with the boy. We'd had a quiet breakfast together, the three of us and the cat, an almost eerily quiet breakfast with none of us speaking except to offer the tea and toast and pass the butter and the honey. I listened to the quietness of the woodland outside the kitchen window, almost like the whispering of a village church or a country churchyard, it reminded me of the long-ago autumn days I'd spent with my father as he chipped and chipped at the headstones and the names of the long-dead people lying beneath them. So we passed the butter and the honey, and I heard the robin again. This time I didn't comment on it. I didn't need to, it was so pure and cool and silvery-perfect. No, it was an absence of sound that caught my attention, if not the attention of the boy and the woman.

The air was somehow empty and still. A sound we'd heard almost incessantly for weeks and weeks was no longer there. The swifts. Their aerial screaming. No more. They'd gone.

I opened my mouth to remark on it. I saw the boy cocking his head to the window. I saw the gulp of his Adam's apple, as he swallowed to clear the mucus in his throat and his sinuses, and listened hard. When our eyes met and he could see I was about to speak, he ducked away, hiding in the privacy of his own hair, to nibble noisily at a piece of toast as if the crunching of it would suffice to break the silence and prevent me from speaking.

And so, into the garden. I followed him down to the pond. He glanced up a few times, and if I'd been expecting a hint of wistfulness that the sky was suddenly so empty, I didn't see it. Odd, after the things he'd said about the birds not leaving, as if it was in the power of the mad mythical swift-boy to hold them back. It was odd to see him appraising the emptiness of the autumn morning with a kind of satisfaction.

'You can help me,' he said, as we came closer to the pond. 'I've nearly finished, but you can help me with the rest of it.'

The smell came to me. It was smell of my nightmares. A brackish slime. Outside, in the open air of the woodland garden, it wasn't so nauseatingly strong as the reek of it which had caught in my nostrils, in my dreams. 'We do it every year, around this time, me and my Dad. It lets the air into the water, otherwise the stuff all dies and goes rotten and sinks to the bottom and whatever...'

He'd been stripping the weed from the pond. When? Maybe at night, in the moonlight, or in the long evenings when his mother and I had been sousing ourselves into sex and sleepiness with gin. 'Do you want to help me finish it off? You'll get very dirty and stinky, but it's kind of fun too. Me and Dad, it's something we do together every year.'

He waded through the tall grasses and rushes at the edge of the water until he was knee-deep, reached through the green-brown surface and clawed at the weed below it. He leaned back with all his weight, and like a fisherman heaving ashore a net replete with his catch, he started dragging out a mat of the stuff. A mat of it, a rug of it, bigger and bigger and more and more until he splashed heavily backwards onto the dry land at the edge of the pond with a mighty carpet of weed, intact in one piece, and flopped it down onto the grass.

'That's what we do!' Heaving with the effort, his face agleam with satisfaction, he said, 'We get tons of it! Stinky! but I kind of love the smell and look! Look! It's popping with insects!'

There was a formidable, almost overwhelming fume of mud and decomposing vegetation: beautiful really, a smell of dying-off and putrefaction, over-ripe with the stench of its own richness. It was the countryside, the autumn, the world. A natural world of life and death and the turning of the seasons. And yes, the mat of weed was fizzing with the myriad creatures which had been dragged into the daylight – countless unidentifiable bugs and beetles and worms, tiny prehistoric beasts which the boy had trawled unceremoniously from the pond.

I helped the boy to finish his job. He'd already cleared most of it, working secretly on his own, while Juliet and I had thought he was in the greenhouse or up in his tower, and I could see a trail of the slimy mats which he'd dragged away and into the woods somewhere. Together, we heaved more of it out of the water and dumped it under the trees. We were dripping wet and lathered in mud. Breathless, barely able to speak after we'd extracted an especially spectacular piece, a great congealed mass of tangled roots and fibres, he'd muttered something about composting it or recycling it in some way. Unlikely, because no one had done any real 'gardening' in the overgrown wilderness of Chalke House for years. But he could use it, he was using it, he mumbled to himself as we hauled it through the trees and towards the greenhouse.

I didn't know what he meant. No matter. In any case, the pond looked better for its autumn 'spring-clean'. The water was a deep, murky, mulligatawny mirror.

So it was done. I got the sense that I was dismissed. We'd spent an hour or two together and that was enough for him. There was such an air of abstraction in his manner, his face was so clouded with his own intense preoccupation, that he could no longer bother to glance at me. When I spoke to him, if only to express a platitude about 'a job well done' or 'a good way to work up an appetite for lunch', it was as though he couldn't bear to have my voice pestering his ears. He didn't want me around any more. He didn't just drift in the direction of the greenhouse; he headed off, quite purposefully, and threw a wary look over his shoulder to make sure I wasn't following him.

Fine with me. I watched him slink into the dense cover of the nettles and cow-parsley. In the ensuing silence, I waited until I felt myself truly and comfortably alone, and I walked further away from the house, deeper into the woodland.

To the car, at the foot of the Scots pine. I hadn't been there for a while.

The Daimler was almost overgrown with grasses and thistles. And the tree had dropped its daily, nightly showering of needles and cones and brittle black twigs. The hearse, like a badger scenting a coolness in the air, was growing a shaggy overcoat to coincide with the end of summer.

I didn't open it up this time. I didn't slide inside and sit behind the wheel and inhale the fragrant memories. At first, I made as if to swish some debris from the bonnet or the roof, but then I hesitated and stepped away. What was the point? The old car, so sleepy and still, so long neglected, was slipping into a slumber of hibernation... or rather, a torpor from which it might never awake. Moribund. What was the point of disturbing it? Time to let go.

An eerie hush. I stared up and up, where we'd seen the swifts hurtling and screaming day in and day out since the very first week I'd arrived, and there was a clear blue silence. Up there, the devil-birds had relinquished their realm and gone away.

Good. The boy, who was clinging to the memory of his dead father with such an obsessive madness that I'd been touched by the strength of his imaginings, would surely see a reason in the birds' inevitable departure. Time to let go.

I found myself climbing the tree. And in a few minutes, before I'd realised what I was doing, I was halfway up, my feet jammed uncomfortably into the notchy branches, and looking down through the sooty prickliness of a one-or-two-hundred-year-old pine tree at the ground below, and onto the roof of the hearse.

Why? I'd just felt like doing it. Like a boy, I'd reached for the lowest branches and swung myself up and up and easily up. No, not so easily; there was pain, every move was a wrenching in my ribs, the torn muscles were being stretched too much, too soon, too raw. But the pain was alright. I felt it moving me, onwards and upwards, I was swarming through the dark, dry branches and they were burning my hands, they smelled black and carboniferous, the venerable tree was a piece of an ancient planet, its roots deep in the rock of England, and it was thrusting skywards from the fossil remains of prehistoric times.

In short, the Scots pine was big and black and old. It hurt and it felt good. I was a man, unnecessarily climbing a tree.

But when I scrambled to the top and emerged onto the bare, tremulous spars of the tree-house, there was nothing unnecessary about it. I felt an exhilaration I hadn't felt on the highest summit of Borneo, or on the pinnacles of the Sarawak caves.

I struggled onto the rickety planks that Lawrence's father had brought up there. I saw the knots he'd tied in the raggedy ropes, and the nails he'd hammered in. In my giddy mind's eye, as I lay stranded on this aerial shipwreck, I could imagine the man up here, I could see him and smell him and hear him, as he lugged the spars into place, as he knotted them tight with the bits of rope he'd brought in his pockets, as he banged in the nails. I lay there, my head swimming, my heart thumping, and I knew that a cooler, braver man than I had built this thing, this jutty bit of planking which was a foothold. More than a foothold, it was a springboard into the sky.

And so I stood up. I was covered in pond slime, but the smell of it drying on my skin was something I'd left far below. It had no connection up here. For the first time in weeks, I could see the faraway horizon, the demarcation in the eastern sky which was the sea; the simplicity of sky and sea and nothing else.

The tree sighed and swayed. I moved with it, unafraid. And I rejoiced in the emptiness of the sky, and for the swifts... the splinters of godliness that had been there and had now taken themselves off, so tiny and brave, on a journey of thousands of miles across mountains and seas and deserts... and which would come back, they would come back next spring to this very place, to the very crannies and crevices and blobs of gluey spittle they'd built in the broken-down greenhouse.

The tree creaked and groaned beneath me. I felt the mud drying on my skin. I listened to the silence of the sky.

But then there was a sudden sound below me, so incongruous that it made me wobble. I sat down hard and took hold of the ropes.

Breaking glass.

I ROLLED OVER and peered down and down, through the branches of the Scots pine. I could make out the bulk of the Daimler, directly below me. And I hadn't realised, because I'd been so absorbed by my communion with the air around me, that I had an unobstructed view of the greenhouse from my vantage point.

The building leaned drunkenly against the slabby chalk cliff. It was almost swallowed by decades of tangling undergrowth, and overshadowed by the dense, late-summer foliage of oak and ash and beech. The panes of glass were remarkably intact, carpeted with moss and years of the rotted-down acorns and keys and mast that the trees had rained onto them; a few holes here and there, where the vine had burst its way out or maybe a resilient sapling was prising its roots into the framework.

I could see something moving inside the greenhouse.

The boy. I could see his body pressed against the glass. In defiance of gravity, he was pressed hard against the ceiling, against the panes in the ceiling. It was like watching a fish swimming lazily through the waters of a neglected pond. He moved slowly, with a strange balletic grace. His outline was blurred, but silvery white, like the upturned belly of a tench, doomed to a death of oxygen-starvation in a stagnant aquarium. He'd smashed a pane. I'd heard it, and I saw the splinters of glass newly-scattered on the mat of moss. And a strange thing... his hand came poking through, into the air of the outside world.

He was groping around, with his fist clenched on something. He must have caught his hand on the broken glass, because it withdrew as suddenly as it had appeared... and then it reappeared, his fist bunched on a wad of some kind of material, and when it withdrew a second time he'd left the wad in the hole.

I lay on the tree-house and I watched. Again, and again, his hand emerged from a hole in the roof. And each time it withdrew, he left the hole stuffed with a wad of grass or leaves or...

Swimming against the mossy-green glass of the ceiling, clinging with his prehensile fingers and toes, he was repairing the broken panes. No, he was blocking the holes where the glass had broken.

'WHAT ON EARTH have you been doing up there? Why on earth did you...?'

Juliet was standing at the foot of the tree when I scrambled down from the lowest branches. I was winded and sore, but more or less intact. The descent had been harder than the ascent, and now my hands were burning more fiercely than before and I was struggling to get my breath.

She went on, seeing that I was unable to speak for the moment, 'I've been watching you. I was looking for Lawrence so I went up to his room, to see if he was there and get his washing and stuff. At first I thought it was him. I mean, I saw someone on the top of the tree and of course I thought it was Lawrence. When I looked through his binoculars and saw it was you, I... I don't know... I was watching you and wondering what on earth you were doing up there...'

It all came out in her stream of words, all the stress in her voice, her worry for me and for her son, and her face was pinched with anxiety. She saw how I rubbed at my hands and wrists, and she took hold of me to massage some strength back into my fingers. I said to her, 'I'm alright, Juliet, I'm fine, I just wanted to...'

She dropped my hands and stepped back. 'You stink,' she said. Her face twisted in disgust, the quick snickering snarl of a stoat or an otter. 'Look at you, you're filthy. And Lawrence's room, it stinks the same, his sheets and clothes...' She narrowed her eyes and shook her head, like an angry and confused little girl. 'What's going on? Can't we just be normal, do normal things, instead of all this mad stuff with birds and climbing trees and wading in ponds and...?' She stared up at me in exasperation. 'I mean, Chris, I thought we got you here to make things calm and straight and, well, normal. But it doesn't feel like that right now ... I mean, where is Lawrence, have you got any idea where he is, or are you too busy climbing trees and...? Where is he?'

I tried to touch her, but she recoiled from me, from the mud on my body and the blackness of the bark on my hands. I heard my platitudes again... when and where had I become so good at them?... in Borneo, my daily patter with the smug Malays and the complacent Chinese and my sweet, deferential students? I heard myself, as at last she let me take hold of her and press her sobbing, shuddering body into my shirt. 'Hey Juliet, he's alright, he's going to be alright, I know exactly where he is and what he's doing. I went up the tree because I wanted to be sure the swifts have gone. It was a kind of project for him, and yes, I know he got a bit too... a bit too wrapped up in it, like a teenager with his own weird perspective on something I'd meant to be just an interest for him. But now the birds have gone. They've gone, and I'll make him see that they had to go, it's quite natural and all's right with the world...'

Her body was calming. She was breathing more slowly. She wiped her eyes on my sleeve, so when she looked up at me she was smeared with tears and pond-slime, a ghastly gothic mascara.

'He's in the greenhouse,' I said. 'The thing with the pond, well, he told me he used to do it with his father every year, to freshen up the water, to let the air in or whatever. So I helped him finish it off. Good clean fun, that's all. He's dragged a lot of the weed to the greenhouse, he said something about compost or something, and right now he's fixing some of the broken panes in the roof...'

I pulled an incredulous face, and elicited a rueful smile from her. 'Yes, I know, teenagers are weird, and Lawrence is weirder than most, if you don't mind me saying so. Nobody's done any gardening around here for years, and suddenly he's got the urge to... well, I've no idea actually.'

I took her by the hand and tugged her along with me. 'Come on, let's go and look. And then the three of us'll go up to the house and get cleaned up and get some lunch. Alright?'

THROUGH THE BRAMBLES and nettles and parsley. The unmistakable perfume of autumn. And a trail of weed from the pond.

The door of the greenhouse was shut. In the gloom of the undergrowth, the panes of glass were barely opaque. I peered through. No movement of the boy. But a shadow moving. A huge black and brown shadow, moving.

I pushed at the door and called out. 'Hey Lawrence...?'

It didn't budge. I pushed harder, with more weight and with my foot at the bottom of it. It grated open – an inch, another inch – with a nasty scraping sound. There were lumps of half-bricks, piled behind it.

'No you... No I don't want you...'

The boy was there. For a second he was leaning against the door, to keep it shut. His face was in the crack, hissing at me. 'No, you can't, I don't want you...!' And then, as it opened wider, 'Get in! Get in!'

And his arm snaked out. It seized mine with a sinewy force and yanked me through. It shot out and yanked his mother, as though she was a rag-doll. And then he was shoving the door shut again and heaping the rubble of half-bricks behind it.

So we were inside. With the boy. And with hundreds of birds.

In one body, like a flock of roosting starlings, the swifts swept this way and that, around the confined space of the greenhouse. One body. It was as though the boy had entrapped a single miraculous creature and it was exploring the limits of its prison in a mood of terrible, pent-up anger. Anger, yes. The thrumming of hundreds of wings and the hurtle of a hundred bodies... the energy in the suffocating space was more than that. It was a rage against imprisonment, a lust for freedom.

The smell? The noise? A fetid, screaming madness...

The swifts were in our faces, in our hair, in our mouths. They moved as one, a panther of birds, sleek and sudden and a marvellous muscle. But then, as we stumbled over the uneven bricks of the greenhouse floor and gazed around us, as I looked up and saw how he'd stuffed the holes in the ceiling with wads of weed from the pond, the creature that the boy had captured seemed to shatter into smithereens. Where there'd been a swooping black shadow, swerving from one corner of the space to another, it broke into pieces.

There was a twittering chaos. The flock fell apart, and a hundred birds blundered and smashed and collided with each other and the mossy green glass. Here and there, one of them spiralled out of control and crash-landed, crippled, sculling round and round on the ground like a dizzy clockwork toy... another, and another, and...

'Let them out!' I yelled at the boy. I had to yell, above the silly hysteria of the birds. It was infectious, and this time no one to quell it but me. 'Let them out, Lawrence! Let them out!' I was moving back to the door to kick at the bricks and pull it, grating and screeching, open.

But he was too quick for me. For a brief, unmanly moment, we grappled together; me and the mythical bird-boy from the shadows of the moon, from the stench of the pond, and he was too strong.

'I told you! he yelled back at me, as he leaned on the door and held it shut. He shouted into my ears, which were baffled by the featheriness, by the sooty-brown chaos swarming around my head. 'They don't have to go, they don't have to! I told, I told you!'

I'M AT THE bus stop. It's a beautiful day. Morning or afternoon, I'm not sure. Early afternoon, I think, the sun is warm and bright in a cloudless sky, lowering to a faraway horizon.

I'm carrying nothing. No bag, not even a jacket or a spare shirt. But when I pat at my pockets, an experienced traveller checking the only essentials I need, I've got wallet and passport and car-keys. Not sure when I'll need the keys. I feel better having them with me, there's some meaning or symbolism in having the keys even though the car is... not sure where the car is. Passport and wallet and keys. Nervous, I don't know, I pat at my pockets and stand at the roadside.

The sky is high and empty. Not a cloud. The country is vast and empty. Not a tree. I'm breathing. It feels good.

The bus. Suddenly it's right in front of me. The door hisses open. Before I can move a muscle or say anything, the fat woman trussed like a turkey in her bus driver's uniform shoots out her hand and grabs me. Snarling ugly. *Don't just fucking stand there, get in and leave that fucking mad bitch and fucking mad boy and fucking get in...*

I'm sitting at the back. I can see rows of people in front of me, their shoulders and their long black hair. They all have black hair. Some of the women are holding children, who swivel their faces and stare at me. There's a man with a cockerel.

I look along the aisle and try to focus on the view through the windscreen. The way ahead is brown and incredibly smooth... as smooth as glass. So smooth and wide that the driver is leaning us all this way and that, through one long sweeping bend after another. So fast, so smooth. I stare ahead, through the long narrow tube in front of me and past the other passengers, and we sway with the swooping rhythm of the powerful machine. Spatter. Sometimes a spatter of brown water hits the windscreen. One swish of the wiper and it's clear. Faster and faster. It's almost like flying.

Bang. A series of juddering bangs. Hit something – a log or a croc? We're rolling. It's all black and brown and people shouting, women and children and a man with a cockerel. Filling with water. Upside down. The shouting stops, and the voices are gurgling, gargling...

Trapped. I'm trapped at the back, at the bottom, there's no way out, no way to go except down and down and darker and darker until it's only a huge swirling blackness and such a pain in my chest that I shout with all my might and a beautiful bright silver bubble blooms from my mouth...

I watch it float away from me. Mine. My air. Leaving me. Leaving me empty.

And then... *Tap tap tap.* Someone, something, somebody is tapping... trying to get in, to get me out... I reach out and bang with my fist at metal or glass or whatever it is, and the tapping is louder, more insistent... and I burst out of my dying place, my coffin, somehow. I claw myself up and up, towards the light.

There's my bubble of air. Mine. My air. I reach for it...

He's sitting on his bed. The window behind him is wide open and there's the estuary, the sea. It looks so cool and grey and the air is so cool and clean that I reach out for it, I take it like a cool silk scarf and reel it in, through the window, and wrap it loosely around my neck.

Tap tap tap. He's sitting on his bed in his room which smells of him, and he's tapping at a headstone. He's propped it up, on the floor of his room, so that he can sit with it balanced between his knees, and he's chipping at it, striking the handle of his chisel with his hammer. Every time he taps, a powder of grey dust puffs into the air and falls like a whisper onto the carpet.

He looks up at me. His mouth is horribly twisted. His chin is shiny with spittle. His smile is grotesque, but in his eyes there's a glimmer of warmth for me and the satisfaction of the job he's doing. He moves his lips, and they ooze another trickle of saliva. He mumbles, but his words are unmistakable. 'Nearly finished. The last letter. And I'm done.'

Sick with fear, for him. Sick in my stomach, sadness for him. I can't see his side of the headstone, only the back of it. But I guess, from the twist of the smile on his face and the light in his eyes, that he's tapping the letters of his own name. A very old man. My father. Ready for death.

'Dad? You're alright, Dad... I love you, Dad...' I move towards him.

Before I can touch him, he speaks again. 'For you. It's for you.'

Sick with fear, for him, for me. I sit on the bed beside him and put my arm on his bony, cold shoulders. Cold, because the wind from the estuary is on his back and I want to take off my grey scarf and wrap it around him. Scarf? There's no scarf, only the shiver of an autumn afternoon. He angles the headstone towards me, so that I can see what he's doing.

It's finished. He leans to it and blows the dust from the last letter. Lawrence Lundy.

DEATH CAMP. IMAGINE a death camp.

I'd been through the house, looking for Juliet and Lawrence. I suppose I knew where they were, but I was hoping to find them somewhere else, in a normal place, doing something normal. So I went through the shabby, comfortable living-room, strewn with cushions, smelling of cat, powdered with chalk dust, a litter of country magazines and glasses and bottles, and slices of lemon, and glasses and bottles... No one there. I went around the back of the house to the holly wood, where a smart silver car was botched all over with a mess of blood, dried to a clotted, congealed kind of scab, as though it was a piece of a bigger car and had been amputated and discarded after some horrific accident. There was no one in the kitchen. It looked normal and smelled of normal things, like toast. I stood and stared around the room. Toast. What a word! I longed for toast, and honey, and sitting at a kitchen table with a woman and her son and eating toast and honey. But there was no one.

I went up to my room. I wasn't there. I went into Juliet's room, where the bed was a tangle of sheets. I felt at them, I smelled at them. I stood at her dressing-table and picked up the hairbrush and picked the hairs from it. I held my breath and stared at the door of the wardrobe and I willed it to open, I stood there and I willed the wardrobe door to open and a man to step out... that the clothes on their hangers would slide apart and he would come out, in his RAF uniform, his face puffy and grey, his eyes glaucous and moist and a slather of sea-water on his lips. But he didn't. Fuck, it would've been something, somebody. I moved to the wardrobe and opened it and I nuzzled my face into the hanging clothes, as I'd seen the boy do, as though it might be the magic sign or the spell to conjure somebody, something, but there was no one. Not even a slithery hand came out, to touch my face with its clammy, rotting fingers.

Even that would have been normal, compared to what I was going to find.

I went up to the tower. I thought I might find the woman and the boy there, in bed together. Or the boy and his father, enjoying some quality time, a dead man and a mad boy chuckling and joshing and exchanging their stories of being dead and being mad. I pushed the door open and there was no one. The room stank of the pond. Indeed, the sheets on the bed, black with mud, were fizzing with the bugs and beetles and worms the boy had brought on his body. High on the ceiling, the model planes hung so still, they didn't move or touch. There was a silence and a smell of death.

Death camp. I knew they were there, but I'd been searching the house in the vain hope that I might find them in a room, talking or eating or doing something in a room like normal people do.

They were in the greenhouse.

A submarine, almost subterranean light. I pushed the door open, I leaned with all my weight because someone had piled a rubble of bricks behind it. They didn't hear me come in, even the grating of the door as I shoved it open.

Juliet was holding the bag. Lawrence was shovelling.

She was a small, thin figure, covered in dust and feathers, and she was bending low and holding open a black plastic bag. Cowed. Beaten. I stood at the door and looked at her and tried to remember her as I'd seen her before – the russet elf of the woods, the red squirrel, the marten, the naked nymph astride me, silvery in the moonlight. No. Not now. She was a figure from a terrible wartime scene. All grey and thin, beaten.

The boy had a spade and he was shovelling the bodies of the birds from the floor of the greenhouse and into the bag. Even as he shovelled them up and launched them with a whispery hiss off the spade and into the bag, another bird, here and there, would drop from the ceiling and onto the floor. I stood at the doorway and looked up. There were still dozens of swifts up there, they were snuggling and twittering together in a furry, feathery, living and breathing confusion of bodies. But, as they fought for space, as they rummaged and scrabbled with their clumsy long wings and negligible feet to find somewhere to cling onto, one of them, and then another, lacking the strength or the will to hang on, would spill away from the murmuring mass of birds and fall... and with no space, no time, to find a purchase on the air, it would spin out of control and land with a poor little slap on the ground. Pathetic, the way it rowed and crawled among the bodies of the birds that had already fallen, as though it might hide among them.

And then the spade. The boy came with the spade and swished them into the black plastic bag. Some of them dead. Some still alive. Swish, swish. Onto the spade, into the bag.

'Can't you see? Are you blind?'

The boy didn't answer. Then he looked me in the eyes. 'Blind?' He echoed my word, as if he'd never heard it before.

And then he said it again, 'Blind...' relishing it this time, with a glimmer of a memory of something bad he'd done. Juliet didn't seem to hear me at all. She was too busy bagging the bodies of the birds that the boy had been shovelling. They had two bags full, one each. I stood back and watched, appalled, an abstracted spectator watching some grainy, black and white footage of a wartime atrocity.

They went out of the greenhouse, bent like slaves under the weight of their bags. I followed them. The woodland was trying to be normal. The robin was singing. A jay shrieked and fluttered through the branches of a horse chestnut, black and white and electric-blue. But then the world, looking down on the boy and his mother so mired in nightmare that they might never awaken, fell still as they went by. The robin stopped singing, although he'd waited all summer to find his voice again. The jay shuffled its kaleidoscopic wings and was silent.

They, the boy and his mother, tipped their bags into the pond.

We'd cleaned the pond. Lawrence, in the night in his pants in the mud, had cleaned the pond. It was a clear brown soup. He up-ended his bag and tipped out thirty or fifty swifts. Juliet did the same, another thirty or fifty birds. They floated on the surface. Some of them rowed with their wings, like water-boatmen or other aquatic insects. The pond was covered with the dead and dying... sailors from a torpedoed battleship, dead or half-dead, or still alive and knowing that the cold or their loss of blood would kill them... or that something terrible and invisible in the darkness would smell their blood and rise from the depths and...

Something did.

There was a slow, oily swirl in the water. Something down there – no need to hurry such a sumptuous feast – was stirring the soup with its ancient, muscular tail. The pike, hypnotic in its primeval ugliness, older than the house and the garden and as old as the pond itself... it swirled through the surface and swallowed bird after bird after bird in a feat of gargantuan greed.

A feeding frenzy? No, the pike was a god of the pond. It didn't do frenzy. It accepted sacrifices from its poor blind believers in the world above its world, and did a relentless, godly gluttony.

For a minute, no more, the water turned and stirred in a rich, brown broth. Until all the swifts were gone. Not one of them was left on the surface. They were swallowed whole, or they were taken down and stored in a shadowy green larder.

I followed the boy and his mother back to the greenhouse. They were like trolls or troglodytes, slaves in a death camp. No good trying to engage the boy or reason with him, nothing I could say would make him change his mind. He had wadded the broken panes so tightly, so thoroughly caulked the ribs and stanchions of the building, that nothing could ever escape it.

Against their wills, against all of their wisdom, the swifts were his prisoners. Just as, in his mother's wardrobe, he had contained the very being of his father. Release... for the birds, for himself and his mother and me... a release from the nightmare was in his power.

Chapter Twenty-Three

FOOTSTEPS ON THE stairs.

This time I'm really awake and listening. Not dreaming. And not just listening. I'm lying on my bed and all of my body is wired, prickling with the energy and adrenaline of listening. I'm awake. I'm not dreaming. My whole being is awake. My blood is awake.

I'm in my own little room.

No food that evening. Not even a sandwich or a burnt sausage. Only gin. No tonic or ice or lemon; all run out. The last of the gin, we drank it neat, in a dreary silence. The boy was... I don't know where he was. The cat was... the cat was trawling the reed beds of the pond for a bedraggled bird. A cockchafer bumbled into the room and into my glass, and as I sat and swayed and soused myself and felt it nipping at my lips with its pincers, it drowned in my dregs. It died, sozzled in alcohol, and I drank the gin it had drowned in, like the disgusting snake-juice and beetle-juice I'd drunk in Borneo. Later... who knows when? Midnight or one or two o'clock? Whenever we'd dropped the sad empty bottle and our glasses onto the floor and abandoned the room to the moths and the bats which whirled through the open windows... I'd slipped into bed with the woman. And she'd snarled at me to fuck off. So I snarled back at her and slipped out of her bed. Anyway, she smelled of bird-shit and feathers; brackish and deadly.

So I'm in my own little room. I hate. Not sure. I hate all of it. Most of it. Not sure. Drunk, really.

I heard someone in the kitchen, opening and closing cupboards. Juliet, hungry, looking for something to eat? Or the boy?

And now, footsteps on the stairs.

Not trying to be quiet, no tip-toe. Pausing and stopping and waiting. Carrying something? As though balancing. Balancing something?

I'm holding my breath. It's fear, and it's listening. I can't breathe and listen at the same time. I hold a breath so long that my chest is hurting. And when, at last, I open my mouth and inhale because my lungs are bursting, I smell something.

Smell. Can you smell in your dreams?

The sweat of a sebaceous body, the rank unmistakable smell of a boy? The mud from a pond, the black and fetid mud that's been dredged from hundreds of years ago, medieval mud smeared on a sweaty teenage boy? The smell of my dreams.

But I'm awake, and this is a different smell. It's warm, it's homely, it's the smell of a rainy autumn afternoon in a kitchen or a classroom.

It's coming up the stairs. A hot smell.

My mind is swarming, and my body is wired so hard it's prickling with listening and can't move. Hot smell. Top of the stairs. My brain is trying to connect, and my body is so charged with the energy of waking and waiting that it's clenched onto the bed.

He comes in. The boy. He looms in the doorway and he stops. Because the thing he's carrying is heavy and it's slopping and spilling. A splash of hot stuff onto the floor.

He steadies himself, balances. He lunges across the room and sloshes the saucepan at me.

I REMEMBER, I rolled to one side and heard the whack of the boiling-hot liquid on my pillow.

Whack! Because in an instant it was no longer a liquid. It was a fist of molten wax, punching into the impression of my head on the pillow.

I felt the splatter of it, on my neck and chest, a scalding-hot skin on my face. On my eyelids.

Another moment, and I was standing, I was a madman flailing around the room, half-blinded and squealing like a piglet and groping in the air for the boy to grab or hit or...

He hit me. There was a clanging impact on the side of my head, the saucepan, still hot. Again... he must have stepped away from my futile fists and slammed the flat hot surface of the pan into my ribs. I could smell him, his body and his breath, and the wax on my face was a dazzling pain. And someone else, the woman was there, the two of them foul with the fume of the greenhouse and their gruesome toil. She was yelling at him and yelling at me. There was a scrummage of naked bodies and a blinding darkness, and all I could do was shove my way through it, connecting a haphazard punch with him or with her and blundering out of the room.

Seconds later, I was under the shower.

My head and face and all my body, drunk and burnt and beaten, I stood until my quivering knees gave way and I collapsed in a heap. I lay there, mewing, and I curled up like a baby, letting the water cascade onto me. For minutes? For an hour? So wounded that all I wanted was to lie with my face in the water and my arms wrapped around my chest, in expectation of more blows, more scalding, more pain.

I felt the wax congealing in my hair and on my skin. With my eyes tightly closed, in a cocoon of blindness, I picked at it with my fingers and it peeled away like a jelly of burnt flesh. It was in my mouth.

THE WATER SWITCHED off. It dribbled and stopped.

She had me on my feet and she was patting me dry with a soft towel. She led me out of the bathroom and into her room, where she put me to bed with such tenderness I might have been a dying child or an old man about to take his last breath. She laid me on the bed, like she was laying me out. I was all but dead, a living corpse. And there, through the small hours of that night, she salved me with her hands, with her lips, with her body.

She applied a cold cream to the burns on my chest and head, where the boy had struck me with the pan. She held a cool damp cloth to my face and neck, and she whispered that my eyebrows and even my eyelids were burnt, but my eyes, she whispered, my eyes were safe. She made me open them, she looked long and deep, and then she let me close them again, because the pain of their searing was too much. She went downstairs and came back with honey, and she smeared it onto my wounds for the antibiotic qualities she said it had. All through the night she held me, she healed me. From time to time she got out of the bed and I heard her go to the window, to feel the coolness of the air and to look out, and so she could come back with her skin as cool as the night.

At last the morning came. I heard the shiver of a breeze in the trees, and the first, gentle, experimental phrases of the robin.

'He's in the greenhouse,' she whispered to me. 'He's my son and he needs me and I love him more than anything, whatever he's done to you and to other people. I love him, whatever he does, whatever he's doing.'

I felt her moving away. I heard her putting on some clothes. She leaned to me and said, 'He's down there, I saw him in the night. I think he was carrying out more of the birds. I guess they're all dead. It's better if they're dead. Then it's over.'

She went out.

Oh god. Oh god. If only.

I lay in my private darkness, with my eyes screwed shut. They were burning, as painful as if the boiling wax had just been poured in. A sound swam into my brain, out of my memory, an early morning sound. The sound of dawn.

No, not the silvery sweetness of the robin or the mellow fluting of the blackbird. No. An expression of such indescribable dreariness that would eclipse all the joy of an English woodland. The mosque, it was in my head. Oh god... god is great, yes I submit I give in I surrender, I collapse under the weight of the sheer repetition, the dinning and relentless repetition, I give in I give in... oh fuck.

I pressed my hands to my ears as hard as I could, as though I might squeeze the noise out, squeeze it dribbling out of my sinuses like a blockage of foul-smelling yellow mucus. At last it stopped. And when I opened my ears again and listened, the robin was singing his cool, clean song. Holier than a dawnful of mosques.

If only it could have been as simple as that. If the swifts would die and the story was over. If the death of the birds would mean an awakening from nightmare, into the daylight of reality. If only...

Chapter Twenty-Four

I HEARD HER shouting for her son, and so I rolled off the bed.

I sat on the edge of it for a few moments and inhaled a series of long, deep breaths. What do they call it, in books, in movies – a kind of Garden of Gethsemane moment? When the hero knows it's near the end and it'll take one more push towards a climax, or else he could just roll over and stay in bed and nurse the wounds he'd already sustained, and honourably... well, honourably, he could just not show up for the resolution of the story?

I was naked. I could hardly see. I didn't feel like a hero. I groped around for my pants or a shirt and remembered they'd be in the bathroom or in my own room and I'd never find them. I crawled to the shower and doused myself, because my body was burning and my face was blistering. No clothes, good excuse...

Bad excuse. I didn't need clothes. In the whole of this story – apart from an early visit to my father, and then a foray into the outside world of the village, to a higher sphere of light and air and a shop with almost nothing in it and a snarling woman trussed-up in her horrid little bus – there were no other people but me and the woman and the boy. Only the three of us. A triangle. And we'd seen each other naked or half-naked enough times; we'd pissed in the nettles, we'd groped into the pond, we'd made love, we'd snuggled and snuffled and smelled each other's bodies, we'd grappled and fought more than enough times not to be coy, or squeamish, or gawky.

I stood up and felt my way down the stairs, through the hallway and the living-room. Out into the garden.

No excuses. I was blinded, I was burnt. Why the fuck would I need clothes?

How marvellous it felt, the cool air on my skin. Through my slitted eyelids I could barely see the light of dawn: it was a grey blur, my eyeballs had been boiled in their sockets like eggs in a pan. But yes, the conventional wisdom was true, that the removal of one sense enhanced the others. So the breeze was bliss on my body, the movement of the leaves in the trees was a murmuring of sweet voices, and the forest was deliciously fragrant. If only... futile to imagine it... but if only I could have blocked out the reality, or unreality, of what I was doing in that Lincolnshire woodland, it would have been joy.

No. It all came back to me, with the voice of the woman. She was calling very loudly, 'Lawrence, Lawrence!' and the tremor of fear in the stress on the first syllable struck a chill in the autumn morning. I stumbled towards the sound. In the confusion of my mind, which hadn't really awakened from the horrors of the night, I jumped to the conclusion that her shouting meant one thing, that she'd gone to the greenhouse and couldn't get in. The boy was inside and had blocked the door so weightily with bricks that she couldn't get in. Indeed, as I fumbled my way through the undergrowth in what I thought was the right direction, I imagined her hammering at the door, shoving on it and hearing it grate and screech on the crumbly obstruction behind it, unable to open it, and knowing that the boy was in there and... and what was he doing in there, something so odd or eccentric or worse, so appalling, that he mustn't allow his own mother inside to see it?

I fell headlong into a barricade of nettles. I banged my face into a rubble of half-bricks and knew I was near the greenhouse. I felt no pain, no hurt to myself, to my own skin or flesh or bones, because, overwhelming any assault or injury to my own being, the terror in my belly was the image I'd had before, when I'd blundered in and seen the boy up there, in the roof, hanging, his throat upturned... and when I'd thought for a grotesque split-second that he'd...

And so now, as I heard Juliet's cries and the wrenching, motherly fear in them, I felt a sickness in my stomach for what the boy might have done... the release he'd sought from his madness, a big beautiful boy dangling himself and throttling himself and inflicting an unspeakable pain on his mother. I almost retched at the thought of what I would find.

Somehow, I was on my feet again. I beat at the nettles with my arms and hands and swept them aside. And forcing myself to let more and more daylight onto my scalded eyes, I struggled to the door of the greenhouse.

It was open. I fell inside.

No one. Nothing. I strained to look up at the roof. No birds, no boy. No frantic woman, who, in my damaged mind's-eye, I'd pictured staring up and up at a horror beyond every mother's worst imaginings.

'Chris, he's not there...' She pounced on me and dragged me outside. 'He's not there... where is he? Oh god, what are you doing?'

She was in a dithering panic; an elfin woman, smelling of cold-cream and honey and bird-shit, desperate to find her teenage son. She appraised me, stark naked, bruised and blinded and bewildered, in the doorway of a derelict Victorian greenhouse, my nudity marked with rude red burns on my face and my chest, my face blistered with a scald of wax. And then, as though I was a dancing bear in a medieval fair, she lugged me away from the greenhouse and towards the pond.

I could feel the cooler breeze from its surface. I squinted into the reflected daylight and saw her moving through the reeds, pushing them aside with her hands, and heard her insistent murmuring, her moaning of her son's name, as if, at any moment, she might discover his body. I tried to follow her, if only to demonstrate some solidarity, to make a gesture of team-work in her search. But she waded ahead of me, deeper, and I could see her up to her knees, up to her waist, feeling into the water for her boy.

Gone... she lost her footing, stepped into a hole in the muddy bottom or over the brink of the shallow ledge, and with a sudden whoosh she sank out of sight, only to reappear and flounder back to the shore, to grab me so hard she collapsed me and fell on top of me.

She was heaving with the shock, she was slithery with mud. Her hair was slick. Her face was a smear of cold green water and hot tears.

'Find him, Chris... Please help me find him! Has he gone back to his room? Where is he?'

At her suggestion, we both looked back towards the house. Chalke House, I narrowed my eyes and swept it from one side to the other as I'd done on my first arrival. It was all grainy, my eyeballs felt raw, although they'd been so cooked. Chalke House – a grand, shabby hunting-lodge, trying to be impressive, with its turrets and its toothy mock-battlements, but looming rather queerly in the morning light. Very English, unique, a gentleman's folly from the 19th century... and...

And a figure at the open window of the tower?

If we'd hoped to see the boy up there and watching us, watching our folly in the pond... or a figure in squadron-blue, raising a hand in a lazy wave...

No, we didn't. I saw that same crawling shadow, the very one which had crawled across the face of the house on the day I'd arrived. But this time, at the end of a summer in which I'd been seduced and smothered in nightmare, there was no one at the window. Even Juliet Lundy, who was hungry with all her eyes to see anything, to see a uniformed ghost or her son safe and sound... she didn't see anyone.

She manhandled me down to the car.

I sprawled against its flanks. It felt huge. I leaned all my weight on its familiar hugeness. Car – too paltry a word. Hearse, too humdrum. Daimler... yes, the name resounded of stately homes and gentlemen's clubs, and, better still, of my father and my childhood, the days we'd spent together in the long-ago but never-forgotten corners of an English countryside.

But something was different. Something in the touch of the dusty, rusting paintwork was different. An energy. Such a strange and unsettling energy that I stood away. And then I reached out and touched it again. Felt it. A hum of energy. It was alive.

'He's here,' I said very softly.

I turned to the woman. She was standing so still, her eyes so dead and empty, that I thought she hadn't heard me. 'He's here, he's inside.'

She just nodded. And she followed me around to the back of the hearse and watched as I opened the door.

It opened silently, on its oiled hinges. No horrible creaking. The thing we saw inside was strange and horrid enough...

The birds, there were dozens or scores or a hundred birds. They were the living, the barely living, harvested from among the dead and brought to this place of death, to live until they died. Purgatory, a limbo between life and hell. There was a crawling, murmuring mound of them, like bees in a hive, a heap of furry bodies bumbling together. The adults were downy black, dusky brown, and the juveniles, which would have relished a miraculous adventure to the Mediterranean and Morocco, or even an oasis in Tamanrasset or Timbuktu ... they were grey and white and a quivering mass of pure energy.

Wasted energy. A stink of wasted life. As I opened the door wider, they started to fall out onto the grass. They slithered out, and they were all broken. They flapped and fluttered – hopeless, purposeless, the utter paradox of what they'd been born to be. They were flightless swifts.

'I still got one.' His great bare legs, and a bare muscular torso. His crowing voice. 'I still got one ...'

The boy emerged.

He'd been lying beneath the rug of birds. They spilled off him. He sat up, with a lunatic grin on his mouth. He saw me and his mother standing in the open doorway of the hearse, and he said, 'I came down in the night, I got the last of the living, and brought them in here.' He giggled horribly, a girly mad giggle. 'In here, a place for the dead, for their final journey.' And then, as he peered closer towards me and I could see the spittle and feathers stuck around his chin and smell the sickly, shitty pungency of the birds on his body, he said, 'Look at you... what the fuck happened to your face?'

And he heaved himself out of the hearse.

Some of the birds stuck to his skin, they clung to him with their feeble feet, as if he, their tormentor, might yet grant them some kind of release. But he brushed them off with a careless hand. He trod carelessly on the cripples in the grass. With a twisted smile on his face, he said, 'Alright Mr Teacher, Mr always-right Mr Teacher...' and I could feel him looming over me, a dark, stale-smelling figure, more like an ogre than a teenage boy. I could feel the chuckling laughter in him, as he said, 'And your pants? What happened to your pants? You come here in your big black car and knowing stuff, and now look at you, you can't see fuck all and you don't know fuck all, and no pants...'

'Lawrence, please...' His mother was there, trying to take him in her arms and comfort him, console him, because, like me when I'd first felt the dangerous tingle from the car, she was afraid of the anger in him. 'Lawrence, please, I love you, I don't want you to be upset. Let's all go up to the house and we can...'

'Upset?' He brushed her off, as if she were an annoying fly. 'You don't want me to be upset because my Dad's gone away and I'll never fly because some stupid spotty student said so, and I blinded some stupid kid and...' He struggled to stop himself, turned to me and leaned close. I could smell his furry, cotton-wool breath. 'Alright, so I can't keep them all. So you were right, you were right, Mr Teacher. It's time to let go.'

And then, grotesquely, he was kissing me.

I could feel his lips on my wounded neck, his open mouth and tongue, as though he was trying to heal my blistered skin with the same secretion of saliva he'd learned from the swifts. He enveloped me in his arms, and I could feel him shuddering, his whole big body sobbing and shuddering, and his hot wet kisses on my neck and my face. And then he enfolded his mother in an enormous, smothering embrace and, 'Oh Mummy, my Mummy, my little Mummy...' he was kissing her and blubbering.

He wrenched himself away, although his mother clung to him as if the wrenching would break her heart. 'See?' He said to me, through the tears in his mouth. 'See? I still got one. That's all I need.'

Clenched firmly but softly in his right hand, he had a swift.

For a moment he opened his hand and revealed the bird, long enough for me to see that it was whole, it was bright-eyed and alert and superbly intact. And then he lowered his weeping head to it, and he was whispering, 'You're the last one, the only one. You can fly, you can fly to the moon if you want to. Maybe I can come with you.'

It opened its wings and held them up. They were perfect. But before it could clap them and try to lift off from his palm, he closed it up in both his hands, with great care, as though it were an exquisite fan made of paper or silk.

He moved from the car to the Scots pine and he started to climb.

'Oh no, Lawrence, no...' she was crying out. But in no time at all, he was ten and twenty and thirty feet above us. He swarmed upwards, knowing the holds from his previous ascents, gripping strongly with his left hand and using his other wrist and arm as a lever as he held the bird in his right hand. As I stared after him, a shower of sooty bark fell onto my face and onto my eyes, so that I had to look away and rub excruciatingly at them with my fists. Juliet was calling after him, 'Oh Lawrence, be careful, be careful...' and to me, 'Chris please, can't you stop him, can't you do something?' And, as I hesitated, she shoved me aside. Before I could try to reason with her, make her see the futility of what she was doing, she was climbing, she was wriggling her way through the branches, panting and mewing and trying to keep up her frantic calls to her son.

She couldn't do it. In a clumsy replay of the time when I'd first laid eyes on her, she tumbled herself back down again. She landed giddily, tearfully, on her knees beside me. Her face was all smudged with bark and moss. She was pleading.

I had no choice but to step forward, as though I might chase after the boy and stop him.

I was naked, barefoot, I could hardly see. Every touch of the tree on my body was like a jab or a poke from a mean-spirited opponent, thwarting all my attempts to close on it. But once I'd achieved the first two or three holds, with my feet jammed agonisingly against the great black trunk and my hands burning, I realised that continuing might be no less painful than slithering down, and so I kept on climbing, until I saw the open sky above me. I was still ten or fifteen feet below him, but I made out the boy kneeling on the spars of the tree-house. He was gripping them and the knotted bits of rope, adjusting to the precariousness as the highest branches swayed in the morning breeze. And then he stood up.

He didn't know I was there. I could have called out to him, I was about to call out, but I didn't. I stopped myself, because I thought that my voice might surprise him and he might fall, and another part of me was saying, with a twinge of guilt, that I just didn't want to. Fuck, I'd done enough. I'd put up with enough turmoil and bedlam and pain. Let the boy do what he wanted, for whatever half-baked reasons, and then he could climb down again. Let me be a disinterested spectator, in this final moment of the story, and then I'd be out of it and away from Chalke House as soon as it was all over.

He stood up and braced himself with his legs apart. He was god-like against the sky. His long black hair fluttered in the wind. Every muscle was defined, in his back and his shoulders, through his thighs and calves to the very splay of his feet on the planks. He looked unshakable. He was a young god of the sky and nothing would unsettle him.

Perfect. Not a cloud, not a whirling of crows, not a faraway vapour-trail. Not a blemish in the infinite blue.

I peered down, and I could just see Juliet, who'd moved away from the base of the tree and closer to the pond, so that she could watch where her son had emerged intact and erect at the very top. The height made my head spin. A bubble of nausea rose into my throat. And by the time I'd taken a breath and peered upwards again, the boy was cupping the swift in both his hands and holding it aloft, stretching up with his arms, on tip-toes, as if he would touch the sky itself.

Simple, really. An act of simplicity and wonder.

The bird opened its wings and quivered them, feeling the movement of the air through its feathers. And then it clapped the marvellous wings, once and twice and a third time, and it arose from the boy's hands.

For a moment, moth-like, it beat around his head, it was in his hair and his eyes and clawing at his face with its tiny feet, but then it spiralled away and rocketed skyward. The sheer vertical speed of it, the power... miraculous. A second later, as my poor eyes tried to follow, the swift had disappeared forever.

And the boy?

He swayed to one side. He brought down his left arm as though to swat into his hair, as though the bird or a memory of it was still distracting him. He wobbled. To compensate, he shuffled his feet and maybe he snagged the ropes with his toes or... His right knee buckled, he dipped to the planks and brushed them with his fingers to try and steady himself.

And a strange thing. The sound he made from deep in his throat was not panic, or fear. It wasn't weeping. It sounded more like a gurgle of laughter. So that when he straightened up again, he did so with such a rush of energy, as though his body were charged with the joy of releasing the bird, that he teetered to the very edge of the platform.

And then he was gone. He spread his arms and lifted his face to the sky, and he was gone.

He barely brushed the branches as he fell. Whatever the source of the energy which had propelled him from the tree-house, whether he'd lost his footing or he'd launched himself after the swift, he spun past me, clear of the tree itself. I watched him fall.

At the same time, I saw in a dreadful millisecond that Juliet had moved back towards the tree. She must have seen the boy faltering and dashed instinctively forward. I heard her scream. I saw her little white face upturned. At the last moment, as he plummeted towards her, I saw her lunge against the side of the Daimler. In a mad, maternal effort to save her son, she was right there, beneath him, when he smashed onto the bonnet.

MY FIRST REACTION... I must admit, was to stay where I was. I clung to the trunk of the tree, I stared down and down, and I listened.

There was no movement, nothing at all, no groans or whimpers. A pair of wood pigeons, which had erupted from the overgrown cliff beside the greenhouse, rattled away on their stiff, grey wings and then there was silence. A mean and wretched thought crept into my mind, and I tried to shoo it out. I was out of reach of the Lundys and I could hide in the dark, prickly branches as long as I liked, or I could climb to the sky and just breathe, on my own. The thought skulked around my brain for a few shameful moments, like a hyena, slavering and hunched, circling a campfire in the dead of night. Until I drove it away. And I steeled myself to climb down the tree.

They were both dead. The boy had broken his mother's bones with his own. Her body was dented into the car. He'd struck her with all his weight, driving his knees into her chest. For himself, his head had found the very spot where her hammer had impacted the windscreen... and he'd punched a greater hole in it, his head and shoulders buried deep into the car itself. When I opened the door, the mess of his face was pooling blood onto the leather upholstery and under the driver's seat.

I found myself walking in a daze, towards the house. I wasn't thinking much. I was overcome by a tremendous weariness, an overpowering torpor. I did everything slowly and deliberately, in the strangely comfortable knowledge that there was no need for speed or heroic action. Juliet and Lawrence Lundy were dead. Nothing would change that.

I turned around the back of the house, with a vague idea of appraising the woman's car. It was ugly, I didn't like it, it was all bloody and horrid, so I tugged at the tarpaulin and covered it completely. I went indoors and wandered from room to room, with the creeping intention of clearing-up or making amends in some desultory way. I picked up bottles from the living-room and dropped them into a bin in the kitchen. Upstairs, I straightened the sheets on Juliet's bed, which were stained with cold-cream and honey and crumbly with the wax she'd peeled off my body. I picked up some of her clothes, folded them and put them into the wardrobe, where her husband's suits and uniform were hanging. I rearranged the combs and brushes on her dressing-table.

In my own room, on the pillow there was an eerie impression of my own head, where the molten wax had cooled into a skin. I touched it, a ghostly imprint preserved for posterity. But then I crumpled it into pieces. Absent-mindedly, I kicked the empty saucepan under the bed.

I went up to the boy's room. It was as untidy as ever, his clothes strewn around and the sheets all rumpled. The model planes swung in the breeze from the open windows. The same... it was just the same as it had been when Juliet had first taken me there and introduced me to her son. Even the cat. The orange cat was lying there, as if this was just another day and nothing had ever changed.

One difference. It was cooler. I went onto the balcony and looked out. I picked up the boy's binoculars and swept them across the horizon of trees, to the rickety planks at the top of the Scots pine, down to the greenhouse and the dim outline of the Daimler. I shivered. The wind from the sea was cooler. It would be autumn, and I was naked.

I found my clothes, a pair of pants and shirt, and carried them downstairs. Of course I called the police, I plugged in the phone and there was a nice lady and she sounded a bit shaky when I told her there'd been an accident and there were two dead bodies, and I tried to reassure her and could someone come as soon as possible? I remember I started to put on... no, I started to think about putting on my clothes. It would have made me feel normal. More than my negligible little business of tidying-up, my shirt and pants might almost have made me feel real again. But no, when I put down the phone, I just dropped the clothes and...

I waited in the woodland for the police to come.

I wandered down there, but I didn't want to go near the car. Ugly. I peered through the trees and saw it, my father's car, which he'd maintained so lovingly. So was that it? The end of its journey? After years of dignified, decorous toil as a hearse, and then a second career as a workshop and a home, it was dumped, with a dead boy's head smashed into the windscreen and the dead boy's mother crushed onto the bonnet. Was that it?

I didn't go near the car. I remember I stood near the pond, and when I saw the green-brown stillness of the water, I thought of the way that the Lundys had tipped the dying birds into it. It made me look up into the sky again, as if I might catch a last glimpse of the swift that the boy had released, or any of the swifts which might still be lingering in Lincolnshire. It made me hurry to the greenhouse. One last, important thing to do...

I suppose that was how they found me, the police, when they came to Chalke House.

They would've driven into the overgrown beech wood, the oak wood, the medieval forest in the valley of the wolds, much deeper and denser than when I'd first arrived in May, with the grasses so tall they could hardly nose their neat, new police cars to the open back door of the hearse.

They would've got out and stared, incredulous. A carpet of dead birds, fifty or a hundred? No, some of them still alive, and crawling and fluttering. A Daimler hearse. Two dead bodies on the bonnet.

And they found me. I was in the greenhouse, I'd climbed the vine and I was clinging to the roof, as high up as I could get. I was pulling out the wads of weed that the boy had put there. A policeman came in, having gazed on the dreadfulness at the foot of the Scots pine, and saw me, a man dangling from the ceiling, a naked man stuck with feathers and spittle. He must have cried out, *what are you doing up there?* And I would've answered, *what does it look like? I'm taking out the weed, I'm opening the holes... how else will the swifts, after their miraculous migration, be able to return to their nests next year?*

Epilogue

THE NURSE LED me up the stairs to my father's room, opened the door and let me in. She'd told me he was weakening, he wasn't eating, he couldn't speak. She said she'd tried to call me on the number I'd used, but it sounded like the phone was disconnected. I followed her upstairs. I was carrying quite a heavy wooden box, and she wanted to help me with the door.

He was propped up in his armchair. A skeleton of himself, swaddled in an enormous dressing-gown. He looked so thin and fragile that he might topple out of the chair if I touched him or the cushions which bolstered him in place. A shrunken man. But his eyes glimmered with warmth and recognition as I moved toward him. I put down the box, leaned to him and kissed his forehead.

I pulled up another chair and sat down, close enough so that my knees touched his. I gently took hold of his hands. They were very warm, and when his fingers closed on mine with surprising strength, I felt a tingle of tears in my eyes.

At first I didn't speak. It seemed enough that I was there, with him. I wanted to say I was sorry I hadn't been to see him through the months of the summer, maybe to express some inkling of what had happened to prevent my coming. But the way he stared at the wounds on my face, as though he might read them, made me pause. I could see in his eyes that he was trying to recall something, a name he'd seen somewhere or read somewhere, or maybe just a word...

The burns on my face, the scalding, had dried into a spatter of red scabs. I'd studied them myself in the mirror, as they'd gradually stopped weeping and become encrusted.

Unmistakably a splatter of liquid, from one side of my face to the other. He was studying it all, and his mind was figuring.

Thinking to distract him, I prised his fingers open so that I could press the keys of the Daimler into his hands. I told him that the car had been great. He folded his hands around the keys, for their familiarity, their age, and everything they signified for him, the places he'd been to and all the work he'd done. I said, would he like to see these? And I opened his tool box, which I'd brought out of the car and carried from the faraway wolds to his room in Grimsby. I was glad, because a light of love and joy and pride gleamed in his eyes as he stroked the smooth wooden handles of his hammers, as he tested the blades of his chisels with the ball of his thumb. The box itself, I lifted it onto my knees so he could smell the oils, the very cloths he'd used to wipe and clean and treasure the tools of his trade.

At last I set the box down and carefully rearranged the tools into it. When I closed the lid, with the sweet little thud of wood on wood he'd heard hundreds of times, I looked up to see he'd lolled his head back on his pillow and shut his eyes. I took his hands again. He squeezed, but his grip was weaker. He was very tired. More than that, he was shrinking into the cushions of the chair. Weakening, the nurse had said.

I sat there with my knees touching his, my fingers holding his. In a strange and marvellous way, he was beautiful. His face was a work of art. No, it was a work of life, the life he'd had. No, more than that. It was the life he'd made.

Behind him, the estuary was silver in the light of an autumn afternoon. A flock of gulls whirled this way and that, brushing their wings on the water. Their voices were harsh and cold. And the air through the window was cold, a shiver of winter I hadn't felt for years.

I thought he was asleep. I unfolded my hands from his hands and made to stand up.

No. He jolted upright, as though a tingle of electricity had passed through his body. His head came off the pillow and his eyes opened wide. He stared at my face, he read the signs on it, and he found the name and the word he'd been reaching for.

He opened his mouth, his lips moved. *Lundy...* two clicks of his tongue. *Wax...* a single puff of sound, as soft as a kiss.

His body sank back into the chair, he shrank into the dressing-gown, he closed his eyes. The effort of remembering had weakened him even more. I didn't stand up. I didn't want to go. I didn't want to let go. I stayed with him as the afternoon grew darker, until it was night and the gulls fell silent, and I felt the warmth and the strength fading in his fingers.